"I don't know you at all."

Devon pulled her lower lip between her teeth after she spoke—as though she, too, wished to take back the words. She put her right hand on the floor to push herself to her feet.

Miguel closed his fingers around her forearm and held her beside him. "Devon, have you given any thought as to why you ended up in my bed that night?"

"Shock. Confusion. Sleep deprivation. I was a little out of my mind, I think."

"Maybe," he agreed, smiling, although it took some doing to produce a grin. Part of him wanted her to say it was because she was still madly, passionately, forever in love with him. "I think we both were."

"I didn't know if my grandmother was going to live or die. I needed comfort. You offered me that."

"Devon, it went past offering you comfort five minutes after we left the hospital." The words came out as a kind of growl and her eyes widened a little with dismay.

"I told you, it was an aberration. We were both a little crazy that night."

Dear Reader,

Babies are such wonderful little creatures. Being able to contribute a story to a series dealing with the women who dedicate their lives to bringing babies into the world was a challenge we were happy to accept.

Midwives have helped women deliver their babies from ancient times, but in the past hundred years, at least in the United States, the craft has fallen into disfavor and is still viewed with skepticism by much of the medical profession.

Today many women are rediscovering the joy of delivering their children with the help of skilled midwives like Lydia Kane and the others at The Birth Place.

Lydia's granddaughter, Devon Grant, has always known she wanted to follow in her grandmother's footsteps, but she's taken a different path to that goal, becoming a Certified Nurse Midwife instead of following traditional ways. Now she's back in Enchantment working alongside Lydia, and old wounds and new secrets add to the tension between the women, tension that's intensified further by their differing approaches to their age-old craft.

The reappearance of Devon's teenage love, all grown up and even more handsome than before, only adds to the complications in her life—and then there are the children she's taken under her wing at the risk of being arrested for harboring illegal aliens...and wildfire on the mountain...oh yes, and a baby born under the stars.

We hope you enjoy reading *The Midwife and the Lawman* as much as we enjoyed writing it. We'd also like to add a special thank you to the great authors in this series (Darlene Graham, Brenda Novak, Roxanne Rustand, C.J. Carmichael and Kathleen O'Brien) whose books preceded ours. It was an honor and a privilege working with all of you.

Sincerely,

Carol and Marian

The Midwife and the Lawman
Marisa Carroll

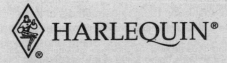

HARLEQUIN®

TORONTO • NEW YORK • LONDON
AMSTERDAM • PARIS • SYDNEY • HAMBURG
STOCKHOLM • ATHENS • TOKYO • MILAN • MADRID
PRAGUE • WARSAW • BUDAPEST • AUCKLAND

ISBN 0-373-71182-4

THE MIDWIFE AND THE LAWMAN

Copyright © 2004 by Carol I. Wagner & Marian L. Franz.

This edition published by arrangement with Harlequin Books S.A.

® and TM are trademarks of the publisher. Trademarks indicated with ® are registered in the United States Patent and Trademark Office, the Canadian Trade Marks Office and in other countries.

Visit us at www.eHarlequin.com

Printed in U.S.A.

For Erika, Jennifer, Allicyn and Matthew
and now for Becca and Nicholas,
and always for Sarah

CHAPTER ONE

HE WONDERED if Devon would ever come to him again.

Enchantment's Chief of Police Miguel Eiden put the decidedly nonregulation thought out of his head as his radio crackled to life. It was the day dispatcher, Doris Fernandez, checking in.

"Chief Eiden, did you copy the transmission from The Birth Place?"

He hit the toggle that opened the receiver affixed to his shoulder, frowning a little at the use of his title. Until a few weeks ago Doris would have called him Miguel. Then he'd still been one of the guys. Now he was the boss, and things had changed. "Roger that, Doris." He'd picked up Devon Grant's conversation with her grandmother, Lydia Kane, on the scanner speaker. He hadn't responded, though. That was the last thing Devon would want.

"Shall I send out a ten-fourteen?" Ten-fourteen was code for a police escort.

The only other officer on duty this shift was Hank Jensen. Hank was six months out of the New Mexico Police Academy. It would be lights and siren all the way back to The Birth Place. Devon would be furious. Madder than she'd be if he showed up. "Negative, Doris. I'm heading back into town. I'll meet her at the Silver Creek Road intersection.''

''Affirmative. I'll notify the clinic that you're available.''

''I'll give you an ETA after I connect with Ms. Grant. Eiden out.'' He stood up but didn't leave the shade of the brush arbor where he'd been sitting with his grandfather, Daniel Elkhorn. ''Gotta go, Granddad. Devon Grant doesn't want to be delivering a baby in the back of her Blazer any more than I do. I'd better see she's got a clear run the rest of the way into town.''

His grandfather stood, too, unfolding his barrel-chested, six-foot frame from his lawn chair, and took a limping step forward. ''This'll be the second baby in two weeks that she's talked the mother out of delivering at home. Not the best endorsement for her grandmother's clinic.''

''How'd you know that?'' Miguel looked at his grandfather over the top of his sunglasses.

''Heard it down at the Legion.'' Daniel stared back at him from eyes that had faded from black to brown with the passing of years, but still seemed able to see right through him. His skin was bronzed and creased as an old leather jacket. His hair was more gray than black now. His nose jutted out from his face like a hawk's beak. Miguel had inherited that nose. ''Course you already know that. You helped her get Ophelia Pedroza to The Birth Place, too, didn't you?''

''It was a breech birth. I don't blame Devon for not wanting to deliver Ophelia way the hell out on the reservation with only an assistant midwife for help. And now Lacy Belton's running a fever. Sounds like it could be serious.''

''Or she could've caught a cold from one of her kids. Makes no difference. Lydia Kane will be fit to be tied that Devon's done it again.''

Miguel didn't have an answer for that. He opened the door of the Dodge Durango the town fathers had seen fit to buy for the chief who'd preceded him and swung inside. The air conditioner wasn't working again. The vehicle had been sitting in the sun and the interior was like an oven. It was nearing ninety this July afternoon, a higher than normal temperature for the altitude. He rolled down the window and made a mental note to have the SUV serviced, which ensured another hour of doing paperwork.

''I'll check back in tomorrow if I can, Granddad. And if you see anyone else prowling around the barn, you stay put inside, you hear? You're not the only one who's had things come up missing. It could be just kids from town or the reservation raising hell, or it could be illegals making their way north to Colorado. Either way, you don't need to do my job for me. Give the station a call. I'll get someone out here, pronto.''

Daniel lifted a hand in acknowledgment—or dismissal, more likely. Sixty years ago he'd island-hopped his way across the Pacific, one of the famous Marine Navajo Code Talkers. Before that he'd grown up on the Navajo reservation when living off the land was the only option for most Native Americans. Even crippled by arthritis and nearing eighty, he was fearless and a crack shot. He wouldn't stay locked inside his trailer waiting for his grandson to come to his rescue. He'd confront the person stealing the eggs from his chicken coop and carting off things from the pile of darn-near junk behind his barn.

Miguel made up his mind to increase the patrols in this part of the township, and the old ghost town of Silverton, a mile farther into the hills. It would mean overtime for his small force, and more than likely another go-around with the town council over the cost. He must have been crazy to take over the job when Chief Hadley up and retired after his wife hit a million-dollar jackpot on an anniversary trip to Reno.

He checked the dashboard clock as he headed back out the dusty track that connected his granddad's place with the main road. It would take him fifteen minutes to reach the rendezvous, but once he crossed the creek he'd have a good overview of Desert Valley Road—the route Devon would have to take to bring Lacy Belton off the mountain.

By the time he got there, he wouldn't have to worry about air-conditioning. He had no doubt Devon's frosty welcome would cool him off just fine.

DEVON SCOWLED IN ANNOYANCE. Even with half of Arroyo County to patrol, it *would* have to be Miguel who showed up to accompany her back into town. Not that she needed an escort. Lacy was doing just fine in the back of her Blazer, and her husband, Tom, was right behind them in his pickup with their two kids, Luke and Angie. But once she'd radioed that she was bringing her patient into the birthing center to deliver, the outcome had been inevitable.

Devon eased over to the side of the road. Miguel was standing, arms folded, beside the big brown Durango emblazoned with the Enchantment Police Department logo. His gray Stetson shading his face, he straightened as she rolled to a halt and lowered her window.

"Everything okay, Devon? Where's your backup?" Miguel knew The Birth Place midwives usually worked in pairs for a home birth.

"No one was available." Lacy was one of Lydia's most loyal patients, and she'd insisted her baby be born at home. So Devon had agreed to attend the delivery alone. Reluctantly. She was a registered nurse and a certified nurse-midwife. She couldn't quite meet Miguel's gaze. She'd choked again and he knew it. "Lacy's running a fever. I felt it would be better if she delivered at The Birthing Place." She was taking the safest course for her patient. She didn't need to feel defensive, but she did.

"I picked up a bug from the kids, that's all," Lacy said from the back seat. She was a little thing, but she'd already had two successful pregnancies. She began to pant, making puffing sounds through pursed lips. Devon glanced at her watch, timing the contraction. "Wow. That was a doozy." Lacy leaned back against the seat as the contraction eased.

"We need to be on our way." Lacy was only about five centimeters dilated, but as this was her third child, her labor would probably progress quickly. The sun had already wheeled far over into the western sky. Once it dropped behind the peaks of the Sangre de Cristo Mountains, darkness would fall like a blanket.

Miguel studied Devon from behind the concealing sunglasses for a few more unnerving moments before nodding his agreement. His khaki shirt and pants were as crisp and wrinkle-free as if he'd just put them on. He looked as if the heat didn't bother him a bit. When she was sixteen and hopelessly romantic, she'd thought his apparent disregard of physical discomfort must be the result of his Navajo and Spanish-conquistador heritage. Now she'd realized it was just as much a function of his stubborn Scot/Irish/German genes. "I'll lead you in." He turned away, gave Tom Belton a thumbs-up and folded his length into the seat of the SUV.

The rest of the trip was uneventful. Lacy's contractions were a steady four minutes apart. Her face was flushed and her eyes bright with fever, but she wasn't unduly stressed. Miguel pulled into the small parking lot at the back of the adobe-style clinic. Devon parked in the space beside him and climbed out of her truck to help Lacy from the back seat. The graveled path into the clinic was screened from the view of the parking lot and windows so that a woman in labor could walk directly into the birthing rooms unseen, even if she was wearing only a bathrobe.

It was one of the many thoughtful details that stamped the clinic with Devon's grandmother Lydia's unique touch.

"Do you need any help?" Miguel asked, coming to stand beside her. Devon had to tilt her head a little to meet his gaze. He'd taken off the sunglasses and she got the full dose of his deep-brown eyes. His straight dark hair held unexpected hints of copper and gold. At least it had in that long-ago summer when she'd given him her heart—and her virginity. These days he wore it military short, a reminder that he was a Marine reservist, as well as a policeman.

Lacy waved Miguel off. "I'm okay." But she accepted Devon's arm around her swollen waist.

Tom Belton wheeled into the last parking space in the small lot. He'd gotten held up at one of Enchantment's few stoplights. The children came tumbling out of the truck and ran to her.

"Are you okay, Mom?" Lacy's son asked.

"I'm fine. I just need Daddy to put his arm around me and help me inside."

Devon stepped aside to let Tom support his wife. She looked up and saw her grandmother standing, tall and straight, just inside the open door that led to the birthing rooms. Lydia's hair was pulled back into her usual bun. She wore khaki slacks and a rough-weave cotton shirt with an open neck and sleeves rolled up to her elbows. On the days she was seeing patients, she often wore long, flowing skirts and rings and bracelets of silver and turquoise. But not when she was attending a laboring mother.

A stethoscope hung around her neck, and under it Devon could see the rare, rose-onyx pendant Lydia was never without. If you looked at it closely, you could just make out the design of a Madonna and child, in the pink and rose swirls at its heart. Except for a few new lines around her mouth and a shadow of fatigue in her blue eyes, Lydia showed no visible signs of the heart attack she'd suffered six weeks earlier.

Behind her grandmother Devon noticed the clinic's accountant, Kim Sherman. Devon still found it hard to believe that the somewhat abrasive and aloof young woman was really her cousin, the daughter of the baby girl Lydia had been forced to give up at birth years before Devon's own mother was born. The discovery had been a shock, but learning Lydia had kept her daughter's birth a secret all those years didn't surprise Devon as much as the others. Lydia was good at keeping secrets.

And because Lydia kept secrets, Devon had secrets, too.

"Lydia, I'm glad you're here," Lacy said, and the relief in her voice was so evident Devon felt color rise in her throat and cheeks.

"Let's take your vital signs and check you out, then we'll decide whether to call Dr. Ochoa and head over to Arroyo," Lydia said in her bracing, no-nonsense voice.

Hope Tanner Reynolds, Lydia's assistant, joined them. "Hope, will you help Lacy get settled? Tom, you and the children are welcome in the birthing room, as well. I need to speak to my granddaughter and then I'll be right with you." The door closed behind them. "Do you have reason to believe Lacy's fever is caused by something more serious than a cold?" Lydia asked without preamble.

Devon took a moment to compose her answer. She always felt as if she was back in college taking an oral exam when her grandmother queried her about a birth.

"Miguel, would you like something cold to drink?

Or a cup of coffee?'' Kim asked, covering the small, telling silence that followed Lydia's question.

''I could use a glass of ice water,'' he responded, taking his cue.

''That's an even better choice. I was just getting ready to empty the coffeepot. It's been simmering away all afternoon. It's probably the consistency of roofing tar by now.''

''Then I'll definitely stick to ice water.''

He followed Kim down the hall, leaving Devon and her grandmother alone.

The clinic was unusually quiet. The office staff had gone home for the evening and there were no expectant mothers in the whitewashed waiting room comparing symptoms, while their children squabbled over the toys in the sunny corner opposite the fireplace, no women in labor being cared for in the other pastel-colored birthing rooms.

''She probably has some run-of-the-mill virus that poses no harm to her or the baby,'' Devon responded at last. ''But without tests I can't rule out a urinary-tract infection or Group B strep, even an amniotic infection, although I don't think that's the case. In any event, intravenous antibiotics would be the safest course to follow.''

''We don't do IVs here.''

''I know. That's why...''

Hope opened the birthing-room door in time to overhear the last of the exchange. Hope had been a labor and delivery nurse before she returned to Enchantment with her sister. She had recently become a licensed midwife under Lydia's tutelage. She was newly and happily married to Parker Reynolds, the clinic's administrator, and helping him raise his son, Dalton. But eleven years earlier, things had been very different. Hope had been a seventeen-year-old runaway from a polygamous religious cult, pregnant and alone. On the night Hope's baby was born, Devon, only a teenager herself, had overheard her grandmother agreeing to sell the infant on the black market. Paralyzed with shock and betrayal at her adored grandmother's unethical actions, she had done nothing to save her friend's baby. Hope had left the area a few days later, and Devon hadn't heard from her again until Hope had returned about a year ago, apparently reconciled to the loss of her child and ready to move on with her life. It seemed Hope had forgiven Lydia for what had happened, but Devon could not so easily forget what her grandmother had done.

She'd kept the secret of that night sealed in her heart for more than a decade, confronting her grandmother with her knowledge only when Lydia decided to step down from the center's board of directors and asked Devon to take her place. Lydia had refused to acknowledge any wrongdoing, insisting she'd done what she had to do to save the center and begging Devon to believe her when she said that Hope's baby had gone to a good and loving home. The issue remained unresolved between them, straining her relationship with her grandmother almost to the breaking point.

"I have a suggestion," Hope said, taking on the role of peacemaker between them as she so often did these days. "It's not routine, I know, but couldn't

Joanna Carson order antibiotics for Lacy? She takes care of both Lacy's kids. She knows her as well as any of the OBs.''

Devon relaxed a fraction. Hope was right. It was a little out of the ordinary to ask a pediatrician to prescribe for a woman in labor. But it was a way out of the standoff.

Lydia's expression remained tight. She fingered the pendant at her neck, a nervous gesture she'd acquired in the stressful weeks since Devon had agreed to move back to Enchantment and practice at the clinic. ''I don't see any other solution, short of sending Lacy to the hospital. Dr. Ochoa would certainly not be receptive to coming here to start the IV.'' Carlos Ochoa was one of the OBs who backed up The Birth Place midwives at Arroyo County Hospital. Their professional relationship was cordial but not close.

Hope shot Devon a glance that said as plainly as words not to mention they were both qualified to administer drugs by IV if the doctor so ordered. That was not Lydia's way.

''I'll call Joanna,'' Devon said, reaching out a hand toward her grandmother. A hug or a touch had always been the signal they used to convey an apology when they'd clashed during Devon's growing-up years. And they had clashed, often. They were too much alike, Devon's mother, Myrna, always said. But Lydia didn't see, or chose to ignore, her granddaughter's tentative gesture. These days the distance between them was too great for a simple ritual to make things right.

''I suppose you must,'' Lydia said, ''if Lacy can

deliver here. It will be less stressful for her and the baby.''

Devon nodded. ''Good. That's settled, then. Let's get back to our mother.''

Lydia smiled at Hope and reached for the doorknob. She didn't give Devon a backward glance.

IN ANOTHER HOUR it would be daylight. Lydia turned away from the window. Lacy Belton, her new daughter asleep in the crook of her arm, dozed on the high bed. Nearby, her husband was stretched out in a recliner that the parents of one of her mothers had donated to the center. The older children were curled up in the corner on an air mattress.

The delivery had taken longer than she'd anticipated, but everything went smoothly. Another life brought safely into the arms of a loving mother, one more small atonement for the sin of giving her own firstborn away.

Feeling every one of her seventy-four years, she turned her thoughts from the past—she knew from long experience there was no comfort there. It was so quiet now she could hear the beat of her heart. Steady and strong. No pain, no shortness of breath. Just weariness, and the ever-present weight of despair. How was she ever going to make things right with Devon? If she'd known that long-ago night that Devon had overheard her making arrangements with Parker Reynold and his father-in-law to buy Hope's baby, could she have done something, anything, to mitigate the damage?

Probably not. Devon was as stubborn and bull-headed as she was. And what she had done was wrong, criminal even, though it had all turned out right in the end—Hope had been reunited with her son. But at seventeen, would Devon have been able to understand her grandmother's motivations, her desperation? She might have. *If only I had known she was there, hiding, listening to every word.*

Hope opened the door and stuck her head inside. "Everyone asleep?" she asked in a whisper, moving closer in her soft-soled shoes. At Lydia's nod, she said, "Come and have a cup of tea."

Lydia cast one last look at the sleeping family, then walked with Hope to the staff room just down the hall. Tom could find her easily if Lacy or the baby needed her.

"Where's Devon?" she asked, blinking a little at the light Hope flicked on.

"I sent her home. She'll have to do most of the prenatal visits tomorrow because you're sleeping in." Hope motioned Lydia to a seat and poured her a cup of her favorite herbal tea.

"I'm not."

"Yes, you are. The cardiologist gave you permission to come back to work part-time. Part-time doesn't mean eighteen-hour days."

"I feel fine."

"You don't look fine," Hope said bluntly. She took a seat beside Lydia, her own mug cradled between her hands. "We can't go on like this, Lydia. The tensions between you, Devon and me are spilling over into our work."

"I'm tired. I really don't want to discuss this tonight.'' Her voice sounded like a tired old woman's even to her own ears.

''You won't want to discuss it tomorrow or the day after, either.'' Hope's tone remained quiet but firm.

''I tried to explain to Devon why I did…what I did.'' The guilt of it still lay heavily on Lydia's soul, and she couldn't say the words aloud without pain. She couldn't say, *I sold your baby to Parker Reynolds.* ''She still holds me responsible.''

''She will always hold you responsible, unless you tell her the whole truth.''

''No. I can't. Not after all this time.''

''Lydia, Parker and I both agree Devon should know that Dalton is my son. You can't let her go on believing I don't know where my child is. My uncle is in prison. I'm not afraid of him anymore. I release you from the promise you made me to keep Dalton's identity secret.'' She reached out and covered Lydia's hand with her own. Tears sparkled in her eyes. ''I thought you'd told her the truth about his adoption months ago.''

Lydia pulled away from the gentle touch. She set the mug down with more force than she should have. Tea sloshed over the rim onto the plastic tabletop. She blinked back the sting of unfamiliar, unwelcome tears. She never cried. ''It's too late. Don't you see? Talking about it isn't enough. It won't turn back the clock. It won't make Devon respect me again. It won't make her love me again.''

CHAPTER TWO

MIGUEL SAT with his booted feet propped on the porch railing of his cabin. He'd "borrowed" a set of old, high-backed wooden kitchen chairs from his parents' garage just so he could do exactly what he was doing now. There was no way you could tip back on two legs and take in the sight of the Sangre de Cristos on one side, and Enchantment nestled in its valley on the other, in a plastic lawn chair. None at all.

He took a swallow of his beer. It was warm. He grimaced and poured the rest over the edge of the porch onto the ground. He liked a beer now and then, but it had to be cold. He didn't drink much. Not with a father and brother who were both recovering alcoholics. He had too many strikes against him with his genetic makeup not to be wary of following the same path.

A hawk cried as it circled overhead. Off in the distance a dog barked, or maybe it was a coyote, although coyotes didn't usually come this close to town. Below him, on the narrow winding road, he saw lights flicker on in a couple of the minimansions that had been built out this way in the past decade.

His cabin wasn't in the same league with those homes. Log sided, it had four rooms and a bathroom downstairs, and space for two more bedrooms and another bathroom beneath the steep-pitched dormer roof, if he ever had the time and money to finish them. But it was his. And so were the five wooded acres it sat on. His heart and his roots were here. The high country, the thin, clear air, were in his blood.

Hunter's blood, Daniel called it. The Elkhorn clan had been hunters since the Diné, as the Navajos called themselves, had come into the Glittering World. Or so the legends told. But Daniel had left the Arizona reservation and moved to Enchantment when he married Miguel's Mexican grandmother and took over running her father's hardware store.

His father, Dennis Eiden, on the other hand, had wandered into Enchantment in the sixties, a war-weary vet out to see the country he'd fought for before settling down. He was a blond, blue-eyed farm boy from Ohio, but one look at Elena Elkhorn and he had stayed. He married her, moved her to Albuquerque. Worked days and went to school nights until he got his teaching degree, then brought her back to Enchantment to settle down and raise a family. He was retired now, throwing pottery and selling it for good money at a gallery in Taos.

And working to stay sober. Just like Miguel's older brother, Diego, a Bureau of Indian Affairs cop on the big reservation in Arizona.

The sound of a familiar engine coming up the road in the twilight wormed its way into Miguel's thoughts. It was Devon's Blazer. He was so attuned to its vibrations that he even woke up in the middle of the night if she drove by to attend a birth.

He dug a plastic bottle of raspberry-flavored iced tea out of the little cooler where he'd stowed his beer and swung his legs off the railing. He jogged down the drive past the stand of pines that shielded his home from the road and waited for her. He wasn't expecting her to come up to the cabin without an argument, but he had a backup plan if she put up too much of a fuss. He patted the pocket of his shirt. It was still there, the sheet of paper with the guest list for Nolan McKinnon and Kim Sherman's wedding-rehearsal dinner. As best man and maid of honor respectively, he and Devon were hosting the damn thing as their gift to the couple. If it was up to him and Nolan, it would have been barbecue and beer, the same as the couple had planned for the reception. Catered by Slim Jim's, the best damn barbecue in the state.

But it wasn't up to him and Nolan.

Devon slowed when she saw him standing by the side of the road. She wanted this party to be perfect to show Kim she was welcome in the family, and she was making herself into a nervous wreck to accomplish that goal. She rolled down the window and looked up at him, no hint of a smile showing on her face. Miguel felt the absence of that smile like a cloud blocking the sun on a cool day. He loved Devon's smile, a slow curving of her lips that grew and widened until it wreathed her face and sparkled in her eyes. "What is it, Miguel?" she asked, weariness underlying her words.

He held out the bottle of flavored tea. "I thought you might like a glass."

She shook her head. "Thanks, no. It's been a long day. A long *two* days, and I've got tons of things to do up at my place." Devon had moved into a tiny cabin a thousand feet farther up the mountain. At night he could just make out her bedroom light from his kitchen window.

"We've got a ton of things to do here, too." He pulled the sheet of paper out of his pocket. "The chef at Angel's Gate needs to know our final numbers and whether we've decided on the chicken or the fish." Angel's Gate was the multimillion dollar ski resort that had opened that spring in the mountains above town.

She flexed her long, tapered fingers on the steering wheel. She had small wrists, dainty and feminine, and slender arms. But she was stronger than she looked. She had to be to catch babies for a living.

Her facial features resembled her grandmother's, but she wasn't as rangy and rawboned as Lydia. Devon was soft and curved in all the right places. She molded herself to him when she lay beneath him. Her honey-blond hair spilled over her shoulders and curled itself around a man's fingers, caressed his cheek when he kissed her throat or traced the roundness of her breast with the tip of his tongue—

"Have you eaten?" He hadn't meant to bark the question at her, but he had to get his mind on something else—fast. She jumped a little in her seat.

"What? Yes. I had an apple and some crackers with peanut butter." She looked a little confused.

"How long ago was that?"

"Between Lena Morales and Winona Preston's prenatal visits. About eleven, I guess."

"It's almost eight. We can't be talking food and menus with you wasting away from hunger. That's no way to make an informed decision. C'mon up. I've got chicken salad and flat bread. I'll make you a sandwich."

"I can't."

"Sure you can. I didn't do the cooking. My mom did. Old family recipe." It was time they got out in the open what had happened between them that night six weeks earlier. She'd been scared and exhausted when he'd come across her in the hospital waiting room the second night after Lydia's heart attack. He'd only meant to offer her something to eat and a place to kick back and relax for a while. It had ended up being much more than that. "It's only for a sandwich, Devon. You don't have to be afraid I'm going to try and get you into bed again."

Her gray eyes met his brown ones without flinching. "I'm not afraid. But I really am too tired to deal with this." She waved the paper at him.

Miguel straightened, putting a little distance between them. It had been his fault that night. He'd let the situation get out of hand when she'd been frightened and alone. Hell, who would have guessed the same fire that had sparked between them as teenagers would flare out of control all these years later? Their coming together had been spontaneous and white-hot, unplanned and unprotected. At least they'd dodged the pregnancy bullet. Although the thought of his baby growing in Devon's belly was a consequence he would have welcomed, it would only have made a complicated situation impossible. He reached out and plucked the sheet of paper from her hand. "Okay, I'll tell him half chicken and half fish and we'll just let people fight it out at the buffet table."

"You can't do that."

"Then we'll order one of each for everyone."

"That'll cost a fortune."

"Money's no object."

"Easy for you to say."

"Then come in and let's take our best guess on who wants what." He stepped back so she could pull into his driveway. She hesitated as though she might still refuse. He held himself still, kept his expression neutral. It had taken him six weeks to get her alone again. He was an officer of the law. He was a U.S. Marine. He had self-discipline. He could do this. He could keep his fly zipped and his hands to himself—if he really put his mind to it.

"THANKS. I NEEDED THAT." Devon pushed her empty plate away. She'd thought she'd be too nervous to eat, returning to the scene of her complete lapse from sanity, but she'd managed just fine. Miguel's mother was a great cook, and her chicken salad, Southwestern style, was the stuff of dreams. She'd eaten the sandwich and a dish of fruit salad besides. She picked up her glass of iced tea and took a look around.

She'd only been in Miguel's cabin that one time, and never in the kitchen. It was neat as a pin. The cabinets were pine and so was the paneling on the walls. The floors were tiled in the same soft sandstone color as the countertops. A traditional adobe fireplace was set in one corner with a drop-leaf pine table and two chairs in front of it. From where she sat in one of those chairs, Devon could look out the window and see part of a cabin farther up the mountain. She hadn't realized Miguel could see her place from here.

Her gaze swung from the view to the man sitting quietly in the other chair, making notations beside names on the guest list. He was frowning slightly while he wrote, winged eyebrows drawn together over eyes as dark as night, eyes that only hinted at the heat and light at his core. She slapped a lid on her thoughts. She wasn't going to go there.

"Okay, I've done the math. Put me and Nolan down for chicken. And your grandmother?" He gave her a quizzical look and she nodded. Lydia didn't like fish. "My mom and dad will probably want the salmon."

"Mine, too."

"Your grandfather Kane isn't coming, right?" he asked next.

"His health isn't good." Lydia and Devon's grandfather had been divorced for many years. He'd never known about Kim's mother, the child Lydia had given away at birth years before he met her. But he was a kind and loving man who would welcome Lydia's grandchild into his family, Devon knew. "Kim and Nolan are going to take Sammy to visit him before school starts."

"What about your uncle Bradley and your cousins?"

"Uncle Bradley and Aunt Irene will be here. Derek and Jason can't make it. They're coming for Christmas instead."

"Fish or chicken?"

She blinked. "I have no idea." She should call her mother and ask, but if she did that, Myrna would insist on coming out to help plan the party. That was the last thing Devon needed. Her mother had a heart of gold, but she was also domineering and opinionated. She loved to run the show, and usually did. The few days she'd been in Enchantment after Lydia's heart attack had been a strain on everyone involved.

"Let's say one of each then. Fish for Father Ignatio. His cholesterol is sky-high." He made a check on the paper. "That leaves you and the bride. Which is it?"

"Chicken for me," Devon said.

"And Kim?"

"I don't know." The trouble was, even though Kim had asked her to be her maid of honor, she didn't know her new cousin at all.

"Ask her in the morning."

"Okay, I will."

Miguel tallied up the numbers. "That's almost a fifty-fifty, providing Kim goes for the salmon, and I bet she will." He was probably right. He was Nolan McKinnon's best friend, so he had a direct line into Kim's likes and dislikes.

"The salmon's five dollars a plate more. Maybe we should just go with the chicken." Devon winced when she heard herself speak the thought aloud. Being responsible for keeping the clinic afloat was beginning to color her thinking in all sorts of ways.

Miguel grinned across the table at her. "Do I detect a little penny-pinching here?"

"We agreed on a budget, remember? I don't want to go over. And aren't Navajos supposed to not be interested in money?"

"The Diné are interested in harmony. Too much money puts you out of harmony with yourself. I don't have that problem." He grinned. "I hear the salmon is excellent. And hey, nothing's too good for Kim and Nolan, right?"

"Right." She smiled her agreement. It was nice to have someone to help make the decisions.

A pager went off. Miguel's hand went automatically to his belt, Devon's to the waistband of her pink scrubs. "It's mine," she said. "I left my phone in the car."

Miguel waved his hand toward the wall. "Use mine."

She stood up a little too quickly and had to steady herself with a hand on the tabletop.

"You okay?" He didn't make even the slightest move toward her and Devon was glad. If he had, she might have let him take her in his arms and...

"Just tired." She punched in the clinic's number.

"The Birth Place," a voice answered.

"Trish?" Devon was a little surprised the clinic's receptionist, Trish Linden, was still on duty.

"Yes, I'm still here. Got some paperwork I wanted to finish up. One of your patients is on her way in.

Carla Van Tassle. She's spotting. Just a little, but she's worried.''

Devon sorted through her mental case file until she put a face to the name. Carla was seven weeks pregnant with her second child. Lydia had delivered her first, a little boy, twenty-two months earlier. "I'll be right there.''

"Wait a moment, Devon, your grandmother wants to speak to you.''

"I thought you were taking the day off,'' Devon said, when Lydia came on the line.

"I did take the day off. I came in to catch up on some charting and to give Lacy Belton a follow-up phone call.''

"I planned to do that a little later this evening.'' Devon felt her neck and shoulder muscles tighten. Lacy's temperature had returned to normal and stayed there after she had received the IV antibiotics Joanna prescribed. She and her baby had left the clinic shortly before noon.

"I'm sure she would still appreciate your call. And you'll probably want to set up a convenient time to check in on her tomorrow, anyway.''

"Yes, I do.''

"I just wanted to tell you that since I'm here already, I'll examine Carla. I'm sure it's nothing serious.''

Spotting early in a pregnancy wasn't unusual, but Devon would have taken a blood sample, checked hormone levels, maybe ordered an ultrasound to be on the safe side. Not Lydia. Not at The Birth Place. Her grandmother had decades of experience, four thousand healthy deliveries to her credit. She relied on her instincts and her personal knowledge of each and every patient that passed through her care.

"I'll be glad to come back." Devon kept her voice even and pleasant. She was very aware of Miguel standing just a few feet away. She was usually pretty good at hiding her emotions—she had to be in her business. But he was also very good at reading people for the same reason.

There was a small silence before her grandmother spoke again. Her tone was unusually gentle. "Devon, I assure you I'll transfer Carla to Arroyo County for an ultrasound if I think there's the least chance this is serious. I'll notify you immediately if that's the case so you can be with her."

Devon took a breath. This was Lydia's way of apologizing for their disagreement over Devon's handling of Lacy Belton's delivery. If only they could do the same with the past. "Thanks, Lydia."

"Good," her grandmother replied briskly. "As I said, I don't anticipate any real problem with Carla, so I'll see you tomorrow. Why don't you take the morning off, come in after your visit with Lacy?"

Devon opened her mouth to say she'd be in at her usual time, and then changed her mind. She could use a few hours to herself. "All right. I will. Good night, Lydia."

"Good night, Devon." She replaced the receiver.

"Everything okay?"

"Yes. One of my patients is spotting a little. She's still early in her first trimester, so it's probably hormonal. The cervix is very sensitive at this point, so it could also be that she and her partner were just a little too energetic in making love.''

Miguel lifted his hands in a time-out gesture. ''Whoa. That's enough.''

Devon laughed. ''I'm sorry. I was thinking out loud.''

He was smiling, but he looked distinctly uncomfortable, and totally, breathtakingly male. Her stomach tightened in response and she felt her pulse speed up.

''That's more information than I really need,'' he said.

''I'll remember that.''

''Are you heading back to the clinic?''

''No. My grandmother is going to check Carla over. She'll call me if she needs me.'' She caught a glimpse of the smooth, bronzed skin of his throat. She had kissed him there that night, and the taste of his skin had been like sunlight and sagebrush. She forgot what they'd been talking about. She forgot what she was going to say next. ''I really should be going,'' she finished in a rush.

''You don't have to run off, Devon.'' He kept the width of the table between them, but she felt as if he was only inches away. She wished he *was* only inches away.

''I…'' She stopped and got hold of herself. ''Would you like me to drop by and check on your grandfather while I'm out that way tomorrow morning?'' They were neighbors. Neighbors did things like that for each other.

''The Belton place is five miles from Granddad's.''

"I thought I'd drive on up to Silverton. I haven't been there since I got back." Silverton was an old abandoned mining town in the hills north of Enchantment. Horseback rides, picnics, a played-out silver mine and false-fronted wooden buildings slowly falling into ruin. It had been one of her favorite places as a girl.

"I don't know if that's such a good idea. We've been getting a lot of calls about stuff coming up missing out that way. Probably just kids, but with the INS cracking down on border crossings, the Coyotes are working their way farther north all the time."

Coyotes, the unscrupulous men who transported undocumented workers across the border from Mexico and sometimes left them to die a terrible death in the desert.

"I'll be careful. Thanks for the warning." But the more she thought about it, the more she wanted to go.

Devon had gotten up as she spoke and was heading into the main room of the cabin, with its whitewashed walls and shiny, wide-planked wood floor. A big fireplace made of river rock stood against one wall, flanked by floor-to-ceiling windows. Hanging on the opposite wall was a gorgeous hand-woven Navajo rug in warm earth tones. Miguel's aunt, Carmella Elkhorn, was a master weaver. The rug was most likely her work.

"Thanks again for the sandwich and the tea," Devon said. "I'll talk to Kim as soon as I check in tomorrow." She reached to open the door.

Miguel circled her wrist with his hand. His grip

was painless but strong. She would have had to use her other hand to pry his fingers loose, and she didn't trust herself to touch him even that much. "We have to talk," he said quietly. "And not about the party."

She started to shake her head in an instinctive denial. They hadn't seen each other a half-dozen times in the past ten years. Before that they'd parted in anger and hurt. Then the first time they were alone together, she fell apart in his arms and into his bed. He must think she'd lost her mind.

She wasn't sure she hadn't.

"I know we have to talk," she said, refusing to meet his eyes. "But not now, please." She was too vulnerable, her nerves rubbed raw by fatigue and the temptation of his nearness. "All I can say now is that I'm very sorry about…that night. And I promise you it will never happen again."

CHAPTER THREE

"SHE'S ADORABLE, Lacy." Devon handed the sleeping infant back to her mother reluctantly. She loved holding babies.

"She looks just like Angie did at that age." Lacy settled the baby on her shoulder. "She's nursing well, too. I was a little worried. I didn't have as much milk as I needed for Angie. I had to put her on a bottle way sooner than I wanted to."

"Any problems this time?" Devon asked, putting her stethoscope and blood pressure cuff back in her tote.

"Heavens no. My milk just gushes."

"No redness or sore nipples?"

"A little," she said with a grin. "She has an excellent sucking response."

"Great. That's what I like to hear. I'll leave you some cream for the soreness. It should help." Devon stood up and reached down to touch a fingertip to the baby's silky cheek. "You did good, Lacy."

"Thanks, Devon. Maybe we'll do it again sometime."

"You're planning on having another baby?" When Devon let herself daydream about a family of her own, she always pictured herself with four children.

She was an only child and had always envied big families.

Lacy nodded. "Not right away. But Tom and Luke want a boy to even out the numbers. And I like the idea of this little angel having a sister or brother close to her own age to grow up with. I hope The Birth Place will still be operating in a couple more years."

"It will be." Devon said what Lacy expected her to, but the truth was she didn't know how long the clinic would stay in business if her grandmother retired. The other midwives were dedicated, but they couldn't be expected to shoulder the responsibility of keeping the always cash strapped clinic afloat.

That would be up to her.

If she gave up her practice and her life in Albuquerque.

That was a big *if.*

"I'll see you to the door." Lacy put her hand on the arm of her chair as if to rise.

"Stay put," Devon said, bending to pick up her bag. "I'll see myself out."

"Thanks. I'm still a little stiff." Lacy settled back into the rocker. "Tom took the kids to town to buy gifts for the new baby with their allowances. They're going to fix me a special dinner and then we're going to pick a name for the baby."

"Sounds like a wonderful evening."

She smiled down at the sleeping infant. "It will be."

Devon's heart contracted. It always happened. She didn't think she would ever grow blasé about watching a mother with her newborn at her breast. "I'll stop back in a few days. We'll fill out her birth certificate then.'' The clinic usually did two follow-up visits after a birth, more if the midwife thought it necessary.

"Thanks, Devon. Say hello to your grandmother for me."

"I will." She let herself out of the cabin into the bright sunshine of the summer morning. The sky was so blue it hurt to look at it without sunglasses, but off to the south was a ridge of dark clouds. One of the thunderstorms she'd heard predicted on the TV the night before? This one looked to be a long way off, and moving away, so it shouldn't spoil her trip to Silverton.

But first she'd stop and pay her courtesy call on Miguel's grandfather.

Daniel Elkhorn had been working as a carpenter on a remodeling project at the clinic when she was fifteen. She had been born and raised in San Francisco, but long visits to Lydia in Enchantment were the highlights of her childhood. That was how she'd first met Miguel—he'd been helping his grandfather during summer vacation. Daniel had been patient with all her questions about Navajo customs and way of life. He never once asked her if her sudden interest in his heritage had anything to do with her very obvious crush on his grandson.

She had no trouble finding the turnoff to the Elkhorn place, although it had been a long time since she'd been out this way. Daniel lived in a mobile home, white with green shutters and a steep-pitched snow roof suspended above it on wooden posts. A

small barn housed a couple of milk goats and a
chicken run. A swaybacked roan horse grazed in a
fenced pasture that would be in shade when the sun
dropped behind the ridge line. A dusty, dark-blue
pickup was parked alongside a newer dual-cab
pickup. She wasn't Daniel's only visitor, it seemed.

Sitting in plastic lawn chairs beneath a brush arbor
was Daniel and a plump woman in traditional Navajo
dress—long-sleeved blouse and long, pleated cotton
skirt with a woven belt. Her hair, gathered into a
heavy knot at the back of her head, was black, barely
streaked with gray. Her jewelry was silver and turquoise. Devon recognized her as Elena Eiden, Miguel's mother. She was holding a spindle, spinning
yarn from a pile of sheep's wool in her lap.

Elena put down her work and rose from her chair.
"Devon Grant? Is that you?" She shielded her eyes
from the sun with her hand.

"Hello, Mrs. Eiden. Yes, it's me."

"How good to see you! Miguel told me you were
back in Enchantment. I was planning to stop by the
clinic. Dad and I have been in Arizona visiting my
daughter and new grandbaby. We only returned to
town a few days ago," she explained, motioning
Devon to an empty chair. "I have pictures for Lydia.
She delivered her, you know."

"I know she'd love to see them. We all would."
Devon felt gooseflesh rise on her arms. She might
have been carrying Miguel's baby, another grandchild
for Elena, if the timing of their night together had
been different. Not for the first time she felt a tiny

pang of regret, not relief, when the thought crossed her mind.

"Father, you remember Devon Grant. She's Lydia Kane's granddaughter." She spoke in English, although Devon suspected she and her father had been speaking Navajo when she drove up.

"*Yah-ta-he,* Grandfather," she said, using the Navajo greeting he'd taught her years before.

"Welcome. It's been a long time since you came to visit and ask questions about the Diné, Devon Grant."

"Yes, it has. I don't have time to come to Enchantment often anymore."

"But now you're here to stay, aren't you?" Elena asked, resuming her spinning. She was a weaver, too, Devon remembered, though not as renowned as her sister-in-law.

"For the time being. I've taken a six-month leave of absence from my practice in Albuquerque."

Daniel let a few seconds elapse before he spoke. It was a sign of politeness among the Navajo, making sure someone was finished speaking before jumping in. "Are you here now to learn more about the Diné?" His face was impassive, but a glint of humor sparkled in his faded eyes.

"I would still like to learn from you," Devon said carefully, shying from his gaze. Obviously the man's advancing years hadn't taken a toll on his mind. He hadn't forgotten that she'd been as much interested in Miguel as about Navajo lifestyles.

"You have followed the Navajo way in honoring

your grandmother's wish that you return to Enchantment.''

"I will certainly stay until my grandmother is fully recovered from her heart attack.''

"How is Lydia?'' Elena asked.

"She's regaining strength and is impatient to be back delivering babies full-time.''

"I heard you went out to the reservation to help Ophelia Pedroza. Not many whites will make that drive for any reason.''

This time Devon had no trouble meeting the old man's gaze. "She needed me.''

"Miguel told me the baby was breech. That you had to take Ophelia to The Birth Place to deliver.''

Devon felt the familiar need to explain her actions and fought it down. The silence stretched out a little longer than good manners dictated. "It was a difficult birth. I'm not my grandmother. I don't have her experience and expertise. For Ophelia's sake and the baby's, I felt they should be brought to the center.''

The two Navajos nodded acceptance of her explanation. Daniel changed the subject. "What brings you this far up the mountain? You didn't come all this way just to say hello to an old man like me.''

"Well, not exactly,'' Devon responded, smiling. "I'm also going to drive on up to Silverton. I haven't been there in years. I used to love to go there.''

"Not a good place to go,'' Daniel said bluntly.

"He's right, I'm afraid,'' Elena said. "Dad's had stuff stolen and whoever's doing it could be hiding out there.''

"Miguel mentioned it.'' Devon wished she'd kept

her mouth shut when she saw the flicker of interest in Elena's face.

"Someone's been in my chicken coop," Daniel elaborated. "Couple nights ago they took off with a hen. It's probably just kids, but if they go after my goats, I'll shoot them."

"You will not," Elena said firmly. "You'll call Miguel. And then you'll call Dennis and me and we'll come and get you, and you can stay at our place until they catch the thief."

"I'll stay here." Daniel's tone left no room for argument.

Elena's lips tightened into a straight line, but she said no more, concentrating on tugging a strand of wool from the bundle of fleece on her lap.

"I'm only going to stay there a little while," Devon assured them. "I just want to see if the place has changed."

"There are ghosts there," Daniel said. It was Navajo custom not to mention the names of the dead in case their malevolent ghosts were nearby. But Devon knew he was talking about Teague Ellis. Teague had been Enchantment's bad boy a generation ago. He'd died in the Silverton mine before Devon was born, his body not found until years later.

"I'm not planning on going into the mine," she said, rising from her chair.

"It's still not a safe place to be right now," Elena said. "Ghost or no ghost."

"I'll be careful." Devon turned to Daniel. "It's so good to see you, Grandfather."

"Come back again, Devon Grant. I am here most days."

Elena once more put down her spinning and followed Devon to her truck. "Thank you for stopping. My father enjoys the company. He misses my mother." Elena did not mention her mother's name in deference to her father's beliefs. Elena herself didn't follow the old ways. Her mother had been Roman Catholic and Elena had been raised in that faith. The heavy silver cross she wore around her neck was proof of that.

"I'll stop by as often as I can."

"Thank you."

Devon waved a last goodbye to Miguel's grandfather, then climbed in her truck and headed up the mountain, following Silver Creek. There was only a trickle of water now. The snow melt was long over and there'd been little summer rain to keep it running free and strong.

The turnoff to Silverton was almost invisible if you didn't know where to look. But she did. She kept Silver Creek on her left and watched for the landmarks she remembered from her teens, the twisted ruin of a huge cottonwood tree on one side, and a big limestone boulder on the other. There was a sign, too, leaning and faded. If you weren't looking for it, it was hard to see. She nosed the Blazer onto the old roadway and shifted into four-wheel drive.

The Silver Jacks mine had never been large or profitable, and Silverton had flourished as a community for only twenty years or so. It didn't exist on any maps, and few tourists found their way up here. Even most of Enchantment's teenagers tended to stay away. It was too far from town to be convenient for a lovers' lane, and since the way in was the only way out, it was even more inconvenient as a place for underage teens to drink beer or smoke marijuana. The thrill wasn't worth the price of getting caught.

A mile or so past the turnoff she rounded a big outcropping of rock and saw the narrow valley that housed what was left of the town. The creek ran along one side of what had once been a street, and dilapidated wooden buildings lined the other side. Here and there one- and two-room cabins with caved-in roofs rose out of the tall grass and young aspens that had grown up around them. Above the town she could see the dark opening of the Silver Jacks mine.

Devon parked the Blazer off to one side of the track, reached behind her and pulled a small collapsible cooler from the back seat. She lifted the hatch and dug a flashlight out of her midwife's kit. She would need it if she wanted to look inside the mine entrance. She walked over to the porch of one of the derelict false-fronted buildings and sat in the shade. The sun was warm on her jean-clad legs, and she could smell the scents of dry grass and pine resin in the cool, thin air. She leaned gingerly back against the weather-beaten porch post, testing its strength.

She listened to the water dance over the stones in the creek bed, watched the sunlight filter through the branches of the cottonwoods that lined its banks and felt a measure of peace. She remembered coming here the summer she was eighteen, trying desperately to understand the dark changes that had come over Miguel when he returned from duty in Somalia. Now, more than ten years later, she understood those changes, what war and death could do to a man. But then she hadn't been wise, only desperately in love, and his withdrawal had broken her heart.

She slipped the cooler strap off her shoulder, deciding she'd eat after she explored a little, picked up the flashlight and started walking along the faint path that led to the mine entrance. She wouldn't go inside, of course—it wasn't safe—but with the beam of the flashlight she could see well into the interior. She wondered if it was still the same as it had been a dozen years ago, a mine entrance straight out of a Wild West movie, wooden supports framing a narrow, gaping hole in the ground that somewhere not too far inside, ended in a deep drop-off where Teague Ellis had died.

Devon stopped walking. A cloud had passed over the sun, darkening the little valley, reminding her that daylight ended early here even in the summer and that dangerous strangers might be close by. The sun came out again, colors regained their brightness and the birds their songs. She turned away from the creek toward the mine, letting her curiosity override her caution. The ground before the entrance was devoid of vegetation. Odd bits and pieces of rusted metal lay half buried in the stony ground. A few old barrel staves stuck up out of the dirt like the rib cages of dead animals. Anything of value, including the silver, was long gone.

Someone had put up a barrier to deter the curious from entering the mine since the last time she was

here. A screen of metal mesh, the sort used for a dog
run or a schoolyard fence, had been stretched across
the opening and secured with heavy wooden two-by-
fours nailed to the mine's supporting posts. But one
of the two-by-fours had been pulled away at the bottom corner, and the wire mesh bulged out, leaving an
opening big enough for a small person or a large animal to crawl through.

Had a coyote made the old mine its den?

Or perhaps a *Coyote* of the human kind?

Devon looked down and saw footprints leading into
the mine. She stopped moving, stopped breathing.
This would probably be a good time to turn around,
get back in her car and drive away. Then she heard
it. A sound like a dry, racking cough followed by faint
sobbing, as though a child were crying, weak and
fearful. She looked down at the footprints once more.
They were very small.

Devon refused to listen to the voice of reason that
was telling her only a fool would step foot inside that
mine with simply a flashlight to defend herself. But
she couldn't ignore a child crying. She jerked on the
wire mesh and it moved grudgingly outward, enlarg-
ing the opening enough for her to get through without
crawling on her hands and knees. She stood for a
moment, letting her eyes adjust to the darkness beyond the oblong area of sunlight just within the opening. A small flurry of movement ahead and a little to
the left attracted her attention. "Hello? Who's
there?" The crying stopped, but another bout of
coughing broke the quiet. "I won't hurt you. It's all
right. I'm here to help."

She switched on the flashlight and took several steps, almost tripping on a bundle of thin blankets spread over what appeared to be an old mattress. She looked around. The flashlight beam picked out a lawn chair by the mattress, one of the aluminum ones with plastic webbing that folded flat, in the same green-and-white pattern as the one she'd been sitting on at Daniel's place. Beside it sat a rusty camping lantern and a couple of plastic plates and foam cups. Next to those were two plastic, gallon milk jugs filled with water. A fire pit had been made in a natural depression in the mine floor.

The sniffling sound came again, followed by a hushed whisper. Devon couldn't make out the words. She thought they might be Spanish, though. "Please come out," she said in that language. "I won't hurt you." More rustling, as though someone was trying to crawl away. She narrowed her eyes. An area of darker shadows loomed on the mine wall. She moved a little more to her right and realized it was an opening to a smaller tunnel branching off the one she was in. Cool air brushed across her face and breasts. Perhaps it wasn't a tunnel, but an air shaft, maybe even the one Teague Ellis had fallen to his death in. Devon dropped to her knees and trained the flashlight on the hole.

Two sets of dark eyes stared back at her from frightened faces. They were indeed children. Girls. Sisters, probably, from the similarity of their facial features. The elder held the younger cradled in her arms. "Go away," she said in Spanish. "Leave us alone."

One look at the little girl told Devon she was the source of the coughing. She was wearing jeans and a dirty Scooby Doo T-shirt. Her face was flushed with fever, her eyes glittering with tears. Her hair, black as night, was a filthy tangle around her face. The older girl's hair was not quite as tangled, but just as dirty. She was wearing a thin, shapeless cotton dress and cheap sneakers.

And she was pregnant. Very pregnant. Even holding the smaller child close to her body couldn't hide that.

Were the children illegal aliens hiding out from the authorities as they made their way north? Were the men that had brought them here still around? She hoped not. The child coughed again and she banished thoughts of Coyotes. *"Soy una enfermera."* Devon's Spanish was not as good as she needed it to be. She switched to English. "I'm a nurse. Let me help you."

No response. Devon balanced the flashlight on a ridge of rock beside her, then hunkered down and held out her arms for the younger child. Suddenly she caught movement out of the corner of her eye and froze. Had she guessed wrong? Was the girls' Coyote still here, after all?

"Jesse," the little girl whispered.

Devon turned her head. A boy, as ragged and dirty as the girls, stood over her. He looked to be about fifteen, not yet a man, but almost. He was thin to the point of emaciation. He wore jeans and a faded red windbreaker over a ragged Dallas Cowboys T-shirt. Her little cooler was slung over his left shoulder, as were the two fleece blankets she'd left folded in the back of her truck.

"Get up," he said in English.

Devon stood, her heart beating hard. He held a length of two-by-four like a baseball bat. He could kill her with a single blow and they both knew it.

"I'm a nurse. I—"

"Get away from my sisters," he shouted. "I'll take care of them. Just leave the flashlight and go. Get out and don't come back!"

CHAPTER FOUR

DEVON HAD NOTHING to defend herself with but the flashlight, and it would be no protection against the two-by-four.

"Get out of here," the boy repeated.

"Your sister needs help. She's ill."

"I'll take care of her." He swayed on his feet.

Devon spoke with all the authority she could muster. "Sit down before you fall down." She reached out and grabbed the two-by-four from his hands. The unexpected movement and the strength of her grip surprised the boy enough that he let go, stumbling backward over the thin mattress and sitting down hard.

Devon rocked backward, too, but didn't fall. She trained her flashlight on the two girls, still huddled in the darkness of the smaller opening. "It's okay. You can come out now."

The older girl did as she was told, pulling the younger with her. Devon moved a few steps away so they could go to their brother. "Put your head between your knees if you feel faint," she told him.

"I don't feel faint," he said, sneering.

"Well, you look faint. Go on, do as I said."

"No." But the defiant word ended on a moan and he dropped his head between his upthrust knees.

The older girl lowered herself awkwardly by his side and laid her hand on his shoulder. "Jesse, are you sick, too?" She spoke in English so Devon responded in the same language.

"I think he's just hungry. When was the last time you had something to eat?"

Jesse didn't answer. The girl looked at Devon and shrugged thin shoulders. "It has been two days for my brother. Yesterday Maria and I ate the last of the chick...the food."

So that was what happened to Daniel Elkhorn's stolen chicken. "Your brother needs to eat. There's fruit and a peanut-butter sandwich in the bag on his shoulder."

"Sylvia," the child, Maria, whispered. *"Tengo hambre."*

So now she knew their names, Jesse, Sylvia and Maria.

"Quiero plátano."

"There's a banana. And grapes and an apple."

Jesse was upright once more, still pale, his mouth set in a tight line. Sylvia tugged the strap of the cooler off his arm, removed the lid and held out half the peanut-butter sandwich to him. He waved her away. "You two eat the sandwich. Just give me some water."

Sylvia bent forward to whisper in his ear, her gaze skittering over Devon before she lowered her head, and when she was done he devoured his small portion in two bites. Devon hadn't heard what she said, but had no trouble guessing she had urged him to eat to keep up his strength so that they could escape as quickly as possible.

She wasn't about to let that happen.

Maria held out her half-eaten banana. "My throat hurts." Again she spoke in Spanish, the language she was obviously most comfortable with.

"I know, sweetie. I have medicine in my car that will help her feel better." Devon directed her words to Sylvia and Jesse equally. Brother and sister glanced at each other and then Jesse nodded slowly.

"You can help her." He used both hands to lever himself up off the old mattress. Devon wondered if it, too, like the chicken and probably the lawn chair, had been stolen from Miguel's grandfather.

Devon held out her hand to the little girl.

Jesse put himself between them. "We'll all go," he said.

Devon nodded. "Okay."

She moved toward the opening of the mine shaft, half expecting to turn around at the entrance and find they'd all disappeared again. But they followed her in silence through the wire screening and down the path to her truck.

Devon lifted the hatch on the Blazer and opened the combination lock on her midwife's box. The box contained everything she needed for a delivery—oxygen, masks for the mother and baby, suction equipment, a laryngoscope to open an airway for the baby if necessary. A second smaller box held her anti-hemorrhage drugs and the equipment she needed to do the necessary newborn tests. She handed Sylvia a sack of hard candy from one of the top compartments and another bottle of apple juice.

Sylvia nearly snatched the sack from her hand but murmured, *"Gracias,"* as she did so. Devon held out her hands to Maria, showing her a bottle of Tylenol. "This will help you feel better."

Maria looked at her brother. Jesse narrowed his dark eyes but nodded permission. The little girl came forward and Devon gave her a Tylenol to swallow with the juice Sylvia handed her. Then Devon lifted the little girl onto the tailgate. She weighed next to nothing. "I'm going to listen to your lungs," Devon explained. She glanced back at Jesse. "Does she understand English?"

He nodded. "Yes. But she doesn't speak it very well yet."

"She was going to be in special English classes in first grade but—" A sharp word from Jesse cut short what Sylvia might have revealed.

Devon pretended not to notice. She'd already come to the conclusion that the children must have spent considerable time in the States, for both Jesse and Sylvia spoke with little accent. She put the tabs of her stethoscope in her ears and put the disk against Maria's chest. "Take a deep breath." The little girl pulled in air, but the breath ended in another cough. Devon moved the stethoscope to the right side and repeated the directive, then she straightened, draping the stethoscope around her neck. The little girl was congested, but not dangerously so. With rest and food she would be fine in a couple of days.

But not if she stayed in the damp and dirt of the abandoned mine.

Maria needed more than a fever reducer and a few ounces of liquid. She needed to be warm and safe. She needed to be where Devon could administer antibiotics if she needed them. "Jesse, your sister needs to be away from this place. Both of your sisters. And you need food and rest, too. Isn't there someone I can contact to come and help you?" She felt like an idiot as she spoke. Would these children be in the situation she'd found them in if there was anyone who could care for them?

"We have no one," Jesse said flatly. He looked more like an old man than a young boy. His dark eyes were sunken into his head, a faint stubble of beard shadowed his chin, and deep lines bracketed the corners of his mouth. "They sent our mother back to Mexico. She died there."

They, Devon deduced, meant the INS, *la migra.* "How did you get here?"

"We have a truck," Maria piped up. "But it's broken." She pointed in the direction of one of the ruined buildings near the mine shaft.

"*¡Silencio!*" Jesse hissed.

Maria began to sniffle and hung her head. Devon put her arms around her thin shoulders and gave her a reassuring hug.

"Just leave us some of the pills for Maria's fever and go away," the boy said, hostile once more. "We'll be fine."

"I can't do that. Maria is too ill. She could develop

pneumonia. You know what pneumonia is, don't you?''

His head came up. ''Of course I do.''

''Let me take Maria to my house and care for her.'' Devon tightened her embrace of the child. ''She needs rest and care. You all do. Come with me.''

''No. Like I said, just give us some of those pills and you'll never see us again.''

''What about Sylvia? A few pills won't help her when she has her baby.'' Devon was at a loss for any other way to break through his resistance.

Sylvia looked stricken at the mention of her pregnancy. She crossed her hands over her belly, not in the instinctive, protective contact with her unborn child that was common to women the world around, but in shame and misery. Sylvia's child was not wanted, had probably been conceived in ignorance or even fear. Had she been raped? Devon hoped with all her heart she had not. Teenage births, especially without prenatal care, could be dangerous for mother and child under the best of circumstances. If the pregnancy was a source of misery and fear compounded by neglect and malnutrition, the outcome could be tragic.

Devon made up her mind. There was no way in the world she was going to leave the ghost town without the children. But if she made any attempt to contact the clinic or Miguel, they would overhear and probably take off running. She had no doubt they'd been hiding in Silverton long enough to have staked out a number of hidey-holes. The ghost town didn't draw a lot of visitors, but it wasn't totally isolated.

To remain undetected for any length of time, they had to have been clever and resourceful.

And if she left with the children and then contacted the authorities, what would become of them? Would they be separated? Deported? Or left to the system of overworked, underfunded advocates for whom they would be just one more set of statistics when all was said and done? She made and held eye contact with Jesse's suspicious gaze. "If you come with me, I won't speak a word to anyone about the three of you." She had nothing to convince him of her sincerity but her words.

Suddenly her radio came to life. "This is Birth Place base to unit two. Devon, are you there?"

She moved around the fender of the truck to answer Trish Linden's query. In the side mirror she saw Jesse swing Maria up off the tailgate as Sylvia scooped up the sack of hard candy and the bottle of Tylenol.

She thumbed the toggle. "I'm here, Trish." She broke the connection momentarily and held out her hand. "Wait, please." Jesse had already carried his sister several yards back up the path to the mine, but Sylvia stopped at her plea. "Just for a moment."

"Devon?"

"I'm still here, Trish. What's up?" Devon hoped her voice sounded normal. Deliberately she turned her back on the three children, praying they wouldn't run.

"Are you anywhere near Silverton?"

"I'm right in the middle of it."

"That's what I wanted to know. I'm going to patch you through to Chief Eiden. He wants to talk to you.

I don't do this very often,'' Trish continued, "so if I screw up, just hang on, okay?''

Miguel couldn't have picked a worse time to try to communicate with her. A series of clicks preceded the sound of his voice. "Devon, do you read me?''

"Loud and clear.''

"I thought you were going to stay away from Silverton.''

"I didn't say that.''

"See anything odd up there?''

"Nothing out of the ordinary.'' She turned to face Jesse and his sisters. The trio stood watching her with dark and suspicious eyes. At least Jesse and Sylvia were watching her that way. Maria had laid her head on her brother's shoulder and looked half-asleep. The Tylenol was probably kicking in, reducing her fever enough to allow her to rest comfortably. It would only last a few hours and then the fever would be back, climbing and becoming dangerously high if she weakened any more from lack of food and water.

"I was going to drive up there, but there's a report of a couple of lightning strikes over near Wolf Canyon I need to check out. Don't want any fires getting out of hand around here.'' Thunder rolled down the valley and echoed in the cracks and crevices of the mountain, adding urgency to his words.

"There's no sign of anyone having been here lately.''

"Thanks, Devon. You've saved one of my guys some time, and wear and tear on the squad cars. Eiden out.''

"Did you copy all that, Devon?" It was Trish's voice again, slightly distorted by background static.

"I got it all, thanks, Trish."

"Thank goodness. I never quite know whether I'm doing it right," Trish fussed. "I just wanted to tell you not to hurry back if you're enjoying yourself. Your two-o'clock called and said her car has a dead battery. I rescheduled her for tomorrow."

"Thanks, Trish. I'll see you at three. Devon clear." She released the toggle and put the radio receiver back in its clip on her visor.

"She called that guy you were talking to 'Chief'," Jesse said. "Does that mean he's an Indian, not a cop?" His lip curled in a sneer. He tightened his arm around Maria. Sylvia began inching away again, moving farther up the path.

"He's both actually," Devon said.

"You lied to him about us."

She nodded. "Yes, I did."

"Why'd you do that?"

Why *had* she done that? She hadn't wanted to lie to Miguel. She wasn't a deceitful person, and she valued honesty in others and in herself. But she didn't regret her action. "I gave you my word," she said.

Jesse held her gaze a few moments longer, then nodded. "We'll go with you."

DEVON RESTED HER HEAD against the glass of her bedroom window. It was very late, long after midnight. She was tired, but she couldn't sleep. She looked down the mountain, noticing for the first time that if the branches of the trees outside her window moved just right, she could see a gleam of light from the direction of Miguel's house. Why hadn't she noticed that before?

He was up late, too, it seemed. Probably because he'd been on patrol around the country looking for signs of wildfire started by the thunderstorms that had rumbled through the valley, producing sound and fury, but not much rain.

She straightened and walked out into the main living area of the cabin. The room was small, but the soaring ceiling gave the illusion of space. Adjacent to her bedroom was a bathroom with both a shower and a tub and a stacked washer and dryer. She could hear the dryer humming away now. She might as well see if the load of towels was dry. She couldn't sleep, anyway.

Next to the bathroom was an eat-in kitchen. She'd stopped by both the grocery and the minimart to stock up on food for the children. She hadn't wanted to arouse suspicion where she usually shopped by buying too much food. The clerk would wonder why a woman who lived alone and ate Lean Cuisine more evenings than not would buy two gallons of milk, two dozen eggs and three loaves of bread. Her refrigerator was full for the first time since she'd moved into the place.

The dryer buzzed and she hurried to silence it. Above her, in the loft, the three children were sleeping, Jesse on an air mattress on the floor, the girls in the sleeper sofa beneath the window. After she'd broken radio contact with Miguel, she'd gone back to the mine with Jesse and his sisters and helped them pack their few belongings and carry them to the old stable where they'd hidden their truck.

But that was as far as she'd gotten. Jesse had refused to let her inside the badly listing building with its empty windowpanes and sagging roof, guessing correctly that she would see the license plate and use it to learn more about them.

They'd ridden into town on the floor of the Blazer, and she fed them cold cereal and scrambled eggs and toast as soon as they'd gotten safely inside her house. By the time she'd found clean clothes for the older siblings—a pair of faded scrubs for Jesse and a high-waisted denim jumper for Sylvia—and one of her smallest T-shirts for Maria, and shown Sylvia how to run her washer and dryer, she was fifteen minutes late for her three-o'clock prenatal. Lydia had not been pleased, but there was nothing she could do about it.

She returned from the clinic at seven to find the children scrubbed as clean as their clothes. Thankfully their hair had only been dirty, not infested, so a trip to Taos for lice shampoo wouldn't be necessary. She couldn't buy that at the pharmacy across from Elkhorn's Hardware any more than she could buy two gallons of milk and three dozen eggs in one stop. People would notice.

She pulled warm, clean-smelling towels out of the dryer and carried them to the couch in front of the fireplace, which she'd filled with silk ferns for the summer. She began to fold them, still thinking of the three children. Keeping them safe and fed and secret was not going to be easy. They were runaways. Probably illegal aliens. She still didn't even know their surname or their ages.

Keeping their whereabouts a secret was breaking the law. Something she had never done in her life.

But she had given her word to three desperate and scared children. And she was determined to honor it. Even if it meant she must keep on lying to everyone she knew.

CHAPTER FIVE

"I BROUGHT YOU SOME TEA." Kim Sherman smiled as she held a steaming mug out to Devon a couple of days later. "I thought you might need a boost."

"I do." Devon smiled back at her cousin, although it took some effort to get her tired facial muscles to produce the desired response.

"I won't keep you from your work." Kim stepped away from the table where she'd placed the mug. "I just wanted to let you know I talked Lydia into going home. I also checked to make sure everything's turned off, put away and locked up except the front door."

"Thanks," Devon said, taking a sip of the tea. "Especially for getting Lydia to go home. She's been here since seven this morning."

"I know. I'm sure her doctor wouldn't approve of the hours she's been working."

"Exactly. I'm glad she listened to you." She was glad, but she also felt somewhat envious of Kim's relationship with Lydia. It was so much better than her own.

"Anything I can do for you? Any billing? I have twenty minutes or so until Nolan and Sammy pick me up." Sammy was Nolan's seven-year-old niece, an energetic tomboy he'd been raising since her parents' tragic deaths. Kim eyed the pile of charts on the table. When she'd first come to work at The Birth Place, her office door had always been firmly closed. But since she'd fallen in love with Nolan McKinnon and been accepted as Lydia's granddaughter, she no longer barricaded herself behind a closed door.

She had also abandoned the well-worn gray cardigan, buttoned to the throat, that she had worn so often in the past. Her clothes were still conservative and businesslike, but the colors were softer, brighter. She'd exchanged her dark-rimmed glasses for contacts, and now Devon saw her own gray eyes staring back at her.

Her eyes, and Lydia's.

"I'm almost ready to call it a day, too. I'm finishing my report of Jenna Harrison's delivery." Devon was working in the all-purpose area of the clinic that served as a storage area and break room. She didn't have an office of her own, and had, in fact, resisted broaching the subject. For once she did, it would mean that she was staying at The Birth Place for good. Admitting that her life, such as it was, and her practice in Albuquerque were a thing of the past.

She hadn't thought much of either in the past few days, she realized.

Kim moved closer, her arms crossed beneath her breasts. "Mother and baby are doing fine, I hope."

Devon didn't have any problem finding her smile this time. "They are." Then the smile disappeared. "It was touch-and-go there for a while."

"You mean she was in danger?" The death of No-

Ian McKinnon's sister and her baby seven months earlier, although unavoidable, had weighed heavily on the staff and, in Devon's opinion, had been a contributing factor in Lydia's heart attack. Devon bent her head to her notes for a moment before looking up at her cousin again. "Not life-threatening. But I was afraid we would have to transfer her to Arroyo for a C-section."

"But you didn't have to transfer her. And I'm sure she thinks her son is worth it."

"I'm sure she does." Lydia had never doubted that Jenna, an older, first-time mother, could complete the labor and delivery without intervention. Devon had not been as serenely confident as Lydia. She never was. When Jenna's progress stalled at eight centimeters and remained there for several hours, Devon wanted to urge her grandmother to move Jenna to the hospital.

But she'd kept her mouth shut, and now she was glad. Lydia had suggested one more session in the huge Jacuzzi that half filled the birthing suite. The warm water and subsequent reduction in pressure on Jenna's lower body had done the trick. Her contractions once more became productive and less than an hour later, her squalling, red-faced and utterly beautiful little boy had made his entrance into the world.

Jenna and her son had remained under the watchful eye of the midwives the rest of the day. Devon had just finished helping her strap her son's carrier into the safety seat of the Harrisons' minivan for the trip home.

"Devon, may I ask you a favor?" Kim sounded oddly hesitant.

Kim had never asked Devon for a favor before, other than the honor of being her maid of honor. Devon put down her pen and gave her cousin her full attention. "Of course," she said.

"I...I'd like to invite someone to the rehearsal dinner if you don't mind. Two people actually."

"Oh, Kim. Did we forget someone? I'm sorry. I don't know how this happened."

Kim waved off Devon's attempted apology. "No, no. It's my foster parents. I...I lost contact with them years ago when they had to move out of the state. Nolan tracked them down for me. And, well, we've been corresponding. I haven't told anyone else about them yet. Even Grand—even Lydia. I wanted to make sure they were interested in seeing me again." For a moment the lost little girl her cousin had been looked out from Kim's eyes. But the ghost was there for only a moment and then it disappeared. "They'll be traveling through the area, and they want to meet Nolan and Sammy. I've invited them to the wedding, but I'm sure they'll understand if—"

"Don't be ridiculous. Of course they're more than welcome."

Devon half rose from her chair and Kim took a small involuntary step backward, then smiled. "No hugging. You midwives are great ones for hugging."

"We are, aren't we. No hugs until the wedding, I promise." Devon felt laughter bubble up, and then a quick tingle of anticipation as she contemplated discussing the addition to the party with Miguel. She hadn't seen him or spoken to him since she'd spirited the runaway children into her home, and the strength of her sudden longing to remedy that situation caught her by surprise. "I think it's wonderful you've found your foster parents again. Do you think they'll want the chicken or the fish?"

THE BIRTHING CENTER appeared deserted as Miguel turned into the parking lot. He eased the big SUV around to the back and noticed Devon's Blazer still in her space. The high-altitude twilight was fading fast, taking the heat of the summer day with it. The sky was clear as blue glass, no sign of clouds anywhere. The leaves on the aspens beyond the parking area were curled on the edges from lack of moisture. The grass beneath his feet felt brittle when he stepped on it. It was only a matter of time before some fool threw a lighted cigarette out of the window of his truck, or a careless hiker started an illegal campfire, and they would be staring a wildfire in the face. And with almost two years of drought behind them, it would probably be a hell of a fire when it got going.

Devon had left a message on his answering machine about the party. Something about two more guests. Probably Kim's foster parents. Nolan had told him he'd tracked them down a couple of months ago. He didn't know much about Kim's childhood, but it must have been tough on her as a kid, her mother dying when she was small, being shunted from one foster home to another. He'd grown up in an intact family, even if his dad did drink too much, and he had aunts and uncles and cousins all over the county, as well as in Ohio. Family was important to the Navajo. In fact, one of the worst things his grandfather could think of to say about someone was that they "acted as if they didn't have a family." But Kim had had no one to look out for her growing up. No wonder she sported as much emotional armor as an armadillo.

He checked the back door of the clinic. It was locked. He left his vehicle where it was and walked around the side of the building. Quietly he turned the handle on the front door. It opened easily and he stepped inside. No one was at the reception desk, but a light came from the records room behind it, and in the break room across the hall.

A movement from the far corner of the waiting room caught his attention. It was Devon, sitting crosslegged on the floor in the children's play area. At her back two big plastic toy boxes were piled full of stuffed animals and pull toys. A wooden table was covered with puzzles and coloring books. A bookcase under the window held what seemed to Miguel to be hundreds of picture books. Devon had a pile of them in her lap, and a couple of dozen more heaped around her.

He stayed where he was in the shadow of the deeply recessed door and let himself enjoy the sight of her. Her hair was caught up in a twist on top of her head, but it was so fine that strands of it floated around her neck and shoulders, catching the lamplight like spun gold. He could see the rise and fall of her breasts beneath the thin cotton of her scrubs. They were blue today, and over the top she wore a printed lab coat covered with fat, naked babies frolicking on fluffy pink clouds.

He suspected that wearing hospital scrubs and a lab coat, even one with fat naked babies on it, was an act of rebellion for Devon. All the other midwives followed Lydia's lead, opting for the earth-mother look—peasant skirts or jeans, sandals or clogs. Not Devon. She was a medical professional with her own style, and she wasn't about to give it up, no matter how often she butted heads with her formidable grandmother.

She raised her hand to cup the back of her neck and arched her back, as though to ease tired muscles. She'd arched her back that way when she'd climaxed that night in his bed, her body tightening around him and spurring him on to his own release. He felt a surge of blood to his groin and decided he'd better make his presence known before his imagination produced a result that would be hard to ignore and damned near impossible to hide from Devon.

He closed the door behind him with enough force that she looked up in alarm, clutching the picture books to her chest. "Miguel! Don't sneak up on me like that."

"I didn't sneak up on you. I moved into an unknown situation with due caution. No telling what kind of suspicious character might be hanging around in here."

"I'm the only one here," she said, and he could tell she was trying hard not to respond to his teasing.

"That's what I mean. Suspicious character." He crossed the tile floor and dropped to his haunches beside her. "Stealing books from the kiddies? I might have to cuff you and haul you down to the station for that."

A tiny frown wrinkled her forehead. "I'm not stealing. I…I thought I'd sort through a few of the worn ones and get some replacements the next time I'm in Taos." She still clutched the books to her chest as though she thought he might take them away from her.

He tossed his hat onto a nearby chair, then levered himself into a sitting position, with one knee drawn up for his forearm to rest on and the other leg stretched out alongside her. "Can't the books wait for another day?" He waggled his index finger at the overflowing bookcase. "There are more books than a dozen kids could read in a week on those shelves."

She wouldn't quite meet his eyes. "People bring them in. They donate them. There are duplicates." She did look tired. Faint circles were smudged under her eyes, and lines bracketed the corners of her mouth. She'd been at the center since five in the morning. He'd heard her truck go by as he was getting in the shower. It was after seven at night now. He should quit teasing her. He changed the subject. "I got your message on my voice mail. What's up?"

She brightened immediately and her smile slammed into his heart. If he hadn't already been sitting on the floor, he would have had to find a chair. "Kim's found her foster parents. Or at least Nolan has."

"That's great. Nolan told me a couple of months ago he was going to try and contact them, but he didn't have much to go on. He said Kim hadn't heard from them for at least fifteen years.''

"She asked if she could invite them to the rehearsal dinner. Of course, I said she could. I hope you don't mind that I did it without consulting you.''

"Did you find out if they want the chicken or the fish?''

"Miguel.'' She slapped playfully at his hand. It was the first time she'd touched him since the night they'd spent in his bed, and he found that it challenged his self-control as much as or more than her beautiful smile.

"Actually, I did ask her which they might prefer. It was a stupid question, because she hasn't seen them or spoken to them since she was a little girl.''

"But I bet she had an opinion, anyway.''

She grinned. "Yes, she did. She thought we should play it safe and go with the chicken.''

"Two more chicken dinners, it is.''

"You don't mind that I okayed their coming without consulting you?''

"I think I've just been insulted.''

Her eyes widened and her grin vanished. "I didn't mean—''

He had to be careful how much he teased her. She was still very touchy about her growing relationship with her cousin. "This is Kim and Nolan's party. I'm happy she's found the couple that meant so much to her after her mother died. You did exactly what I would have done.'' He leaned forward and was saddened that she drew back, even if it was only a fraction of an inch. "Surely you know me better than that after all these years, don't you, Devon?'' He hadn't meant to take the conversation into personal territory, but the words had refused to stay unspoken.

''I don't know you at all,'' she whispered, and pulled her lower lip between her teeth as though she, too, wished the words unspoken. She put a hand on the floor to push herself to her feet.

He stopped her by wrapping his fingers around her forearm, holding her beside him. ''Devon, have you given any thought to why you ended up in my bed that night?''

She drew in her breath sharply, then said, ''Shock. Confusion. Sleep deprivation. I was a little out of my mind, I think.''

''Maybe,'' he agreed with a small smile. Part of him had wanted her to say it was because she was still madly, passionately in love with him. ''I think we both were.''

''I didn't know if my grandmother was going to live or die. I needed comfort. You offered me that.''

''Devon, it went past the comfort stage five minutes after we left the hospital.'' The words came out as a kind of growl and her eyes widened a little.

''I told you, it was an aberration. We were both a little crazy that night.''

Devon had been out of his life for a decade. But the moment she'd walked back into it, he was the same moonstruck teenager he'd been a dozen years before. There was something he had to know. Something he wasn't sure she herself knew yet. ''Are you planning on staying in Enchantment?''

''I haven't made up my mind. Lydia and I have

such differing styles, there are days when we can't say two words to each other without getting into an argument.'' She dropped her head and began tracing circles on the cover of one of the picture books. ''My practice and my life are in Albuquerque.''

''Does that life include a man?''

Her head came up. ''Do you think I would have slept with you if there was?''

''You might have if you were as frightened and lonely as you said you were.'' The question had been nagging at him over the past weeks. He didn't want to think about another man making love to her. She was his. She had been since she was sixteen and she had let him make love to her for the first time—the first time for both of them, although he'd never told her that, either. Damn, he *was* losing his mind. He didn't have a single claim on her. He'd never told her he loved her. Instead, sore in heart and soul when he returned from the mess in Somalia, he'd pushed her away so hard she'd never come back.

Maybe if he'd been older, more mature, he could have handled it better. But he'd been almost as young and green as she was, idealistic and filled with foolish notions of romance and happily-ever-after. He'd expected her to know, without his saying a word, how troubled and disillusioned he was. How the things he'd done or couldn't do had tarnished his soul. He'd counted on her, and the love he felt for her but had never been able to express, to somehow magically heal him. Of course it hadn't. So he'd pushed her away and curled into himself in misery. And broken her heart.

He should tell her now about the hurt and horror of that godawful place and what it had done to the naive, gung-ho kid he'd been, how it had torn him up inside for more years than he wanted to remember. Maybe then they could get past it, move on to the beginning of a future together. But it didn't seem right to talk of death and destruction in this place of hope and beginnings.

She waited so long to respond to his comment that he thought she wasn't going to. At last she said, "There was someone, but we broke up months ago. At Christmastime."

She had been in Enchantment for Christmas. It had been the first he'd seen of her in a long time when, decked out in his dress blues, he come by to retrieve the carton of toys the center was donating to Toys for Tots. She'd said hello, that it was good to see him. And her smile had rocked his world just as it had since the first day he'd seen her, a gawky, golden-haired, horse-mad fifteen-year-old. He'd managed some kind of reply and thanked his lucky stars he'd been in uniform. It put a little needed steel in his backbone.

"What was he?" he asked now. "Doctor? Lawyer? Indian chief?"

"You're the only Indian chief I know. He was a doctor. Third-year cardiology resident."

"Your idea or his to call it quits?"

She sighed. "Mine. He was a great guy, but not the man I wanted to spend the rest of my life with." Who was the man she wanted to spend the rest of her life with? A small-town cop with a few rough edges?

He had to ask one more question. "Did you love him?"

"No," she said quietly. "And no more questions from you."

"Okay, it's your turn. Ask away." He found himself holding his breath. Would she ask why he'd broken her heart so long ago? Would she give him the chance to explain?

She didn't bring up the past. "No need to. Your life's an open book in this town."

He gave an exaggerated groan, hiding his disappointment. "Hell, I should have known that."

"Your mother wants more grandkids, so she's hoping you'll find the right girl to marry soon. I heard that from Trish Linden. And rumor over the tea mugs has it Theresa Quiroga left town after you broke her heart."

"Whoa! That's not true. She took a job with the state highway patrol. More money. Great benefits." Theresa Quiroga had been the night dispatcher at the station. He'd dated her a few times, but it hadn't gone anywhere. He didn't sleep with women he worked with, and she'd accepted that. And to tell the truth he hadn't been much interested in sleeping with her once he heard that Devon was moving back to town.

"And at the moment you're not dating anyone."

"Okay, okay. That's what I get for living in the same town for my whole life." He looked down. The tanned skin of his arm was dark as mahogany against the pale gold of hers.

She was quiet for a moment and he felt the muscles

tense under his fingers. "Miguel, I have to lock up now."

"Sure." He rose to his feet, bringing her with him. "Have you eaten? How about joining me for a sandwich at the Sunflower Café?"

"Jenna Harrison's husband ordered in pizza and tacos for everyone. I couldn't eat another bite."

Miguel bent down, scooped up the picture books and piled them in her arms. He waited, hat in hand, while she turned off the lights and locked the front door. "Not even a cup of coffee?" he asked as they walked around the building to where their vehicles were parked.

"I can't. I have to wash my hair." She smiled at the skepticism he couldn't keep from showing on his face. "Truly. Another time—"

"Sunday night, then."

"What?"

"Dinner. Sunday night. I have to work the rest of the weekend, but I'm off duty that night. We'll go up to Angel's Gate and order the salmon and chicken and a bottle of wine. Sort of a test case for the party."

"I—"

"Don't say no, Devon. We won't end up in bed again. Hell, I promise I won't even ask for a goodnight kiss."

"I wasn't going to say no. And I'm not afraid of ending up in bed with you—I've told you that before. I'd like to have dinner with you, but just so you know, Lydia has two mothers who are due any day. I may have a delivery to attend."

He traced a fingertip over one of the fat babies

adorning her lab coat just above the swell of her breast. He heard her quick little intake of breath and had to swallow hard before he could trust his own voice. She'd agreed to the date. He just had to go on playing it cool and hands off. Thank God he hadn't given in to the impulse to pour his heart out a while ago. She wasn't ready for that. Not yet. "If the stork decides to make a deposit, I'll take a rain check. Otherwise I'll pick you up at seven."

CHAPTER SIX

As SHE DROVE to her cabin, Devon's thoughts were full of her coming date with Miguel. *Date.* Two people coming together for the purpose of romance. She shouldn't think of it that way. Why had she agreed to it? A date with him was a dangerous undertaking. No matter how many times she told herself, told him, they wouldn't fall into bed together again, she knew she was only stirring the air with her words.

The entire time they'd been sitting on the floor of the play area like children, her mind had been filled with anything but childish thoughts. The memory of his arms around her, the way his body had pressed her to the bed, filled her so completely, had made her heart pound so she feared he'd hear it. She'd felt as thrilled as she had at fifteen when the handsome young Navajo had asked her out to a movie.

But she wasn't that shy and infatuated young girl anymore. And he wasn't the same sexy jock she'd given her virginity to in the back of his truck. But neither was he the angry, bitter young man whose withdrawal had broken her heart two years later.

Miguel had matured into the man she'd always envisioned he would become. The one who'd comforted her and held her that night several weeks ago when she'd been so alone and afraid. But care and comfort had quickly turned to heat and passion and swept away all logical behavior. Still, tonight they'd been alone and the same madness could have overtaken them but hadn't. They'd talked and flirted a little and she'd agreed to his dinner invitation, nothing more. So perhaps she was overestimating the danger, if not the attraction, and Sunday evening would just be an enjoyable dinner with an old friend.

The thought was oddly disquieting, and disappointing.

The cabin was quiet when she walked in minutes later, her arms laden with picture books. Faint light came from the loft. The children would be up there, watching the small TV the owner had installed in the multipurpose space. But they could also be gone, disappeared out of her life as quickly as they'd entered it. Devon half expected the possibility each time she left the house.

"Maria," she called. "I brought you some new picture books to read." For a few more moments, the silence prevailed, then Maria's elfin face appeared over the railing of the balcony.

"*Hola,*" she said, smiling. "Do they have lots of pictures?" As she had grown stronger, she spoke in English more often.

"Lots of pictures. And I brought you a coloring book and crayons, too."

A moment later she came clattering excitedly down the narrow stairway. She was wearing new jeans and a SpongeBob SquarePants T-shirt. Her night-black hair was pulled back from her face by sparkly little clips Devon had picked up at the drugstore.

All three of the children had new clothes, or almost-new clothes. Devon had made a trip to Taos to a couple of second-hand clothing stores and picked up jeans and shorts and shirts for Jesse and Maria, and a granny dress for Sylvia. She'd even found a pair of maternity shorts, and along with a couple of oversize T-shirts, the teen would have an adequate, if limited, wardrobe for the rest of her pregnancy. Devon had checked shoe sizes before her shopping trip, so she'd also purchased sale-priced running shoes and underwear.

Maria jumped off the bottom stair and skipped over to Devon. She held out her hands for the picture books and crayons. *"Mil gracias,"* she said, her eyes shining.

"You're welcome. Have you eaten?" It was past eight now. Devon's stomach was growling.

"Sylvia made us spaghetti. It was good."

"I saved some for you," Sylvia said, leaning over the loft railing. "I hope you like it."

"Thank you, I'm sure I will." To Maria she said, "Would you like to take your books into the kitchen and keep me company while I eat?"

Sylvia chose to descend the steep stairs, too, and her movements were cumbersome and slow. The pink T-shirt she wore over the maternity shorts complemented her olive skin and dark hair. The baby was still high beneath her slight breasts, leading Devon to guess she might be as much as a month from term.

"Is Jesse watching TV?" Devon asked her, depositing her shoulder bag and the sack that held Maria's coloring book and crayons on the round oak table opposite the refrigerator.

"He's sleeping."

"He's always sleeping," Maria seconded. Jesse had been more emaciated and exhausted than his sisters. He had done all of the scavenging and most of the chores involved in their nomadic life. That much Devon had learned from Sylvia, and from Maria's much less circumspect comments. She also suspected he'd shorted himself on the meager meals they'd had.

"He's still tired from everything you've been through. He'll catch up on his sleep in another couple of days and be fine." Devon spoke with confidence. Already his thin face seemed a little fuller and his body more robust.

"I'm tired of sleeping." Maria chose a blue crayon and started coloring a picture of vaguely tropical looking fish swimming among fanciful seaweed and coral. The change in Maria's physical condition was even more pronounced than Jesse's. Over the past few days, her fever had abated and the congestion in her lungs had cleared up, leaving her bright eyed and smiling.

Sylvia insisted on serving the spaghetti and she placed a plate of it in front of Devon. The sauce smelled delicious. Devon wound the pasta around her fork and took a bite. It tasted as good as it looked, spicy and rich with a hint of heat. "This is wonderful. I can't believe it came from a jar," she said, taking another bite.

Sylvia looked pleased. "I added a few things. I

found some spices in the cupboard. I hope you don't mind.''

''Of course I don't mind.''

''My mother taught me how to cook,'' Sylvia said quietly when Devon was finished.

''She must be a very good cook. And a good teacher.''

''She was,'' Sylvia whispered, and tears filled her huge dark eyes.

Suddenly the spaghetti lay heavy in her stomach. She picked up her plate and took it to the sink, motioning Sylvia to come with her. The kitchen was small and they couldn't move very far from Maria at the table, so Devon kept her voice low. ''Are you certain your mother is dead?''

''Yes. My cousin in Phoenix had a letter from my grandmother in Mexico.'' Sylvia wiped away a tear. ''And now we've heard nothing more for almost a year. My grandmother was very old. I think she's dead, too.''

Sylvia begun running water in the sink. She added a squirt of dishwashing soap. Her hand was trembling. Devon reached out and covered it with her own. ''How long were you living with your cousin?''

''Since my mother was deported.'' Sylvia tugged her hand from beneath Devon's, rejecting the sympathy, and began washing dishes.

''How did that happen?'' Devon backed off a step, giving the girl the space she needed, then picked up the dish towel and dried the plate Sylvia had just placed in the rack.

''One of the other cooks at the restaurant where

she worked turned her in. They were jealous of how good a cook she was.''

''How was it that you and Jesse and Maria weren't sent back with her?''

''We were away. Visiting my cousin in Phoenix. We stayed there. My mother thought she would be able to get back into the country right away, but it didn't happen. She got caught twice and sent back. Then she wrote that she was sick, but not to worry. She would be better soon. And then…then the letters stopped coming.''

''And things weren't going too well with your cousin?''

''Jesse didn't like staying there. The school wasn't good. Before he took honors classes and was always on the dean's list. In Phoenix there were gangs and drugs. I was scared for Maria to go to that school.''

''And what about you?''

''I like school, but I'm not as good at math or science as Jesse. I like history. And I love to read. So does Maria. Or she will when she learns how.'' A frown dragged down the corners of her mouth. ''I don't know how we'll be able to send her to school when it starts in September. Not unless we can find—'' She stopped abruptly and began wiping up the cupboard.

Devon put her hand on the girl's thin shoulder, and this time it wasn't shrugged off. She turned her gently to face her. ''Who are you looking for, Sylvia?''

''My aunt. My father's sister. She…'' Sylvia glanced toward the doorway as though she was uncertain whether to confide in Devon without her brother's permission. "We think she works at a ski place around here. We weren't sure of the name, though. Angel something. That's all."

"Angel's Gate?" Devon asked.

Sylvia lifted her hands. "We don't know. My cousin's wife thought maybe it was Angel Fire, so we went there first. She wasn't there, and the people at the resort called the police because they didn't believe I was eighteen and thought we shouldn't be on our own. We had to leave in a hurry. But before that happened, someone told us about Angel's Gate here." She glanced in Maria's direction. The little girl paid them no attention, her tongue stuck in her cheek as she searched for just the right-colored crayon.

"So did you go there?"

"No." Sylvia wiped very hard at the granite countertop, moving the cloth in ever-widening circles. "We got lost. The truck started smoking and making rattling noises. Then we saw the sign to Silverton. We thought it might be a real town." Memories darkened her eyes to obsidian. "I hated that place. I didn't want to stay there, but we couldn't get the truck started again."

"How long were you camping out in the mine?"

Sylvia shuddered. "Two weeks. I don't want to go back."

"You don't have to. I'm going to Angel's Gate Sunday evening," Devon said. "I'll make inquiries about your aunt."

"You'll do that for us?"

"Yes." Devon had made her decision to hide the

children days ago, and this was only the next logical step. "What's her name?"

"Sylvia, no. Enough talk." Jesse was standing in the kitchen doorway, hair rumpled, a shadow of beard darkening his chin. Devon had bought him a razor and shaving cream on her trip to Taos, but she suspected he thought the beard made him look older and so far he hadn't shaved.

"Jesse. Come see my picture," Maria said, holding up the picture book. *"¿Es muy linda, no?"*

"Yeah, it's real good." He smiled at his little sister and crossed the small kitchen to lean over her chair and take a closer look. Around Devon, Jesse projected street-smart toughness, but with Maria he gave himself away, and Devon could see glimpses of the happy boy he must once have been.

"I'm hungry. I want something to eat." Maria gave her brother a beatific smile, then looked over to shower its brightness on Devon and Sylvia. The happiness in that one smile banished the doubts tormenting Devon. She was doing the right thing in hiding the children. It would all work out. She would see to it.

"You just finished dinner," Sylvia said. She folded the dishcloth and hung it over the edge of the sink.

"Deseo uvas," Maria pointed to the bowl of fruit Devon had kept on the table since they arrived.

"Of course you may have some grapes," Devon said. "Why don't you take them upstairs to eat while you watch TV? I need to talk to your brother and sister, and it's really boring stuff." She wasn't about to let Jesse and Sylvia change the subject yet again.

She needed to learn more about their situation. And of even greater importance to learn were the particulars of Sylvia's pregnancy. But at the moment that required more trust on the teen's part than she'd yet been willing to give Devon.

"SpongeBob," Maria said, pointing to her T-shirt as she gathered up her coloring book and crayons. "Can I, Jesse?"

"Sure, but don't turn it up too loud." When she looked confused at his words, he put his finger to his lips. *"Silencio."*

When Maria disappeared up the stairs to the loft, Jesse faced Devon, his arms crossed over his chest and his jaw thrust forward. "What do you want to talk about?"

"I want to talk about what we're going to do about the situation you three are in."

"What can *you* do to help?" Jesse asked with a sneer.

"She's already helped us so much," Sylvia interrupted. "She's fed us and given Maria medicine to make her well and bought us these clothes."

"All right," Jesse said, "she's helped us. But what else do you think you can do?"

"I don't know," Devon said truthfully, "yet. But unless you tell me everything, it's a sure bet whatever I try to do for you won't be enough."

"Our parents are dead. We don't have green cards. We're on the run from my cousin who let his jerk boss's son get my sister pregnant. What else do you need to know?"

"Kyle wasn't a jerk. He was good to me."

"He's a jerk. He was never going to marry you. His rich grandfather won't pay his way into Harvard if he's dragging an illegal Mexican girlfriend and little brown baby along with him."

"He said he loved me," Sylvia whispered. Huge tears welled up in her eyes and ran down her cheeks. "He promised we'd always be together."

Jesse softened at the sight of his sister's tears. "He didn't mean it. That's why he's a jerk. He ran off to Los Angeles to his grandfather as soon as he heard you were pregnant. I'm only telling it like it is, Sylvia."

"I know." The hurt and humiliation in the words touched Devon's heart.

"This Kyle whoever-he-is and Sylvia may be too young to think about getting married," Devon said. "But he must be made to accept responsibility for the baby if he's the father." She'd like to get her hands on the spoiled foolish boy that had fathered Sylvia's baby and give him a piece of her mind.

"Yeah. Right." Jesse didn't bother to hide his scorn. "How long do you think my sister would be allowed to stay here if she goes after him for money?"

"I don't know," Devon said.

He gave a disgusted snort and snapped his fingers. "About that long."

Sylvia's head came up. "She's only trying to help, Jesse." Tears continued to stream down her cheeks. "I'm scared, Jesse. I don't know anything about babies." She covered her face with her hands and began to sob harder. Devon wrapped her arm around the girl's shoulders.

"It's all right, Sylvia. I'll help you have the baby. Everything will be all right." She gave her a little squeeze. "I'm very good at delivering babies. It's what I do, you know."

Sylvia nodded and her sobs diminished slightly.

Jesse's hands clenched into fists on the back of the chair, but when he spoke again, it was without anger. "She can't get us green cards, Sylvia. She can't keep Family Services from breaking us up, notifying *la migra,* sending me and you back to Mexico. Taking Maria away from us."

"Maybe I can't," Devon admitted, "but I'm damn well going to try."

"How?"

"First of all we need to come up with a reason to explain why you're here with me. You can't stay secretly holed up in the loft. And you can't just head out on your own again."

"Why not? We got from Phoenix to Tucson to Taos on our own. We found out where Aunt Lucia's probably working. We stayed in the mine for over two weeks with no one finding us."

"And Maria got sick," Sylvia said. She'd stopped crying, but stayed within the comforting circle of Devon's arms. "If Devon hadn't found us, she could have died."

"You did the best you could," Devon said. "But now your best isn't good enough. Sylvia needs to have medical care for herself and the baby."

"And if the baby is born here, maybe they won't send us back."

Devon wanted to reassure her, but she couldn't. "I don't know what will happen, Sylvia. But I'll find out. What's most important now is getting you some medical attention. I'm going to tell everyone that your mother was my friend in Albuquerque. That you're staying with me while your cousin, your guardian, is visiting sick relatives in Mexico." The more truth she could weave into her deception, the better chance she had of it succeeding. At least for a while. Neither Miguel nor her grandmother would be easy to fool for long. She ignored the renewed uneasiness her words engendered and kept on talking. "What about your father? Could he help?"

"He's dead, too," Jesse said flatly, but without the rancor of his earlier words. "He's been dead since we were little. And Maria's father? We haven't seen him since she was a baby."

"Okay. Forget that. And you don't think your cousin—"

"No!" Jesse spat.

"He's not a good man," Sylvia agreed.

Devon could feel her trembling. Another door closed. She had no option, it seemed, but to continue with the deception she'd just hatched.

"Okay, then we'll go with my plan. I'll tell my grandmother that you'll be arriving soon. And that Sylvia is pregnant and needs care. You don't need to tell anyone anything more than what we just discussed. Understood?"

"Will the others, your friends, the cop you talked to, will they believe you?"

Devon nodded firmly. "They have no reason to believe I would lie to them."

Jesse watched her awhile longer. She gave him back look for look. "Okay. We'll stay."

"It's settled then. And now I think you had better tell me your last names, or my grandmother will know something's up the moment we walk through the clinic door."

Brother and sister exchanged a glance. "Our name is Molina," Jesse replied. "Maria's is, too. My mother said my father would not mind her having his name. He was a good man."

"And your mother's name? I...I need to know if I'm to tell my grandmother she was my friend."

"Dolores," Sylvia said softly.

"And your aunt is Lucia Molina."

"Yes."

"Have you checked the telephone book?" Devon asked.

"I checked first thing. And called information, too. She's not listed."

Devon hadn't expected it to be easy.

"Okay. Tomorrow I'll tell my grandmother that you're all coming to stay with me. Then we'll go to the clinic and introduce you to her and you can stop spending all your time in the loft watching TV." Devon was glad it was summer. She wasn't ready yet to deal with the logistics of enrolling three undocumented children in Enchantment's school system. She wasn't certain she'd be in Enchantment at summer's end herself.

"We need to go get our truck," Jesse said.

Devon shook her head. "There's no place to hide it here. You'll have to leave it where it is."

For just a moment she felt a cold wave of fear wash over her. She was building a wall around herself that grew taller with every lie she told. If she wasn't careful, it would cut her off completely from everyone she knew and loved—just the way the lies that Lydia had told about selling Hope's baby all those years ago affected their relationship to this very day. Had her grandmother felt this same fear, this aloneness? And had she ignored it as Devon intended to do?

She wasn't going to change her mind. She wasn't going to confide in another soul, not her grandmother, not Hope Reynolds, not Miguel. Especially not Miguel. She had given the children her word that she would protect them and keep them together. She was doing the right thing for them. That was all she needed to know.

CHAPTER SEVEN

"THE DOPPLER READING on Karen Fineman definitely indicates two distinct heartbeats. She's having twins," Katherine Collins, one of Lydia's longtime employees, announced to the room full of midwives. Devon's smile, like everyone else's, was genuine and spontaneous.

The staff meeting was being held after hours at the clinic. There had been no opportunity during the day. Hope was seated beside Devon on the couch. Trish Linden was behind the reception desk at her usual spot. Kim sat primly on a straight-backed chair near Lydia's, taking notes on a pad in her lap. The center's other midwife, Gina, and their nurse, Lenora, were out assisting a birth. The only man in attendance was Parker Reynolds—Hope's husband and the center's administrator. He leaned against the high counter of Trish's desk, a little apart from the women.

"I believe Lupe Skyhunter was the last," Lydia said, "and her little ones will be three come September." Lydia's memory for the births she attended was phenomenal. Devon had only been in practice three years, and already she had to consult her journal to place some of her earliest babies.

"Karen and her husband were quite surprised by

the news, although I suspected multiples might be the case on her last visit," Katherine admitted. "To make sure, I've recommended she go to Arroyo for an ultrasound test."

Heidi Brandt, Katherine's longtime partner, spoke next. "Karen's husband isn't as committed to a midwife birth as Karen is." Heidi was short and plump and, like Katherine, middle-aged. Dressed in a denim jumper and sandals, she looked like the Peace Corps volunteer she once had been.

"I will probably also recommend Karen make an appointment with Dr. Ochoa," Katherine went on. "This is her third pregnancy and she's excited about a midwife birth, but she's also very nervous. It's not a good combination, especially with the possibility of complications that always arise in a multiple. I've promised to be there for her when her time comes, but this is one case I'm afraid I'm going to have to turn over to the medicos." She leaned back in the worn leather armchair where she'd been sitting with Heidi perched on the arm. She wasn't smiling anymore. None of the midwives liked to turn their patients over to an OB/GYN, even Dr. Ochoa, who had more respect for their profession than many doctors.

"That is, of course, your privilege," Lydia said with a sideways look at Devon. If Devon applied for privileges at Arroyo County Hospital and they were granted, she could oversee Karen's case. But Devon had made no effort to formalize her association with the hospital administration beyond a courtesy meeting with Dr. Ochoa.

"That brings us to our last two items of business,"

Kim said before the silence grew uncomfortable. "Trish has the monthly totals for office visits and deliveries and then I have some new business to discuss."

"Thanks, Kim," Trish said. "First, I've updated the clinic Web site this week, and if I do say so myself it's looking pretty good. Check it out when you get a free minute or two."

"I've already been there," Heidi sang out. "It looks great and you spelled everyone's name correctly." Applause and laughter greeted her endorsement.

"Thank you," Trish said, looking pleased. "Okay. Where was I? Oh, yes. Monthly statistics. We've logged one hundred forty-six office visits, including prenatal, postnatal, reproductive health visits and childbirth classes. Devon has agreed to take over Joanna Carson's New Mother classes, since Dr. Jo wants to slow down a little what with the baby coming and all. Your next class begins two weeks from Wednesday, Devon. We have seven mothers-to-be signed up."

"Thanks, Trish. I'm looking forward to it."

"We referred eleven patients to Celia Brice for counseling or family guidance. We've got eleven births to report so far, twelve when Gina and Lenora get back, with six patients due in the next ten days. Four boys and seven girls. Two have been home births. Nine delivered here at the clinic. We've been busy, ladies."

"Amen, to that," Katherine intoned.

"Just a reminder that the state inspectors are scheduled for sometime next month, so please all of you make sure your charting is up-to-date.'' She swiveled in her chair to check out the calendar on the wall behind her. ''The next full moon is Tuesday, so everyone have a nice quiet weekend and be ready for the fun and games.'' More laughter greeted her words. An age-old tenet of midwifery, and indeed every maternity ward Devon had ever been in, held with the maxim that full moons always produced babies. Sometimes lots of babies.

''Thanks, Trish,'' Kim said. ''Lydia? Anything you wish to add?''

Lydia stiffened slightly, but shook her head, indicating Kim should continue.

''What I have to report concerns the subject of ultrasound testing.'' Being on the board of directors, Devon knew the clinic was as solvent as it had been for several years, but there was no money available for such a major expenditure and possibly never would be. ''I've found a sonography firm in Taos that we can contract with that'll give our patients a better rate than Arroyo County. They accept most insurance plans and they employ a sliding fee for uninsured patients. I've worked out a deal with them that insures our clients enough of a savings to justify the extra time spent in traveling. If any of you recommend your mothers have the procedure, or if they just want to learn the baby's sex, I can help you make the appointment.'' She leaned back in her chair with a small, satisfied smile on her face. Saving money for the clinic and the patients was something of a crusade with her cousin, Devon had come to realize.

"Recommendation of the procedure is still completely voluntary on your parts, just as it has always been," Lydia said. "But perhaps it's time to formalize our policy on the matter. More and more of our patients want to know the sex of their babies before they're born, and if that knowledge contributes to the mother's well-being and we can get her the best price available, then I have no problem with it. Are there any questions?"

Heidi and Katherine shook their heads in unison, although from their expressions Devon deduced neither of the two traditional midwives was enthusiastic about the idea. Had Lydia done this for her? Endorsing an area of technology that she considered alien to her craft so that Devon would feel more comfortable utilizing it in her practice here? Was it one more attempt to bridge the gap between them?

If it was, could she take it several steps further and confide in her grandmother about the children? Lydia had seemed to accept her out-of-the-blue explanation for taking them into her home, although at the last moment she'd gotten cold feet and not mentioned Sylvia's pregnancy. Lydia had made herself available to see Devon's patients so that she could carry out her ruse of going to Albuquerque to pick them up. But to confess and confide all the details of what she had done the past few days required a leap of faith Devon wasn't yet ready to make.

"Very well, then," Lydia said. "I'm sure you all want to get home to your families. Have a nice weekend."

Katherine and Heidi left together with Trish after

a barrage of questions about her visitors that Devon did her best to answer. They were trusting, big-hearted women. She wasn't surprised that they would take her announcement in stride. All of them would have offered the children sanctuary at a friend's behest, and they saw nothing unusual in Devon's doing so. Kim followed the others out the door, inviting Maria to come and play with Sammy when she was settled in.

Devon bent to retrieve her shoulder bag, which had dropped out of sight behind the couch. When she straightened, she saw that Parker and Hope had made no move to leave the room.

"There is something we all need to talk about," Hope began.

"Hope, no." There was a pleading note in her grandmother's voice. She clutched the big woven bag she carried as a purse to her chest.

"We've put this off too long," Parker added. He was a handsome man with a ready smile, but tonight he looked somber. And Hope wouldn't meet Devon's gaze. "Sit down, Lydia. Devon." He motioned Devon to her seat as Lydia dropped heavily onto a chair.

"What is it?"

Hope spoke next. "It's about my baby, Devon. The child I gave up for adoption. I care too much about both of you to let you go on thinking the worst of Lydia's actions that night."

"I understand—" Devon began automatically.

"No, you don't. Or only a little. Beginning with

the fact that you didn't even know my baby was a boy, not a girl.''

"Not a little girl? Not Autumn?'' Over the past decade, she'd thought of Hope's baby at different times, always identifying her with the name Hope had picked for her—Autumn. Now Devon focused on her grandmother's face, but Lydia stared past her at the empty grate of the fireplace. "You lied to Hope about the baby's sex, as well?'' Devon hadn't meant to let the harsh words slip out but couldn't stop them.

"I thought it was for the best,'' Lydia said. She was still clutching the woven bag with both hands. Old regret and new weariness echoed through her words. "If I had told Hope her baby was a boy, she would have been convinced she could keep him safe from her uncle and the polygamist cult he's involved in. It would have been too difficult for her to raise a child alone, so I let her go on thinking the baby was a girl. At risk from the Brethren.''

Hope's voice was gentle, serene. "You were right, Lydia. I was young and alone. I had no education, no money. No resources. I would probably have grown so discouraged I would have returned to my family.'' Her voice dropped to a whisper. "To the control of the Brethren. And my son would have been as much in their power as a daughter would have been. I know that now.''

Parker drew Hope close and said, "Devon, Hope's child is my son, Dalton.''

Parker's son? She'd always assumed Hope's child had been taken out of state, or at least away from Enchantment.

"When did you find out the truth?" she asked Hope.

"After I returned to Enchantment last year. Devon, believe me, I had no idea you knew anything about what happened the night Dalton was born. Lydia never told me you came to see me or that you overheard her...and Parker's father-in-law discussing the adoption until recently."

"He was the man with you in your office?" Devon asked Lydia.

"Yes."

"I was there, too," Parker added.

"I only overheard bits and pieces of what was being said. I...I didn't know you were there at all, Parker."

"Nor I, you," Lydia said very softly.

"As I remember, my father-in-law did most of the talking," Parker continued. "He was, and is, a powerful and influential man, Devon. A hard man to say no to." Devon felt a little shiver. She'd never forgotten the voice she'd overheard. A man's voice accustomed to command, cajoling and threatening by turns. Would she have been able to refuse his demands to hand over the child if she'd been in Lydia's place?

She turned back to Hope. "All these years your baby was right here in Enchantment?"

"Yes." Hope reached out from the comforting circle of her husband's arm and pulled Devon closer. "Loved and cherished just as I prayed he'd be."

"Dalton made Vanessa's, my former wife's, last months on earth happy ones, Devon. Hope, and

Lydia, gave us what she wanted and needed most in the world.''

''Why didn't you tell me the truth before tonight?'' Once more Devon focused on Lydia's strained features. She had learned to live with the ache of their estrangement, but this was a new wound and a painful one.

This time Lydia met her gaze head-on. ''I gave Hope my word.''

''You didn't trust me enough—'' Devon stopped abruptly. Trust. She couldn't trust anyone with her secret about the three children she'd taken into her home, either. Too much was at stake.

''We asked Lydia to keep Dalton's parentage a secret because of the damage it could do to The Birth Place and to Lydia and my father-in-law's reputations,'' Parker said.

Hope nodded agreement, adding, ''But mostly because we feared that my uncle might try to come for him. He's a terrible man, Devon. I told you back then how frightened of him I was, remember?''

''I remember.'' Devon had ached for Hope, but in her innocence she'd never really understood how badly Hope had been scarred by her upbringing in the repressive society of the Brethren.

''Now he's in prison and not likely to ever be free again. When I realized that Lydia hadn't told you about Dalton, I released her from her promise.''

''How long ago was that?'' Devon addressed the question to Lydia. She was appalled at herself, but once more old hurts so long repressed insisted on being voiced.

It was Parker who answered. "As soon as we could be sure Hope's uncle and the Brethren were no longer a danger. That was a week or so before Lydia's heart attack."

"I meant to tell you," Lydia whispered.

"But you didn't. Why?"

She shrugged and Devon saw how old and frail she looked. "It doesn't matter anymore," Lydia replied.

"No, I suppose it doesn't," Devon said, but she didn't mean it and they all knew it was a lie. "I'll honor my grandmother's promise to you, Hope. I'll keep Dalton's parentage a secret for as long as you want me to."

"I never had the slightest doubt of that. You were my only friend in those days, Devon. I haven't told you how much that friendship meant to me when I had no one else in the world. What your grandmother did then was what she thought best for all of us." She leaned forward and rested her cheek against Devon's. "Talk to her, Devon. Make it all right again, please," she whispered. "Your grandmother loves you and respects you more than any other person in the world."

Devon returned the hug. "I think it's time you and Parker went home to your son." Hope looked at her with stricken eyes, but said no more.

"You'll see that your grandmother gets home safely?" Parker said.

"Of course."

Parker and Hope left by the front door. Devon heard the lock turn behind them and moments later their car drove away.

Lydia remained seated. "If only I'd known at the time that you overheard my conversation with Parker's father-in-law that night, so many things would be different between us."

"I was afraid to say anything. I didn't want you to get into trouble."

"It was the second-hardest thing I've ever had to do. The hardest was to give my own child, Kim's mother, away." Devon had no desire to see her grandmother suffer from memories even more painful than those that had been dredged up in the past few minutes.

She held out her hands to her grandmother. "Let's go home. We can talk in the morning when you're not so tired."

"I won't be able to sleep." Lydia made no effort to rise. She reached out and took Devon's hands between her own. Devon knelt at her feet. Her grandmother's touch was ice-cold and her fingers trembled like aspen leaves in a storm. "You do believe I was acting in Hope's best interest, as well as my own, don't you?"

"Yes," Devon whispered.

"You shocked me so that day in my office when I asked you to take my place on the board and you told me you had known all along. But at the time Hope had no idea where her child was. I couldn't tell you any more than I did. I...I had to remain silent."

"I understand. It's all mended now."

"Is it?" Lydia had picked up on the uncertainty in her words. "Can we go back to what we had when you were sixteen and thought I had hung the moon?"

"I'd like to try."

"But it might be too late." Lydia sighed and disengaged her hands from Devon's. "I knew it would be difficult for you to give up your life and come to take over the clinic. But I didn't think it would be impossible. Now I can see why you thought it would be."

"I gave up the lease on my apartment," Devon said. "I arranged to put my furniture in storage. I'm going to stay in Enchantment, at least for the time being."

The flare of hope in Lydia's eyes made Devon's breath catch in her throat. "Then you do forgive me for what I did?"

"I forgave you a long time ago." Devon had forgiven, but she hadn't forgotten, nor had she understood. Now with her deception heavy on her conscience, she felt the weight of Lydia's burden on her own shoulders.

"I've only ever kept two secrets from you in my entire life, Devon. That I gave my own child up for adoption so many years before and the truth about Hope's baby. Keeping the first secret cost me my marriage, and sometimes, I fear, the best parts of my relationship with your mother and uncle. The second cost me your respect. I swear I will never lie to you again."

Devon looked across the lamp-lit room to the last glimmering of twilight beyond the windows. Tears clogged her throat and stung her eyes. She needed her grandmother now more than she ever had. She needed her wisdom and guidance with Sylvia's pregnancy.

She needed someone to confide in about all her other worries and fears. Lydia had promised she would never lie to her again, and Devon believed her.

But Lydia was still recovering from her recent heart attack. Devon couldn't add to the stress she was under by confessing her own secrets.

CHAPTER EIGHT

DEVON LOOKED OUT over the valley beyond the low wall that followed the edge of the terrace. To her left were the ski slopes of Angel's Gate. To her right a view of Mount Wheeler, backlit by the setting sun. The resort's restaurant was a beautiful setting, especially now with the sunset gilding the tops of the ridges and night shadows on the march down the opposite slope.

Their dinner had been excellent, the chicken subtly flavored and tender, the salmon moist and flaky. The wine, the same vintage they'd chosen for the party was very good, also. She'd had two glasses, something she almost never did. But tonight she had no mothers ready to go into labor and Gina and Hope were on call, so she had no need to worry about an emergency summons from the clinic.

"Okay, tell me what's up with these kids you've taken in."

"What?" Devon was startled by Miguel's question. She shouldn't have had that second glass of wine. It had lulled her into a sense of well-being that she hadn't felt in a long time, and left her vulnerable to attack. In reality the question was asked in a tone of friendly curiosity, not confrontation. It was only her guilty conscience that made it seem otherwise.

He poured the last of his beer into his glass, but didn't lift it to his mouth. She could watch his hands forever. He had big, hard hands, but they could be gentle, too, coaxing and caressing a woman's body....

"The kids you brought up from Albuquerque," he elaborated. "Tell me about them. How old are they? How long are they going to be staying with you?"

"I...I don't know how long they'll be staying. Several weeks at least." She took a sip of wine and tried to gather her scattered thoughts.

"They'll want to be back home when school starts, I suppose."

"Yes. But there's a complication." No one had met the children yet. No one knew that Sylvia was pregnant. Not even her grandmother. Nothing had changed between her and Lydia since the night Hope and Parker had told her the truth about Dalton's parentage. There had been no miraculous, instantaneous healing of the rift between them. Years of silence couldn't be mended overnight. And beyond that there was the fundamental difference in the way they viewed their profession. Those differences were evident every time they stepped into a birthing room together. Lab tests, ultrasounds, fetal monitors were the backup technology that augmented Devon's midwife and nursing skills. To Lydia they were unwanted and unnecessary interference in the most natural and woman-affirming process on earth. Tears and a hug were even less likely to bridge that gap than they were the other one.

"Another complication beyond these three orphaned kids being left alone while their cousin heads to Mexico for an unspecified length of time? You must have been very good friends with their mother to take on such a responsibility."

Devon couldn't quite meet his steady gaze. She looked down into the golden liquid in her glass. "The kids need me. I'm all they have right now." That simple and undeniable truth that took precedence over all the rest. The children needed her. She was able to look at him now. Her voice was stronger too. "Sylvia, the oldest girl, is pregnant." Suddenly she was eager for his advice. No one she knew was more level-headed than Miguel. She leaned forward a little, her hands wrapped around her wineglass. "She's barely sixteen. The boy who's the father has ducked and run. She's terrified of giving birth, and I'm not sure exactly what to do next."

Miguel gave a low whistle and settled back in his chair. She waited, growing accustomed once more to his silences and to the inner discipline that kept his face free of easily read emotion. "The kid ought to be held responsible for what he did. But what's right and what gets done are usually two different things."

"She's not sure of her due date, although I think it will be soon. I'm not even certain she'll be here to deliver." As hard as she'd tried, she hadn't yet earned Jesse's complete trust. He was proud and protective, and he was scared of being sent back to Mexico, a country he hadn't seen since he was a small child. If he got spooked and took off, the girls would go with him, regardless of how close to term Sylvia might be.

"You mean the cousin might not be gone all that long?" Miguel asked, and she imagined his tone was more probing than it had been a moment before.

Reality pricked her again. She had to weigh each word before she spoke, every time she spoke, or she would give herself away. "Yes, that's what I meant. Sylvia needs stability right now. And medical care. I hope the cousin can be persuaded to leave the kids here with me." What was she thinking? Miguel was the last person on earth she dared confide in. One thing she did know about him was that his duty as an officer of the law would dictate he turn the children in to the proper authorities if he learned their true circumstances. They would be taken away from her, probably separated. Right or wrong, she couldn't let that happen. She'd never felt quite so alone in her entire life.

"Is the girl healthy?"

Devon relaxed a fraction. The sun was down now, the sky a wash of pink and gold high above, shading to gray and indigo along the far ridge tops. She shivered a little as the mountain chill crept over the retaining wall and curled around her ankles. She was glad she'd worn a dress with a jacket. "As far as I can tell, she's had no prenatal care at all. She hid the pregnancy as long as she could."

"That's not unusual, is it?"

"No." Devon sighed. "It's actually pretty common."

"Why didn't the cousin see she got care when he did find out?"

"It's all come to a head in the last few weeks. And to top it all off, the boy's father is his boss."

Miguel's dark brows pulled together in a quick frown. "That's not much of an excuse."

"I didn't think so, either, but then, it's not my job on the line."

"But when it's your flesh and blood who's been wronged." Navajo tradition set great store by family ties, she knew. And so did all the varied cultures that made up Miguel's complex heritage. He would be a good husband. A good father. She had always been aware of that about him, someplace deep down inside her.

"The kids don't have relatives to turn to right now. They only have me." A waitress came through the sliding doors and began lighting candles on the tables. Only two other sets of diners occupied the terrace this evening, and both those tables were several yards away. Devon looked up as she approached. So far she'd seen no middle-aged Hispanic woman who fit the description Sylvia had given her. This waitress, although one she hadn't seen before, couldn't be the kids' aunt, either. She was too young, and Anglo besides.

"Anything else that I can get you?" she asked. "Another glass of wine. Perhaps a nightcap? Or coffee?"

"I could use a cup of coffee," Miguel said to Devon. "Unless you need to get back to the kids."

"No. They're okay. They're pretty self-sufficient. I'll have coffee, too. Decaf. Black."

"I'll have the high-octane," Miguel directed. "Black."

"I'll be right back." The waitress collected their empty glasses and the beer bottle, retreating back into the main dining room where candlelight glowed on the tables and a fire blazed in the massive fireplace across the room. If she had been alone, Devon would have asked the friendly young waitress if anyone named Lucia Molina worked at the resort, but that was impossible with Miguel sitting across from her. She would have to come back to Angel's Gate alone to make her inquiries.

And what if Lucia was also an illegal? Would she bolt and run when confronted with the knowledge that her nieces and nephew were abandoned and seeking her aid? Would she be able to care for them if she didn't? It seemed that every way she turned, the situation grew more complicated. She shivered with a chill that didn't come from the night air.

"Would you like to go inside to have coffee?" Miguel asked, observantly catching her slight shudder. "It's getting chilly out here."

He didn't look cold. He looked warm and solid and sexy as hell. He wasn't wearing a tie, and his shirt was open at the neck. A dark jacket and khaki slacks completed his outfit. His skin was copper against the white of his shirt, and his eyes were as dark as the valley shadows. His hair had grown a little from the almost buzz cut he'd been sporting when she arrived in town. It would be thick and silky against her fingers, soft against her breasts and the skin of her belly as they made love.

She wasn't cold anymore. She was on fire. And she couldn't take one more step down that imaginary road or she'd be lost.

"It *is* chilly," she said. "Let's go inside."

The waitress reappeared with their coffee and led them to a small table near the fireplace. The warmth of the flames felt good. Devon held her coffee cup between her hands and let her eyes wander the room. There were only two other waitresses in view, and neither of them fit Sylvia's description of her aunt. Devon couldn't stop the disappointed sigh that escaped her lips.

"I think it's time I took you home."

"Oh, no. Really. I don't want to leave." She could have kicked herself for sighing so audibly. She hoped the warmth of the fire could account for the heat she felt rising to her cheeks. "I mean, I'm sorry. I...my mind wandered for a moment."

"It's been wandering for more than a moment. What are you thinking about? The party?"

"Yes. The party." It had been at the back of her mind, so it wasn't completely a lie. "I think it will be wonderful here. It's all coming together nicely." In fact, she'd spent almost no time at all on party preparations since the children had arrived. Thank goodness there were only minor details left to be decided.

Details that gave her an excuse to come back here again.

She managed a smile and was pleased that it felt natural, not forced. "I'm going over the plans one more time with the people here. Probably next week, and then all we have to do is sit back and relax and enjoy.''

''I like the sit back, relax and enjoy part.''

''Me, too.'' She took another sip of her coffee. It had cooled as they talked. She made a little face.

''Do you want your coffee warmed up?'' he asked. ''I'll call the waitress over.''

She shook her head. ''No. I've had enough. Any more and I won't be able to fall asleep, decaf or not.''

He signaled the waitress for the bill and five minutes later they were standing outside under the vaulted portico waiting for the valet to bring out Miguel's truck. The bulk of the building rose up behind them, as sturdy as the rock and cedar from which it was hewn, its windows glowing warm against the darkness.

''My mom's dying to get up here and check this place out,'' Miguel said.

''It's spectacular. I think everyone will be impressed.''

The truck rolled up and Miguel helped her into the passenger side.

''Mind if we take a little detour on the way home?'' he asked, settling into the driver's seat.

She stiffened a little, turning her head to study his face in the last glow of twilight. What was he asking of her? He had promised this evening wouldn't include anything physical and she meant to hold him to his word—for both their sakes. ''I don't want to be too late. The kids—''

''This won't take long.'' A few minutes later he turned the truck off the main road onto a track that was barely visible, rutted and apparently seldom used. Devon wrapped one hand around the armrest and braced the other on the dashboard. The truck had four-wheel drive—without it she doubted they would have made it more than half a mile up the steep slope he'd turned onto.

They drove in silence, fir boughs scraping both sides as the track narrowed, and now and then a branch dragged across the windshield. ''Miguel, where in heaven are you taking me?''

''Exactly.'' She could see him bare his teeth in a grin, and then he stopped the truck. ''Heaven. Or as close as you can get around here.'' He got out and came around the hood to open her door. ''It's only a few yards. You can make it even in those shoes. There's something I want you to see.'' He held out his hand and she took it. This place was obviously special to him, and the certainty in his voice left no room for doubt.

Miguel led the way and Devon followed in his footsteps, not trusting her night vision as he did his. It was a short climb, but almost straight up. He pulled her over the last few feet, brushed aside the boughs of a wind-sculpted pine and drew her up beside him. Devon sucked in her breath at what lay before her. They were close to the edge of the ridge line. Not ten feet in front of them the rocks dropped away into nothingness. But it was what lay beyond the sheer drop that held her spellbound.

Half of New Mexico spread out beneath them, or so it seemed. Far off in the distance, Taos was a pale shimmer in the black velvet sky. Closer by she could see Enchantment's streets laid out in a grid of lights. Around them, here and there on the mountainsides, tiny pinpricks of gold, like fireflies twinkling in the darkness, marked houses and cabins. One of them would belong to Miguel's grandfather, and somewhere hidden in the folds of the mountain was the old ghost town of Silverton. If she turned her head far enough, Angel's Gate shone like glory above them. And higher still, dwarfing all else, the dark bulk of Mount Wheeler. There was more moisture in the air at this altitude, and the scent of pine and cedar swirled on the night air.

"How did you ever find this place?" She turned her head from the beauty of the view and looked up into his eyes, as dark as the eastern sky.

"My grandfather brought me here when I was very young. I camped out in the pine grove back there off and on when I was a kid. It's a hell of a bike ride when you're ten. But when I really started spending a lot of time on the mountain was when I came back from Somalia."

The summer after she'd graduated from high school. The summer she'd thought he would ask her to marry him.

Miguel tugged gently on her hand, inviting her to sit with him on the large, flat boulder that marked the edge of the cliff. Her eyes had adjusted to the night and she no longer felt as if she might step into nothingness if she moved her feet. Devon lowered herself to the rock, feeling the slight warmth the stone still held from the afternoon sun, and the more compelling heat of the man beside her.

"Is this where you kept disappearing to all that summer?" she asked at last. It was hard for her to talk about those days, even now. They'd been inseparable before that time. She'd written to him every day he was in boot camp and when he'd gone overseas. She'd dreamed of him every night, even forgoing her senior prom because he couldn't come to San Francisco to be her date.

"It was the only place I could feel at peace."

"You never brought me here." They'd made love in the back of his pickup, on the banks of Silver Creek, but never here on the mountain. His special place.

"I wanted to."

"Would it have made a difference?" She spoke her thoughts aloud before she could stop herself.

He didn't answer for a moment. "No," he said finally. "I couldn't even help myself for a while there."

In those days she'd understood little of what was happening in that faraway, war-torn African country. She'd known only that people were dying of famine and clan wars. She had been proud that Miguel was there to help feed the hungry and keep the warlords at bay, but self-absorbed teenager that she was, she'd resented his being taken from her, duty or no duty. Now, of course she knew more. That it had not been so simple or straightforward a mission and it had ended in tragedy, and what surely to a proud Marine, had been defeat.

She listened to the sounds of the wind in the firs and the lonely whistle of a freight train on its way to

Santa Fe that carried up to them from the valley below as she waited for him to speak again.

"I stayed up here three days straight once."

She nodded, remembering. "I was a nervous wreck worrying about you, but I never knew where you'd gone." It had been over the Fourth of July. He had stood her up for the town picnic and the parade and fireworks.

He picked up a pebble and pitched it into the void. Devon listened, but she didn't hear it land. "If it helps any, my mom tore a strip off my hide when I got back to town."

"I think I remember throwing a glass of lemonade in your face for the same reason."

"I remember."

"You just turned on your heel and walked away." She had raged and sobbed and clung to him by turns, too young and inexperienced to know how to reach him, and she regretted it to this day.

"I needed to get my head on straight. The trouble is it took a hell of a lot longer than three days to do it. By the time I could talk about it, you were gone and I didn't know how to get you back."

"Tell me about it now."

For a moment she wasn't sure he would. Then he began to speak, slowly, without anger or bitterness. "Somalia wasn't like any place I've ever been. Every time we went out on patrol, we'd be mobbed by little kids begging for food. Only, we couldn't give them any because as likely as not their big brothers were waiting around the corner to ambush us when our guard was down. Do you know what it's like to hold a gun on a kid? And know you might have to use it?" His voice cracked and he was silent for a long moment, pitching another stone over the cliff. "No law and order. No electricity. No water. Teenagers riding in the back of pickups with machine guns bolted to the beds. And God help us, they knew how to use the damned things." His voice had hardened and Devon shivered beneath her light cotton jacket. She wrapped her arms around her knees and looked up at the stars, so many the sky seemed carpeted with them. "Every time we went out on patrol, someone got killed. Usually a couple of them, but sometimes our guys, too."

Miguel turned his head and seemed to search her face. "That wasn't the way it was supposed to be. Some of the older guys had been in Desert Storm. They knew who the enemy was. They had the resources and the backing they needed to get the job done. But this was different. Politicians dropped us in there and two years later they pulled us back out after a lot of good Marines and Army Rangers were killed, and the place is still a hell hole." He shook his head. "It wasn't storming the beach at Normandy. It wasn't raising the flag on Iwo Jima. My grandfather was a Code Talker. His buddy, Manny Cordova won a Silver Star on Okinawa. My dad was Recon in Vietnam. I was Meals on Wheels, and the people we were trying to keep from starving to death would just as soon shoot us as look at us." He rested his forearm on his knee, and she could see his hand ball into a fist. "For a long time I couldn't handle it—there, or when I came home."

"So you avoided me."

"I avoided everyone. I got past it, though. I finished my hitch. I put what the Marines taught me to good use, got my degree in criminal justice and joined the force here in Enchantment." He reached out and brushed his fingers across her cheek so lightly she barely felt it. "But by then it was too late for us. You were gone. I'll always regret it was you I hurt the most."

"No more than I hurt you."

"Coming back to you was all I thought about while I was over there. I lived for your letters. I made plans for us for when I got back."

"Not plans, Miguel. Dreams. I had them, too, but they were only dreams. They couldn't stand up to real life." She'd been infatuated with the tall young Marine. With the romantic fantasy of a Navajo warrior, but not the stark reality of the angry, disillusioned young man who returned to Enchantment that summer.

Miguel leaned forward. She could still feel the heat of his body and she wanted to be wrapped in his arms the way she'd been those long-ago summers, and that not-so-long-ago night. He must have read her mind— it was too dark for her thoughts to be visible on her face—for he asked quietly, "Were you in love with me?"

"We were too young to know what love is," she responded, but the statement lacked the conviction she meant it to have.

"Maybe it wasn't love," he agreed, and she felt sadness steal into her heart. She'd thought he loved her, too, then. She'd been certain of it. "But it was as close as I've ever come. And it was a lot more than a teenage infatuation. I think we proved that a few weeks ago."

She lifted her fingers to his lips, stopping his words. "We agreed we wouldn't bring that night up again."

"You're still single. You told me about the doctor. Have there been other men in your life?"

"One or two."

"Has there been anything to compare to what we had back then?"

Images of the boys she'd met in college, the young doctor she'd tried to make herself believe she could love. None of them had come close to filling her thoughts and her heart as Miguel had done. "No," she whispered, unable to stop herself from speaking the truth.

"For me, either." He was so close now they were touching. He put his arm around her and angled her even closer to his body. She made no attempt to stop him. She wanted to be close to him. She wanted to be in his arms. His aftershave was subtle and enticing, and if she closed her eyes and breathed deeply, she thought of sagebrush and sunshine, scents that would always remind her of him.

Miguel turned and kissed her with a slow, drugging thoroughness that left her breathless and shamelessly seeking more. Devon turned so her breasts were against his chest and wrapped her arms around his neck. The hair at his nape was thick and soft as silk. Her good intentions, her promises to him and to herself to not let things get out of control evaporated like mist in the sunlight. She had ached to be held like this since that night in the spring.

He ended the kiss and she clung to him for a moment, breathless and floating, her eyes closed against the sparkle of starlight within and without. "The past is behind us," he said. "We're not the kids we used to be. We're adults. We know our own minds. We deserve another chance, Devon." His voice wasn't quite steady. His hands on her arms weren't quite steady, either.

But sanity had returned with the end of the kiss, and she knew she couldn't give him the reply he wanted. She shook her head. "My life is as out of sync as yours was all those years ago, Miguel." How she longed to tell him so much more. He had grown into the kind of man she knew he would be. Strong, loyal, full of integrity and the capacity to love. But what had she matured into? A woman who was filled with myriad self-doubts and conflicts. A woman who was breaking the law, even if for the best of reasons.

And he was a cop whose first responsibility was upholding the law.

He laid his finger against her cheek and turned her head to face the valley. "Your future could be right down there, the same future as mine."

She closed her eyes against the longing for what he offered, love and home and family. But she couldn't tell him everything that weighed on her heart, and she wouldn't begin a relationship based on a foundation of lies. She swallowed hard against the tears that threatened. "I can't see anything but starlight and shadows. I—'' She gasped as he pulled her to her feet. ''What's wrong?''

''Fire,'' he said, pointing. Devon narrowed her eyes and looked in the direction he indicated. Way off in the distance, halfway up the mountainside, she saw a dot of orange light that separated into two, then three smaller pinpricks as they watched. ''Some fool idiot has gone and started a fire out by Manny Cordova's place.'' He gripped her arms and gave her one more hard, quick kiss. ''Okay, you're as mixed up as I was all those years ago. I'll give you that. I rushed my fences tonight.'' He jumped down off the boulder and held out his arms so she wouldn't have to scramble down on her own. ''We'll work it out later. But get this straight, Devon. I'm not a confused eighteen-year-old anymore. I'm a man and I know what I want. Understand?'' It wasn't a question, it was a command, and she responded with an automatic nod. ''And one more thing you should know about me. I usually get what I want in the end.''

CHAPTER NINE

DEVON WALKED to the window of Dr. Joanna Carson's office, past the ornate wooden desk and heavy, stained-glass lamps, holdovers from Joanna's predecessor, and opened the equally dark and heavy drapes. The view from the pediatric clinic was almost the same as the one from The Birth Place just half a mile father along Desert Valley Road. She scanned the mountainside for signs of smoke. There wasn't any, thank goodness. There hadn't been all morning, but that hadn't stopped her from watching. And worrying. The fire had indeed been at Manny's ranch. Miguel had skidded to a stop at the foot of her driveway last night, leaned across her to open the passenger door and promised he'd let her know how things were going as soon as he had a chance. Then he'd roared off.

That was more than twelve hours ago. The fire had started in Manny's chicken coop and spread through the dry grass in his pasture, but it had been out for more than half that time. She knew that because she'd listened to the police scanner for most of the night. Miguel had probably been too tired to call and was sleeping in this morning. *Miguel in bed...* The image of him naked, his arms wrapped around her, his erection pushing hard against her was vivid enough to make her catch her breath. She raised her fingers to her lips, thankful she was alone. Beyond the door, Joanna's waiting room was full, and the sound of children's voices, some happy, some querulous with fever, drifted down the hall.

One of the laughing children was Maria, whom Devon had just left in the play area. Joanna had given the little girl a clean bill of health. The congestion in her lungs was cleared up. Maria had answered Joanna's questions without hesitation and shown little fear of the stethoscope and otoscope that the pediatrician wielded with gentle skill.

Dr. Jo, as most of her patients called her, was examining Sylvia now. Ideally Devon supposed she should have made an appointment for Sylvia with Dr. Ochoa, but he couldn't work her into his schedule for at least ten days, so Joanna had agreed to check her over. Devon turned from the window as the exam-room door opened and Sylvia stepped outside, followed by Dr. Jo, whose pregnancy was almost as advanced as Sylvia's.

But there the similarity between the two ended. Joanna's face was alight with joy and contentment. Sylvia's was dulled with anxiety and the hint of tears. Joanna spoke first. "Sylvia's doing well. She's slightly anemic and underweight, but iron and a vitamin supplement, and a couple of fruit shakes a day should take care of that in no time."

"Good," Devon said.

"The baby appears healthy, at least as far as I can ascertain without further tests," Joanna continued, her smile losing a little of its radiance.

"I don't want to go to the hospital for tests," Sylvia insisted. "I hate hospitals."

"We don't have to make that decision today," Devon said gently.

Joanna spoke carefully, her voice clear but pitched not to carry beyond the spot where the three of them were standing. "I don't think you should delay too long. Sylvia is unsure of her due date. I'm a pediatrician, not an OB/GYN, but I estimate the baby is within a month of term. She needs to be making plans for her delivery and for the baby's future. You're very lucky to have Devon for a friend, Sylvia. She can help you with both those decisions."

"Yes, she is a very good friend," Sylvia said evasively. She looked past Devon and Joanna, refusing to meet their eyes. "Where is Maria?" she asked.

"She's playing with the other children in the reception area."

"I'll go to her."

"All right." Devon had known Sylvia was ambivalent about her pregnancy, but she was acting as if it didn't exist.

"You can tell Nicki, my receptionist, to give Maria an extraspecial treat," Joanna said. "She's an angel of a patient."

"Mil gracias." For the first time Sylvia smiled. "I will do that. I think she's very special, too."

Devon wasn't certain how to proceed. She'd hoped Joanna might have better luck breaking through to Sylvia than she had over the past week, but that evidently wasn't the case.

"I'd like to speak to you if you have a few minutes,

Devon.'' Joanna held open the exam-room door so that Devon could precede her into the room. It was small and painted lemony-yellow. A colorful wall-paper border of children playing in a meadow covered the wall just below the ceiling. Propped in a chair in the corner, a big teddy bear wore a surgical mask and cap. Paper booties adorned his feet and a stethoscope hung around his neck.

Devon moved to the exam table, resting both hands on the headrest. The paper covering crackled beneath her fingers. ''First let me say I appreciate your seeing Maria and Sylvia at such short notice.''

''I'm glad to do it. As I said told you earlier, Maria is fine. She's slightly underweight, but otherwise she seems quite well-adjusted. No signs of abuse or de-liberate neglect. She's very sad about her mother's death, of course, but she obviously adores her brother and sister, and close family ties are always good rem-edies for grief. I do recommend that if she's going to be staying with you for any length of time, you send for her medical and immunization records.''

It was as close as Joanna had come to asking out-right if she had any kind of legal claim to the children. She wondered if her friend suspected they might be undocumented? If she did, she didn't ask. It was the same at The Birth Place. It didn't matter to Lydia whether the women under their care were illegals or not. Joanna Carson obviously felt the same way.

''I...I'll do that.'' But how *would* she? The one thing the children were adamant about was that they wanted nothing to do with their cousin and steadfastly refused to divulge either his name or address. Would their family doctor forward the records without his permission? Did they have a family doctor? Yet more complications she hadn't anticipated that day in the old mine.

Joanna's next statement echoed Miguel's words from the night before. "You've taken on a big responsibility with these children, Devon. Especially Sylvia."

"I know I have. But...I had no choice." Devon couldn't quite meet Joanna's searching gaze. She was tempted to tell Joanna the truth. Doctor-patient privilege would protect her confidences, but she kept her silence, knowing it would put Joanna in an awkward position. She changed the subject to give herself a moment to order her thoughts. "How are you feeling, Joanna? You certainly look the picture of health." Before Joanna came to Enchantment, she'd lost a baby at birth. For that reason she was considered a high-risk patient and so was not under the care of the midwives at The Birth Place.

Joanna took her cue. She giggled and the sound warmed Devon's heart. "I *am* the picture of health. We *both* are. As a matter of fact—" she fished in a drawer and pulled out a familiar black-and-white image of an unborn child "—here he is. Isn't he beautiful?" She looked up at Devon, eyes shining with love and confidence. "All the necessary equipment. Arms, legs, fingers, toes. And most wonderful of all, an absolutely perfect, healthy heart."

"Oh, Joanna, that *is* wonderful news. I'm very happy for you. You're going to have your hands full with two in diapers, though."

"Max is so precocious she's almost potty-trained already, and she won't be two until November." Michelle, "Max" to friends and family alike, was Ben Carson's daughter. She was a dark-haired, brown-eyed charmer, heading into her terrible twos. Maybe that was why Joanna seemed to think it wasn't so out of the ordinary for Devon to have taken three children into her home. Joanna had embraced Ben's extended family with open arms.

Devon smiled down at the baby's image. "I swear he looks just like Ben."

Joanna laughed again. "That's what I told Ben, too. He's so proud, Devon. He's already got a pony picked out for him, and I'm not even due until after Labor Day."

"He'll need a pony if he's going to grow up to be a rancher and a horse trainer like his daddy."

"Indeed." Joanna leaned against the counter, one hand on the swell of her stomach. Her expression grew serious. "It's going to take more than a sonogram image of her baby to solve Sylvia's conflicts about her pregnancy," she said softly.

"I know. I'd appreciate any help you can give me."

"I think it would be helpful if she were to talk to Celia." Celia Brice was the therapist who had her office in The Birth Place.

"I've already tried to get her to talk to Celia. She refuses."

Joanna lifted her shoulders in a shrug. "I'm not surprised. She's lost her mother. She's been uprooted from her home. She's pregnant by a boy who deserted her. With time and patience, she could find the strength to make the right decisions for herself and the baby, but I'm afraid time's the one thing she doesn't have in abundance.''

''I agree.''

''I have one other suggestion,'' Joanna said, turning to open the door.

''What is it?''

''Talk to your grandmother. If anyone can get Sylvia through this pregnancy with the least amount of emotional and physical trauma, it's Lydia.''

THE SAME SOUNDS of women's and children's voices that permeated Joanna's office greeted her when she walked into The Birth Place a few minutes later. Maria held Sylvia's hand and looked around her with interest.

''Are all those ladies going to have babies?'' she asked, looking up at Devon, her dark eyes round with wonder.

''Yes, all of them,'' Devon confirmed with a smile.

''Wow! Do you have any babies here today that I could play with?''

Devon shook her head. ''No, I'm afraid not today. But there are dolls in the toy box over there. And lots of books to read.''

Maria swiveled her head toward the play area. ''I'll read a story to the doll baby,'' she said. ''Is it okay, Sylvia?''

''If Devon says so, it's okay.''

''I want you to meet my grandmother, Sylvia. Wait

here a moment and I'll check with the receptionist and see if she's free.''

The waiting room was bathed in sunlight and was filled with pregnant women. Devon could see Sylvia's gaze skitter across a half-dozen gravid bellies, and hesitantly her hand rose to rest on her own swollen stomach. Devon turned to the reception desk. ''Trish, I'd like you to meet my friend, Sylvia Molina. And that sweetie over at the toy box is her sister, Maria.''

The receptionist smiled and held out her hand. ''Hello, Sylvia. I'm very happy to meet you.'' Not by the flicker of an eyelash did she betray any surprise at Sylvia's condition.

''Thank you,'' Sylvia replied.

''Trish, is my grandmother with a patient?''

''She just finished with her appointments. She's having a cup of tea in her office.''

''Could you see that we're not disturbed for a few minutes?''

Trish rolled her eyes at the buzz of activity that surrounded them. ''I'll do my best.''

''Thanks, Trish.'' Devon turned to Sylvia. ''Her office is this way. My grandmother knows everything there is to know about having a baby.''

Sylvia's expression was mutinous. ''I...don't want to talk about babies.''

Devon could feel Trish's eyes on her. She spoke softly but firmly. ''I know you're afraid, but once we talk to my grandmother, you'll feel better, I promise.'' She held out her hand. ''Come on.''

Devon knocked lightly on the door of Lydia's of-fice. She hoped Sylvia didn't notice that her hand was trembling a little. She should have handled this differently. She should have spoken to Lydia privately about Sylvia's condition, not blundered in on her this way. But these days she always seemed to handle things badly when it came to dealing with her grandmother, so why should today be any different?

"Come in."

Devon opened the door and stuck her head inside. "Lydia, I'd like you to meet my friend, Sylvia."

Her grandmother was standing at the window. Watching the mountainside for signs of the fire at Manny's place, no doubt, just as Devon had been doing off and on all morning. "Of course I'd like to meet your new friend. Come in." Lydia turned, her eyes widening momentarily as she took in Sylvia's pregnant form. She schooled her expression instantly and smiled as she set her big earthenware mug of tea on the edge of her desk. She moved toward them, her sandals tapping on the tiled floor. She was dressed for seeing patients today, in a flowing brown skirt and matching tunic tied at the waist with a soft woven belt. Her graying hair was braided in a single plait down the middle of her back. Silver bracelets jangled on her wrist, and silver chains hung around her neck. The Madonna pendant, as always, lay next to her skin, close to her heart.

Devon saw Sylvia glance around the room, taking in the hand-thrown pottery on the tables that flanked the leather couch, the Navajo blankets that served as throw rugs, softening the hardness of the tile floor, the dozen of framed photographs of family and friends, and of mothers and babies, that filled every spare inch of desk and bookcase.

"Sylvia Molina. This is my grandmother, Lydia Kane. She owns The Birth Place. She's a midwife. *A comadrona. Ella es muy hábil.* She's delivered thousands of babies."

Lydia held out her hand. "*Buenos dias,* Sylvia. I hope you like it here in Enchantment."

"*¡Mucho gusto!* Thank you. It seems like a nice town." The teen stood with hunched shoulders, her hands folded in front of her as though trying to hide her pregnancy.

"It is. Are your brother and sister with you?"

"My sister is playing…out there." Sylvia gestured in the direction of the waiting room. "My brother didn't come with us."

"Jesse took the old bicycle we found in the storage shed into town. He says it needs inner tubes for the tires. I told him if he could find them anywhere in Enchantment, it would be at Elkhorn's Hardware."

Lydia motioned to the worn leather couch. "Tell me a little about yourself, Sylvia."

The teen's eyes flashed again, but not with fear. "I'm going to have a baby," she said defiantly.

Lydia chuckled. "I can see that, my dear. Come sit down, and we'll talk about it." Sylvia hesitated, then moved forward, as though drawn by the authority in Lydia's voice. She lowered herself awkwardly onto the cushion, holding herself stiffly as if expecting a blow. Devon perched on the edge of Lydia's desk, letting her grandmother take command of the conversation. Joanna had been right. Lydia was wonderful at drawing her patients out. If she was going to stay in Enchantment, take over the clinic as Lydia wished her to do, then she might as well learn from the master.

The realization that she *was* staying surprised Devon. Yes, she had given up the lease on her apartment and put her things in storage. She had made up her mind to resign from the practice in Albuquerque. But was she ready to completely rethink her approach to her practice of the profession? To embrace Lydia's philosophy of woman-centered, female-empowered childbirth to the exclusion of years of medical training and technical expertise? She only hoped she was making the right choice.

"I don't want to have a baby," Sylvia said, and dropping her head into her hands, began to sob. "*Madre de Dios*. I don't want to have a baby."

Lydia laid her hand on Sylvia's knee. Her voice was still calm and authoritative, but it had gentled. "I know you feel very alone right now, and afraid. That's natural, but so is having a baby. You'll be fine and so will your little one. Devon and I will help you every step of the way."

"No, no, no." Sylvia pounded her fist on the arm of the couch. "What am I going to do with a baby?" She was crying as though her heart would break. Tears dripped from her chin and made dark spots on the cotton sundress Devon had bought her in Taos the week before. "My boyfriend ran away. He won't answer my letters or take my calls. How can I go to school and take care of my brother and sister and a baby, too? How can I get a good job if I quit school?

If I go back to my cousin, he will make me give the baby away, and I don't know if that's what I want, either. Oh, why did my mother have to die?''

Lydia put her arms around Sylvia's shaking shoulders. She looked at Devon over the girl's bowed head, her eyes questioning. Devon heard the words as plainly as if her grandmother had spoken them in her ear. "How did you come to be responsible for this troubled woman-child?" Devon felt a jolt of pain. She still couldn't confide the children's circumstances to anyone, her grandmother included. Lydia looked and acted like her old self, but she was still recovering from a serious heart attack. Devon refused to add any more stress to her life. She would handle this alone, just as she'd been doing since she decided to take the children into her home.

Then Lydia smiled, and Devon's pain went away. It was a smile of approval and pride, a smile that said, *You've done the right thing.* It had been far too long since Devon had felt that approving warmth.

Lydia turned her attention back to Sylvia. "Losing someone we love is never easy. But Devon and I are here to take care of you. We'll help you have your baby.'' Lydia's voice faltered for just a second. Her hand went to the locket hidden beneath her shirt, then lowered to her lap. The uncertainty in her voice had been so slight Sylvia didn't notice, but Devon did. "We'll help you make the decision to keep her, or to give her to the right couple to raise and love as their own. But the decision doesn't have to be made today, you know.''

Sylvia lifted her head, brushing at the tears on her

cheeks. "I pray every night that I will do the right thing. But I'm still so afraid."

Lydia motioned for the box of tissues on her desk. Devon offered them to Sylvia, who plucked two out of the box, wiping the tears from her cheeks. "Do you know when your baby is due?"

"Doctor Jo said in a few weeks. She asked me when I had my last period. I can't remember exactly," she said a little desperately. "It was in October." She looked down at her hands twisting in her lap. "The last time…the last time I was with my boyfriend was at Halloween."

Lydia patted her hands, stilling their restlessness. "That's okay. We can make a good guess." She lifted Sylvia's chin with the tip of her finger. "But I think it is going to be soon, Sylvia. Three or four weeks at most."

The girl nodded. "Yes, I think so, too. I feel odd sometimes. Strange. There isn't any pain, but my stomach…" She lifted her shoulders in a shrug. "It feels different and the baby doesn't move so much."

Once more Devon and her grandmother exchanged looks over Sylvia's bowed head. Braxton Hicks contractions. The precursor to true labor, another sign that Sylvia's baby would be born soon. "That's normal, too, Sylvia," Lydia explained. "Your body is preparing for the baby to be born. Devon can answer all your questions. We can even arrange for a test at the hospital so you can see if the baby is a boy or a girl."

"Will it hurt?"

"It doesn't hurt. Devon is a *comadrona,* a midwife,

too. And a nurse. She will explain everything you need to know.''

"My baby will be okay?" But the tears had stopped and so had the restless twisting of her hands.

"You will both be fine. It'll take a couple of days to arrange for the sonogram. We don't do them here, but in the meantime, would you like to hear your baby's heartbeat?"

"His heartbeat?"

"Yes. We can do that here and now." Lydia stood up, resting her fingertips on the swell of Sylvia's stomach. "I'll make a bet with you. I bet I can tell you if the baby is a boy or girl just from the sound of its heartbeat." Lydia would be able to deduce a great deal more than that as she listened to the heartbeat. She could make an estimate of the size of Sylvia's pelvis, the position of the baby, if it was under any stress, all without upsetting Sylvia any more that day.

"You can do that?"

Lydia smiled. "Indeed I can. I'm right at least half the time."

It took Sylvia a moment to get the joke, then she smiled. "Devon, are you as good as your grandmother at this, too?"

"No," Devon admitted. Midwife lore held that male babies' heart rates were faster than girls', but it wasn't something she relied on in her practice in Albuquerque. Most mothers opted for sonograms and knew what sex their baby was from early on. "I haven't had nearly as much practice as my grandmother."

"Are you making a challenge of this, Devon?" Lydia's gray eyes held a sparkle of mischief as she ushered Sylvia out of her office to the exam room across the hall. Devon was so surprised to find she was being teased that she opened her mouth to retort, but nothing came out. "Well, Devon, let's see how good you are. Do you remember anything I taught you all those summers ago?" Lydia asked, turning in the doorway.

"Everything," Devon said, and followed them out of the room. "I remember everything."

CHAPTER TEN

MIGUEL PUSHED his chair away from his desk and stood up. He was too damn tired to deal with the stack of paperwork Doris, the dispatcher, had piled on the desk before he even walked through the door. The burn on the back of his wrist hurt like hell, too, and that didn't help his concentration any.

He grabbed his hat and headed for the front door of the police station. Maybe some exercise and fresh air would take his mind off the pain in his hand. Doris was at her usual place behind the counter that separated her from the front door of the city building and the good citizens of Enchantment. She looked up from the computer screen when he walked by. "Heading home, Chief?" she asked.

"Nope. Just thought I'd take a turn around the town square. Foot patrol."

"You look like you could use a nap, and maybe a couple of pain pills."

"I'm okay." He hated taking pain pills. They helped the pain but made his brain fuzzy.

"You don't look okay," she said with her customary bluntness. Doris was a no-nonsense single mother who had put two kids through college with no help from the drunken bum she'd married. She'd been with the department twice as long as Miguel, and knew where all the bodies were buried, and what it took to keep everything and everyone working smoothly. In other words she was indispensable. "Take your radio. Both Lorenzo and Hank are out in the hills on calls. I'm holding down the fort alone."

His radio was clipped on his belt. She could see it as plain as day. She was just letting him know who really ran the Enchantment Police Department—and it wasn't him.

"Okay, I get the hint. I'll take the Durango. That way, if anything comes up I'll have my wheels." So much for his half-hour stroll.

She nodded her approval and went back to her work.

It was a hot sunny morning and traffic was light. He'd stop by his parents' house first and tell his mother about the burn on his wrist before she heard it at the market or the hairdresser and went looking for him at the hospital.

"Hey, Miguel. Got a minute?" Nolan McKinnon was waving at him from the sidewalk in front of the newspaper office. Miguel sighed and pulled into an empty parking spot two doors down. He lowered the window and waited for his friend to jog over.

"I thought you got everything you needed last night out at Manny's," Miguel said as Nolan leaned into the passenger side of the big SUV.

"I got a couple of good pictures and I damned near got my eyebrows singed off when that bale of straw next to the barn caught fire, but I didn't get any memorable quotes from the chief of police,'' Nolan said with a grin.

Miguel narrowed his eyes and gave his friend a closer look. Sure enough, his left eyebrow looked a little sparse. ''Hope to hell that grows back before the wedding,'' he drawled. ''No way am I going to the drugstore all decked out in my tux and getting you an eyebrow pencil to fill it in. That's above and beyond the call of duty for a best man.''

Nolan frowned a little. ''God, do you think Kim would make me do that? The wedding's not for a couple of weeks. Does it show that much?'' He examined himself in the side mirror. ''How long does it take for eyebrows to grow back?''

Miguel shrugged. ''No idea. What do you need to know?''

Nolan gave himself one more critical look, then pulled a small tape recorder out of his pocket and flicked it on. ''The usual. I already got fire-safety quotes from the fire chief. Now I need the usual warning about the ban on outdoor burning and campfires.''

''Okay, you got it.'' Miguel grinned. ''The usual. And you can add it's a federal offense to start fires on public land without the proper permits.''

''That's it?''

''Yep.'' Miguel was still grinning.

''Want to tell me how you got that burn on your wrist?''

''I had a lousy fire extinguisher in my truck and I paid the price for it. I'm heading down to the hardware to buy a better one.''

A chirping sound came from Nolan's shirt pocket.

He flicked off the tape recorder and fished out his cell phone with two fingers. ''McKinnon here.'' He lifted his shoulders in an apologetic shrug. ''I'll catch up with you later, Miguel.''

''You know where to find me.'' He backed the Durango out of the parking space and continued on around the square. After he saw his mother, he needed to call Devon and make arrangements to meet somewhere private. He didn't quite have the nerve to show up at The Birth Place and talk to her in front of a dozen other women. He'd all but proposed marriage to her the night before up there on the mountain, and it was going to make for awkward conversation.

He slowed at the crosswalk in front of the courthouse and caught a glimpse of Manny Cordova heading into the hardware store across the square.

''What the hell's that old coot doing in town already this morning?'' He hadn't left Manny's place up on Switchback Road until 3:00 a.m. At that point, his granddad's crony, also an ex-Marine, was still patrolling his fence line watching for hot spots and blowing cinders. That's how Miguel had gotten the burn on his hand, from a flaming ember of dry grass that had landed along the fence line as he was driving up to Manny's place.

He hadn't stopped to get his patrol car after dropping Devon at the foot of her driveway and hightailing it out of town. That was how he learned that the fire extinguisher he carried in his truck wasn't worth a bucket of warm spit. Hell, a bucket of spit would have been more effective. He'd given it a toss into the bed of the truck and then went at it with his coat.

By the time one of the Enchantment volunteer firemen saw what was happening and drove up to lend a hand, a blazing tangle of dried grass had wrapped itself around his left wrist and branded him. When it was all over, there hadn't been enough of his sports jacket left to bother picking up out of the ashes. He couldn't do much about the jacket right now. That would require a trip to Taos. But he could replace the fire extinguisher.

Miguel pulled into a parking spot in front of the hardware that his maternal great-grandfather had started in the 1920s. Daniel had retired and sold the business to Miguel's cousin Joe about fifteen years earlier, but he still helped out around the place. His granddad was probably working today, since Joe and his family were off at his cousin's to help get ready for their daughter's *kinaalda,* the days-long, coming-of-age celebration that traditional Navajos gave when young girls in the family entered womanhood.

His boots thumped on the weathered boardwalk that fronted the store. He took off his sunglasses and gave the vintage Schwinn Corvette leaning against the storefront the once–over. The bicycle was in sorry shape, but new handle grips and seat, and a little work on the chrome would make a world of difference. Even in its present dilapidated shape, the bike was worth a pretty penny. He hadn't seen one like it around town. He wondered whose it was. Since the owner was most likely inside the hardware, he'd soon find out.

Someone had made an attempt to wash the display window in the not-too-distant past, but the glass was so old and wavy you still couldn't get a good look at what was inside. Not that it mattered. His cousin hadn't changed the merchandise in the window in as long as Miguel could remember. When he opened the door, the old-fashioned bell above his head jangled, alerting whomever was behind the counter. The place smelled of horse feed and leather, as well as the linseed oil Joe used on the wooden floor. Like the display window, the crowded aisles and overflowing bins hadn't changed much since he'd worked for Joe and made deliveries in his grandad's '51 Ford pickup the summer before he went to boot camp.

The summer he'd first made love to Devon.

Hell, he couldn't seem to keep his mind off the woman for more than ten minutes at a stretch. Especially when she'd sounded so lost and confused when she turned down his half-baked proposal up on the mountain last night.

Even without his sunglasses the place was gloomy and dark. Miguel gave the store a quick survey, the habit of eight years in police work. His grandfather was behind the counter, Manny in front. Halfway down the third aisle from the left, where the bicycle parts and tires were kept, was a young Hispanic kid, tall and rangy, with the beginning of what might one day be a pretty good-looking mustache fuzzing his upper lip. He gave Miguel the same kind of once-over he was getting and looked away, just a hair too quickly, so as not to look guilty doing it.

Enchantment was a small town. Miguel came across most of the high-school kids at one time or other during the year. He'd never seen this boy before. It didn't take Sherlock Holmes to figure out he must be one of the kids Devon had taken under her wing. He fit the description she'd given of him. Miguel watched him for a moment longer, then shifted his attention to the two old men. He lifted his finger and pushed the brim of his hat back on his head. "Manny, I thought the EMTs told you to take it easy for a day or two. You swallowed a lot of smoke."

"This old jarhead don't know what the word *rest* means," his grandfather growled from his accustomed place behind the long wooden counter that fronted the store. His expression was serene, but Miguel knew him as well as anyone and he caught the flash of concern in his old eyes. "Looks like you got yourself singed up there, too," he remarked, nodding toward the bandage.

"Don't move as fast as I used to," Miguel said, dismissing the injury.

Manny eyed the bandage, as well. "Sure sorry about that, Miguel."

"My own fault," Miguel said. "I should have let the guys in the turnout coats take care of it."

The fire could have gotten out of control, with tragic consequences, and all three knew it. Two years of drought and a town surrounded by thousands of acres of government forest land that hadn't been logged or even thinned out in Miguel's lifetime was a recipe for disaster. They'd dodged a bullet last night, but the next time Enchantment might not be so lucky.

"Manny's looking to buy a new incubator for them chicks he's having delivered today. He's going to have to set it up in his kitchen now since he went and burned down his chicken coop trying to get it to heat up one more time.''

''It heated up all right,'' Manny said, dropping his head to hide his shame. ''*Madre de Dios,* I thought my whole place was going up in smoke.''

''We're all just lucky the wind wasn't blowing last night,'' Daniel said. ''And while we're at it. You're too old to be raising chickens, you old coot.''

''You still got chickens out at your place last time I looked,'' Manny shot back. ''At least no one's been stealing mine out from under my nose.'' The kid in aisle three dropped a tire pump with a bang that brought three sets of eyes to bear on him.

''Sorry,'' he mumbled, and set the tire pump carefully back on the shelf.

Manny drew himself up as straight as a recruit. ''I'm gonna keep my own birds so I can make *huevos rancheros* whenever I want them. I make pretty damned good *huevos,* hey, Miguel? You used to come up to my place and eat them with my boys, remember?''

''I remember,'' Miguel said with a grin. From the corner of his eye he saw the kid was watching him again. He turned his head and the boy immediately focused on the inner tubes in front of him.

''Trouble is,'' Daniel said in his slow, deliberate way, ''don't have no incubator on hand. Gotta be special-ordered. Best I can think of is for Manny to get him a big old lightbulb and hang it over a box for the chicks when they get here.''

''Too hard to regulate the temperature,'' Manny

said, shaking his head. "They'll be okay during the day, but it gets cold at night up there on the mountain. And if I keep a lightbulb shining on them, they'll drive me *loco* peepin' away all night long."

"How about a heating pad?" Miguel suggested. "They got waterproof ones over at the drugstore. Lots of temperature choices, too. Put an old feed sack on top of it and they'll be fine until you can get your incubator."

Manny's eyes narrowed as he thought it over. "Hey, that just might work. You're one smart Indian, Miguel. And then when the chicks are old enough to put outside, I'll have a new heating pad to keep me warm at night."

"You'll need it for all the aches and pains you're going to have putting up a new coop. Want me to add a roll of chicken wire to your bill while I'm figuring it up?"

"Nope," Manny replied. "Most of the fencing's still good. I'm not lettin' it go to waste so you and Joe can get more money outta me."

Miguel turned away from the two old men. They would go on squabbling and telling tall tales of the old days for hours if no one else came into the store to interrupt them. He walked down the aisle toward the Hispanic kid, who stiffened his shoulders and turned to face him. The guarded expression on the boy's face alone was enough to set off Miguel's internal radar. The kid had something to hide. He held out his hand. "Hi. I'm Miguel Eiden, chief of police. I don't think I've seen you around here before today."

The boy hesitated, then shook Miguel's hand. "I'm not from around here," he said. "I'm...I'm staying with a friend."

Miguel nodded. "What's your name?"

Again the boy hesitated. "Jesse. Jesse Molina."

"Looking for inner tubes for that Schwinn out there?"

"Yeah." Jesse looked as embarrassed as any other fifteen-year-old male would who had to admit to riding a bicycle at least three times older than he was.

"Don't see bikes like that often anymore."

"Yeah." Jesse glanced toward the window. "Some wheels."

"You'd be better off selling it. Some polish on the chrome and that bike'd be worth a fair amount to a collector. Or just to someone old enough to remember when Eisenhower was president."

For a moment the dark eyes brightened as if considering the possibility, but then the guardedness returned. "It's not really mine. My friend's just letting me borrow it while I'm staying with her."

It wasn't Devon's bike, either, Miguel surmised. It probably belonged to the Zimmermans, the elderly couple who owned the cabin she was renting. Miguel leaned forward and the kid took a step backward so fast he almost tripped over his own feet. Miguel pretended not to notice. "Probably nothing out here that would fit that relic, but there might be a couple of old inner tubes in the back that would do. Hang on a minute and I'll ask."

"You don't have to do that." The boy's voice bristled with pride and embarrassment. "I don't have any money with me to buy them, anyway."

Miguel nodded. "Won't hurt to look and see if they're back there for when you *do* have the money."

"Yeah, I guess."

"What do you need, Miguel?" Daniel had come out from behind the counter. He was dressed Navajo style this morning, a dark purple velveteen shirt over blue jeans, cinched around his ample middle with a belt of elaborately worked silver circles. Daniel must have plans for the evening. He wouldn't wear his best clothes to work at the hardware on an ordinary day. Miguel cast his mind over the town's schedule of events and service-club meetings that Doris printed off for him on a calendar sheet every Monday morning. Tonight was the regional meeting at the American Legion. His grandfather was sergeant-at-arms. Miguel should probably try to make that one himself if nothing happened to keep him from getting off duty on time.

"He's looking for inner tubes to fit that old Schwinn bike outside. Think there's anything in the back room that would do?"

Arms folded across his chest, Daniel surveyed the boy down the length of his nose. Jesse kept his gaze at the level of the silver clasp of Daniel's bolo tie. "Might have a couple. My nephew don't throw much of anything away that might have use in it yet. I'll go look."

"I already told the chief here I don't have no money."

"We could work something out. Don't get much call for that size no more."

"Listen, old man. I told Marshal Dillon here I don't have any money. And I don't have any way to get any, *comprende?*"

The kid pushed by Daniel, knocking him slightly off balance. Miguel reached out with one hand and grabbed the kid by the shoulder. "That's no way to talk to someone who's only trying to help you."

"I don't want your help. I don't care about that old bicycle. I have a—" He shut his mouth so fast Miguel could hear his teeth click together. He wriggled to be free. "Let me go."

"Not until you apologize to my grandfather for your smart mouth." Miguel tightened his grip on Jesse's shoulder enough to let him know he meant business. The kid was almost skin and bones, not much muscle and no fat. Not as skinny as some of the teens in Somalia that smiled one minute and pointed an AK-47 at you the next, but pretty close.

"I ain't apologizing to nobody."

"Okay, have it your way. We'll go down to the station. Pushing an eighty-year-old man comes close to assault, the way I see it."

The boy went deathly still. "I didn't mean to push him. It...it was an accident. Look, just let me go. I won't come back in here. I won't bother you no more."

"What do you say, Granddad?" The kid was shaking like a leaf. More with fear than anger, Miguel guessed.

"Accidents happen."

"*Lo siento.* I'm sorry," the kid said, his voice cracking.

Daniel inclined his head in gracious acceptance of the grudging apology. "If you decide you want those inner tubes, just let me know."

Just then the bell over the door jangled and Devon stepped inside. A dark-haired, dark-eyed little girl held on to her hand, hopping from one foot to the other. Devon's head was turned. She was smiling at something the very pregnant teenager behind her was saying.

Her head turned back and she blinked. "Jesse? We saw the Schwinn outside, so we thought we'd come in and see what—" She stopped. Her smile was replaced by a frown when she saw that Miguel was hanging on to a handful of the boy's T-shirt. "Miguel? What's wrong? What's going on here?"

CHAPTER ELEVEN

"I TAKE IT THIS IS ONE of the kids you've got staying with you," Miguel growled, giving Jesse a little shake.

"Yes, he is." Devon felt a wave of near despair wash over her. This morning she'd gotten Sylvia to agree to at least minimum medical care. She and Lydia had worked together as a real team to accomplish that goal. Maria was healthy and happy and looking forward to a play visit with Nolan's niece, Sammy Davidson. Later she had planned to take Sylvia or Jesse with her to Angel's Gate in another attempt to locate their aunt. She'd been feeling pretty good about the way she was handling things. And now she'd walked in on what looked like an arrest. "Jesse, what did you do?"

"Nothing."

"Jesse here's got an attitude problem," Miguel said. At the moment he looked nothing like the funny, sexy man who'd taken her to dinner and kissed her on the mountain. He looked like the hard-eyed Marine who'd returned from Somalia and broken her heart. "He needs to learn some respect for his elders."

"I have respect," Jesse shot back. He was stiff and

trembling, but he made no effort to free himself of Miguel's grip. "I told the Indian I was sorry."

"Try 'Mr. Elkhorn,'" Miguel said in that cop's voice that sent cold shivers up and down Devon's spine. Maria let go of Devon's hand and wrapped her arm around Sylvia's thigh, hiding her face.

"Mr. Elkhorn." Jesse swiveled his head to look up at Miguel. "But I don't have much respect for the cops in this town," he muttered. Miguel's eyes narrowed, but not before she saw a spark of amusement behind them.

"No more smart talk." He tightened his grip on Jesse's shirt.

"It's all just a misunderstanding, Devon," Daniel intervened. "Miguel, let the boy go. He said it was an accident and I believe him."

"Thanks." Jesse shrugged his thin shoulders to resettle his shirt as Miguel released him, then took a quick, prudent step sideways. That was when Devon noticed the bandage on Miguel's hand. Her heart lost its rhythm for a moment. He must have been hurt up at Manny's. Was that why he hadn't called her?

"I just came in here to see if they had any inner tubes for that old bike. I thought if I got it to where I could ride it, I could maybe find some odd jobs or something." He shoved his hands in the back pockets of his faded jeans. "When I told the old...Mr. Elkhorn I wasn't going to buy them because I didn't have the money, the cop here didn't like my attitude."

"I still don't," Miguel informed him, but his voice wasn't quite as hard as it had been.

"Do you have inner tubes to fit the bike, Daniel?"

Devon asked, pulling her eyes from Miguel's bandaged wrist.

"I do. I told the boy we could work out some payment if he wanted them."

"I don't want to owe anyone anything."

"That's not good business sense, *hombre*," Manny interrupted. "Take the credit and the inner tubes. How else will you get up to my place to help me with the chicken coop?"

"What?"

"I'm telling you I'll hire you to work on my chicken coop if you want the job. Can't afford to pay more than minimum wage, but I'll feed you while you're there. Is it a deal?"

"You're offering me a job?"

"*Sí,* isn't that what I just said in plain English?"

Jesse's face tightened. His pride was hurt and he longed to say no. His emotions were easy to read, but the realization that he couldn't afford to turn down the opportunity to earn some money was equally easy to decipher. "Thanks. I'll work hard."

"I guarantee you will, *hombre*," Manny chuckled. "It's a deal, then. We'll start tomorrow."

"Okay, I'll take the inner tubes. I've got a couple of bucks for a down payment." Jesse fished two worn dollar bills out of the pocket of his jeans and handed them to Daniel.

The old man didn't refuse the money and Devon was grateful for the sop to Jesse's pride. "I'll make you out a bill and a receipt for the down payment. You might as well come with me. Might take a few minutes to put my hands on them inner tubes in the storeroom.''

Manny motioned Jesse to follow him. ''You can help us load the stuff I need on the back of my truck. I'm too tired to do anything else today. Tomorrow I'll pick you up at seven sharp.''

''I'll find my way.''

Miguel snorted. ''Better take him up on the offer. It's uphill all the way to Manny's place.''

''Listen to the Indian—don't never turn down a ride if your path lies up a mountain.'' Manny chuckled at his own witticism. ''Is that okay with you, Devon?''

''Yes,'' she said. She'd had so many other things on her mind she hadn't given much thought to the kids' lack of money. Now she realized what a worry it must be to Jesse and Sylvia to be completely without funds. ''Thank you for giving Jesse the job.''

''De nada, señorita.''

''Keep your eye on things for a minute, will you, Miguel?'' Daniel requested as the trio headed for the storeroom.

Maria whispered that she wanted to go home, but her words barely registered with Devon, who found her eyes once more drawn to the bandage on Miguel's wrist. She held out her hand and he placed his palm on hers. ''What happened?'' she asked.

''I needed a bigger fire extinguisher,'' he said. ''That's what I'm doing here now, looking for a new one.''

She lifted her eyes to his face, noting for the first time the drawn look around his mouth, the fine lines at the corners of his eyes. "It was close to getting out of control up there last night, wasn't it?"

"But it didn't."

"Thank God. How bad is your burn?"

"Second-degree. A couple of blisters, I might even get a scar out of it. It hurts like hell."

She didn't want to think of him in pain. "Did you ask for pain medication? They shouldn't have sent you home from the E.R. without a prescription. I…"

He grinned down at her and she realized she was still holding his hand. She released him and wrapped both hands around the strap of her shoulder bag.

"Yes, they gave me pain medication. I didn't take it. It makes my head feel like it's packed in those funny little foam peanuts. Can't do my job like that."

Maria emitted a faint giggle and peeked out at him from behind Sylvia's leg. Miguel dropped to his haunches. *"Hola, señorita. Se llama Miguel."*

"Hola," Maria whispered. "I'm Maria."

"¡Mucho gusto!"

"You're a policeman. Jesse said never, never talk to policemen." She ducked back behind Sylvia's skirt.

"I'm Devon's friend. Does that make a difference?"

She looked out at him once more and shook her head. "You were mean to my brother."

Miguel stood up. "Looks like I struck out there, too." He held out his hand. "You must be Sylvia."

She hesitated a moment, then shook his hand. "Yes."

"Welcome to Enchantment."

"Thank you." When Sylvia spoke, her tone was polite but her expression was guarded. Devon's spirits sank a little lower. Having Miguel for a friend was going to cost her some of the trust she'd worked so hard to earn with the girls. Their brother's trust was probably a lost cause.

Jesse appeared with a box containing the inner tubes. "The old guys are back there arguing about a roll of chicken wire," he said. "Let's go. I'll change these when I get back to your place." He refused to look at Miguel.

"We can put the bike in the back of the Blazer," Devon suggested.

"I'll ride it back. There's enough air in the tires now to get that far."

"All right." She was ready to agree to almost anything to get them out of the hardware store. Miguel still looked all cop when he glanced in Jesse's direction. She didn't want any more words between them. "Goodbye, Miguel."

"Later," Miguel said, and even to Devon's ears the single word sounded ominous.

To Jesse it would constitute a threat.

She drove the girls straight home. She'd meant to take them to the drugstore for Sylvia's vitamins and iron supplement, and then to the grocery to restock the refrigerator. She had four patient appointments scheduled for the afternoon and a beginning Lamaze class to teach that evening. That left very little time to explain her relationship to Miguel to the suspicious siblings—especially when she didn't understand that relationship herself.

Sylvia hustled Maria into the house and settled her in front of the TV, coming back into the kitchen where Devon was checking to see if she had all the ingredients for tuna salad. She opened the fridge and stared inside.

"Is Jesse back yet, Devon?"

Devon shook her head. "It'll be slow going coming up the grade on low tires."

"Yes, I suppose so."

"Is tuna salad okay for lunch? Does Maria like it?"

"Sure." The children never complained about what she fed them. "There are chips and cookies in the pantry. And apples and celery in the fridge."

"What about mayonnaise?"

"There's a new jar in the cupboard to the left of the sink." Sylvia knew more about where things were located in her kitchen than Devon did. She had never worried much about what she ate, or when, before they came. Now she found herself looking forward to the meals Sylvia prepared. "There's a box of raisins there, too. My mother always put raisins in her tuna salad."

"Sounds great."

Sylvia took the one good knife from the drawer and the cutting board from the counter. She rinsed the celery and began to chop, curling her fingers under to keep them from harm's way, just as Devon had seen chefs on the cooking channel do. The girl had real talent. Should she speak to her about the possibility of culinary school after she graduated? But then she swallowed her words. She had no business encouraging Sylvia in any future paths she might take. She had no legal claim to the children at all. By rights she should have called Protective Services or the INS days ago.

"That policeman in the store today who was hassling Jesse. He's the one who called you on the radio the day you found us in the old mine, isn't he? I recognized his voice." Sylvia kept on working adding raisins and a few walnuts, from a bag Devon had found in the freezer, to the celery, tossing them in a crockery bowl she pulled from the highest shelf of the cupboard.

"Yes." Devon pretended to concentrate on opening the tuna can and draining off the water.

"He's your friend?"

"Yes, he is." She wasn't about to volunteer any more. What could she say? Their relationship was difficult to define. It had started as a teenage infatuation, then…not-quite-everlasting love.

"You've known him for a long time?" Devon had told Sylvia and Jesse a little about the summers she'd spent in Enchantment with Lydia while she was growing up.

"We dated when we were teenagers. Then he went off to the Marines and I went back to San Francisco. I didn't see him for years until I moved here."

"But there's something still there between you."

"Goodness, what makes you think that?" She was standing with her back to the girl, looking for the milk in the refrigerator, grateful that Sylvia couldn't see the shock that must surely show on her face.

"You were trembling when you saw that he was hurt and examined the bandage on his hand."

"I was surprised and worried, that was all." Devon grabbed the milk and an apple and put them on the table without turning around.

"I used to feel like that with Kyle," Sylvia said, her voice sad but steady.

Devon was grateful for the chance to move the subject away from Sylvia's astute observation of her feelings for Miguel. She turned to the sink. "Do you want Kyle to know about the baby?" she asked as she handed Sylvia the mayonnaise jar.

"I don't know. Maybe? I haven't wanted to think about it." She was silent for a little while before she spoke again. "He should be responsible for her, too." Lydia had decreed after listening to the heartbeat that Sylvia's baby was a girl.

Devon wanted to ask if the baby's father was an American citizen. Most likely he was. Would that make a difference in Sylvia's immigrant status somewhere down the line? She had no idea, and at the moment didn't know where to begin to find out.

Maria appeared in the kitchen doorway. "I'm thirsty," she announced in Spanish, something she hadn't done for the past few days. It was an indication of how upset the encounter in the hardware store had left the child.

"Sit down. I'll pour you a glass of milk," Sylvia said, wiping her hands on a towel.

"I'm hungry, too." Maria had her arms wrapped around a floppy, yarn-haired baby doll that Devon had spotted at a yard sale on her way home from the clinic one day. The doll had come with two different sets of clothes, a blanket, a bottle and pacifier. Maria kept it with her day and night.

"Lunch is almost ready."

"Where's Jesse?" She'd reverted to English now and stood on tiptoe to look out the window. "Isn't he coming back?"

"He'll be here in a few minutes. Here's your sandwich and an apple. You can have a cookie when you finish it."

Maria eyed the sandwich suspiciously, then bent her head to sniff it. "Tuna fish?" She made a face.

"You like tuna fish," Sylvia said firmly.

"What are those?" She pointed to a raisin.

"Raisins. They taste good."

"No. Yuck." Maria said just as firmly as her sister and began to carefully remove each and every raisin from her sandwich.

Sylvia looked at Devon, lifted her shoulders in a shrug that said far more than words and smiled. Really smiled for the first time that Devon could remember seeing. She was a very pretty girl when she smiled.

The back door opened and Jesse stood on the threshold, the sunlight spilling around him like molten gold. He was hot and sweaty from the uphill ride from town, and the angry look he'd worn at the hardware store was still in place.

"Hi, Jesse. You look hot," Maria said, once more speaking in English. "Do you want some of my milk?"

"No. Not right now. I need to talk to Sylvia." He

jerked his head toward the area behind the house. "Come on."

Sylvia hesitated, looking at Maria.

"I'll stay with her," Devon said. She picked up the package of Oreos on the counter. "Would you like a cookie, Maria?" As she hoped, the offer diverted the little girl's worried attention from her brother and sister.

Devon walked to the sink and looked out the window. Jesse was doing all the talking. Sylvia stood quietly, head bowed. The window was closed and Devon couldn't hear what he was saying. Maria asked for another cookie. She wasn't smiling anymore, but clutching the doll tight to her chest. She took the cookie handed her and sat quietly eating it. Devon turned back to the window. Jesse was gesturing to the west, up the mountain toward Silverton. Sylvia gave her head a violent shake. She put her hands over her ears. That was enough for Devon.

"I'm going to see what Jesse and Sylvia are talking about. You'll be okay here, won't you?" The little girl looked at her with solemn eyes and nodded.

Devon opened the door and took the gravel path to the base of the pine tree where Jesse and Sylvia were so deep into their argument they didn't hear or see her until she was standing beside them.

"Want to let me in on the discussion?"

"We're leaving," Jesse said flatly. "I don't like that cop. He's going to start nosing around here for sure."

"There's nothing he can find here that would harm you," Devon said quietly.

"He's Devon's friend," Sylvia said. She wasn't crying, although her eyes were wide and apprehensive.

"Yeah, her real good friend, I'll bet. I saw how you looked at him. You got—"

"That's enough, Jesse," Devon said.

"No. I'm in charge of my sisters. I'm not going to get us picked up by the INS and put on a bus back to Mexico. We've got no family left there at all if our grandmother's dead. Maria's never even been there. America is our home. We'll go to Denver, maybe. Or Las Vegas. I'll bet I could get work at a hotel in Vegas."

"Not without papers you won't," Devon said. She tried to remain calm, the voice of reason, but it was difficult. The thought of the three children homeless and on their own in a city like Las Vegas was chilling.

"There are ways to get papers." His voice was cold, determined. "I'll ride the bike up to the mine and get the truck started somehow. You get our stuff together, Sylvia. Be ready to go when I get back."

"No, don't," Devon said. "Wait." But what right did she have to make them stay? All she could do was call the authorities, call Miguel and set in motion the events Jesse had just described.

Jesse ignored her as she feared he would. He spun on his heel, but Sylvia reached out and grabbed him by the arm. "I'm not going. And neither is Maria."

"You can't stay here." He jerked at her hand, but she held on.

"We are staying here. I believe Devon. She won't tell anyone the truth about us. Even...him."

"We can't take that chance."

"What about *Tia Lucia?*"

"We'll figure out how to get in touch with her when we find a place to stay."

"A place to stay?" Sylvia's laugh was ragged, near hysteria. Devon longed to comfort her, but she stayed silent. Jesse wouldn't listen to her, but he might be persuaded by his sister. "Another mine shaft with the cries of ghosts keeping us awake all night?"

"That was only the wind. It will be a better place than the mine."

Tears ran down her cheeks, but she ignored them. "You can't promise that. I'm not going. Neither is Maria. Today I heard the baby's heartbeat. She's alive inside me. She's going to be born. Soon. Devon and her grandmother know this." She dropped her hand from his arm and laid it on her distended stomach. "I know this. I want my baby to be born here. With Devon to help me. Please, Jesse."

"The cop—he'll figure it out. Or the old Indian will find the truck—"

"Just until the baby is born, Jesse. Please."

He was still as tense as a coiled spring, but the fight had gone out of him. "All right, we'll stay."

CHAPTER TWELVE

THE SIGN THAT MARKED THE ROAD to Silverton had
fallen over again. Miguel made no effort to stop and
right the rickety wooden post. The fewer people who
found their way up here the better as far as he was
concerned. Too damned dangerous. The whole place
should have been bulldozed over when they found
Teague Ellis's body at the bottom of the mine shaft.

He made the turn onto the access road. While he
was out here, he might as well check the place out.
The big SUV was almost too wide to maneuver
through the second-growth pine and aspen. He kept
his speed under five miles an hour. He didn't need
any of the city council stopping him to ask where he'd
come by the big scratch through the center of the
town logo.

Miguel parked the truck just past the plank bridge
that spanned Silver Creek and relayed his location to
Doris at the station. "Ten-four, Chief," she replied.

"Anything going on in town I should know
about?" he asked, resting his wrist on the steering
wheel. It didn't hurt as much as it had the first couple
of days, but it wasn't healed enough to go without a
bandage yet.

"Melvin Whitehorse backed into Striker Martin's

Jeep at the corner of Paseo and Sage. Just a fender bender, but Melvin's claiming Striker was stopped dead in the middle of the street. He's threatening to sue. I sent Hank Jensen to take care of it.''

"Why would Striker be stopped in the middle of the street?'' Miguel wondered aloud before he realized his mike was still open.

"Probably checking out the Widow Barkley's driveway for competition. I heard Earl Lazenby's been very attentive…''

Miguel didn't respond to the observation. Too many people monitored the police band with their scanners. Doris had a penchant for knowing more about what was going on in the town than was good for her, and she grabbed any opportunity to talk about it.

"I'll be ten-seven for the next fifteen minutes or so. I want to check out the old mine entrance and make sure it's still secured. Eiden out.''

He turned off the engine and climbed out of the truck. He'd walk the rest of the way in. No need to advertise his presence to anyone who might be snooping around the place. No birds sang in the trees that lined the almost dry creek bed, although that might be due to the hawk circling high above him. Nothing moved along the main street of the abandoned town except dust devils, the small tornadolike whirlwinds that had fascinated him as a child, and still drew his attention when he spotted them swirling across the landscape.

He and Diego had played out here as kids. Hell, half the kids in town had spent summer afternoons playing war among the derelict buildings. Then he'd gone to war for real, more than once now, when you counted his stints in Bosnia and Afghanistan, and he didn't know if he'd want a kid of his own playing that same game.

A kid of his own.

He hadn't thought much about settling down and starting a family over the years, his mother's not so subtle hints aside. Not until lately. Not until after the night with Devon when part of him had hoped she would be pregnant from it. Now he thought he understood why. That part of him, the part of him that made lifetime commitments, was waiting. Waiting for Devon to come back to Enchantment.

Miguel climbed the steps of the old hotel. One pane of the big front window remained intact. If he wasn't an officer of the law he would be tempted to heave a rock through it himself. He pushed open the big double door and looked inside. Dust and broken bits and pieces of furniture, animal scat, bird droppings. Nothing had disturbed the dust for a long time. He hooked his thumbs inside his belt and surveyed the rest of the town from the sagging wooden porch. Quiet as the grave.

He turned his steps to the mine opening. As he climbed, his thoughts circled back to Devon, the way the hawk circled above him. He'd always been able to talk to her. Even as a hormone-laced teenager, he'd been able to spend time with her that wasn't all about sex. They'd laughed together, hiked together, planned their futures together. He was going to be commandant of the Marine Corps. She didn't want to climb the corporate ladder like her mother and father. She was going to be…exactly what she was now. A midwife. Except she was going to be the world's best midwife and her grandmother's partner at The Birth Place.

Something changed between Lydia and Devon that summer. He'd never figured out exactly what it was, but he had his theories. Hope Tanner had given birth about then and disappeared for ten years. Now she was back and married to Parker Reynolds. And if you asked him, Parker's son looked an awful lot like his new wife. He doubted too many other people had made the connection, but it was his business to watch faces, and body language, and he'd done a lot of it over the weeks Parker had asked him to keep an eye on his place while Hope's uncle, a scumbag member of the Brethren cult, had been out on bail.

Lydia, Parker, Dalton. And now Hope. What had gone on between the three adults back then? And how much did Devon know?

The details of those days had stayed fresh in his mind because it was the first time he'd made love to Devon. He'd been awkward and probably a little rough. Hell, it was his first time, too. He'd tried not to hurt her. Tried to make it good for her, but once he was inside her, the thinking part of his brain shut down and his body took over. Afterward he'd held her and she cried and said it was fine, wonderful, but he knew it was not. He promised to make it up to her.

And things did get better. He grinned. Way better. But nothing like that night a couple of months ago.

He wasn't a gangly kid anymore, and she wasn't a half-scared, half-aroused teenager. She was all woman. And she'd taken as much as she gave before she'd fallen asleep in his arms. It had been good, better than good, and this time he wanted her forever. He tried to tell her that up on the mountain. He hadn't done a very good job of it, but next time he would.

He was still smiling when he got to the mine entrance. The wire fencing was loose at the bottom corner, but there weren't any footprints visible on the stony ground. He unhooked the big flashlight from his belt and shone it into the darkness on the other side. Nothing. No sign anyone had been inside for years. He'd been very young when Teague Ellis's body had been found, but that hadn't stopped him and his brother from speculating about it when they were old enough. Had he been a skeleton? Had animals scattered his bones? Was his *chindi*—the evil spirits that the traditional Navajo believed were all of a person that was left behind after they died—still hanging around in there?

He turned to head back down when he caught a flash of reflected light. Something inside the half-opened door of the derelict barn below the mine was brighter and shinier than anything that had been there for the past seventy-five years had a right to be. He switched the heavy flashlight to his left hand, wincing at the pain from the still-tender burns as he curled his fingers around it, and opened the flap on his holster. Better safe than sorry this far out in the sticks.

He moved to the left, out of line of sight of the sagging door, coming up on the barn from above. He took off the big, gray Stetson and laid it on the ground beside the window, then looked inside. A pickup truck that had seen better days was parked there. The back end was half-full of odds and ends of camping gear, a couple of plastic garbage sacks that might contain sleeping bags or blankets, and what looked a lot like the mattress and folding chairs his granddad had reported missing a month ago.

Miguel slipped inside the door and scouted the pickup. He tried the passenger door. It wasn't locked and opened easily enough. He checked the glove box. It was empty. He wasn't surprised. He switched on the flashlight, checked under the seat. Clean as a whistle. Someone had taken a lot of care to clear out anything that might identify the owner.

Including the license plates, Miguel discovered, as he checked the back of the vehicle. It would make it harder to track down the owner, but not impossible. He strongly doubted it had been reported stolen from anywhere close by, though.

He decided not to call in to Farley's Garage and have it towed.

Whoever owned it would probably be back sooner or later. Not many cars traveled this road, and few of the ones who did got past his granddad's place without attracting his attention. He'd stop by on his way back to town and ask the old man to let him know when someone did come up this way.

He jerked on the drawstring of one of the plastic bags and looked inside. An old lantern, a beat-up skillet and cooking pot and not much else. The familiar logo on a fast-food sack caught his eye. He lifted it out and opened it, and found it filled with napkins and straws, little packets of ketchup and salt and nondairy coffee creamer. A miser's hoard of freebies—or a hungry person's gleanings from a restaurant's condiment bar? A cash-register receipt was stuck between two napkins. He picked it up. It was dated a week or so before his granddad had started noticing things missing. The restaurant's address, printed at the top, was in Phoenix. Hell of a distance to drive for a hamburger. He upended the sack and a plastic figure rolled out. A doll, maybe three inches tall, a fairy princess of some sort, with a sparkly magic wand in her hand, and long blond hair. The kind of thing a little girl would get in a "kiddie" meal. He picked it up and put it in his pocket.

He had an idea who'd driven the truck up here and why it had been abandoned. But he was going to keep it to himself just like his suspicions that Dalton Tanner's birth mother was his new stepmother. If Hope and Parker wanted the town to know the truth of Dalton's birth, they'd tell everyone in their own good time.

And if Devon wanted him to know the truth about the three kids living under her roof, he hoped she'd tell him soon, before he had to do something official about this truck, and their being in Enchantment.

DEVON CLOSED THE DOOR to the birthing room quietly behind her, although it would take more than a closed door to keep the echo of Carla Van Tassle's sobs from her ears.

Lydia came out of her office and waited, arms

folded. "She miscarried?" Lydia's usually brisk tone had softened to a near whisper.

"Yes," The affirmation sounded more like a sigh. "She woke up with cramps this morning and when they got worse and she began to bleed again, she called me. I've been with her ever since."

"How's she taking it?"

"She's pretty upset, but she understands that some pregnancies can't be sustained. Still, it was a shock. She's had no other symptoms except that early spotting."

"And because of me, she didn't have an ultrasound." Lydia looked old and tired, and her gray eyes were sad. Miscarriages were inevitable in some pregnancies, but they were always wrenching—for the midwives, too.

"There's no guarantee it would have shown that the baby was not developing correctly. And it certainly wouldn't have prevented the outcome. The miscarriage was spontaneous. Carla should be able to conceive again with no problem. Although I'm sure Dr. Ochoa will agree with me that she should wait a few months, for her emotional well-being as much as her physical healing. Celia's with her now, and she'll give her all the counseling she'll need later. And we'll be here for her, too."

"I suppose you're right." Lydia didn't sound convinced, and her uncertainty wasn't like her, either.

"I know I am." Devon hoped her confidence wasn't misplaced. Carla and Rick were young. They already had a fine healthy little boy. They would heal from their sorrow and go on to produce beautiful babies. It was only a matter of time.

Was that what was bothering Lydia? That she might be running out of time? Devon rarely thought of her grandmother as old, but she *was* getting on in years, and her heart was no longer reliable. Was Devon's indecision on taking over the clinic adding to her anxiety?

Lydia touched the tip of her finger to the medallion at her throat—seeking solace, Devon knew. "Still, the ultrasound…"

"Wouldn't have changed a thing." Devon laid her hand on Lydia's arm. "Why don't you go home and get some rest? We have a full day of appointments again tomorrow. It seems as if half of Arroyo County is having babies this month."

Lydia looked at Devon's hand on her arm. "Yes, it does seem that way. Devon?" She looked up and managed a smile.

"Yes?"

"Oh, nothing." Lydia apparently changed her mind. "I forgot to tell you your mother called a couple of hours ago while you were with Carla. She and your father have decided to come a few days early for the wedding."

Devon tensed. The last thing she needed was her well-meaning but incurably nosy mother complicating the already difficult situation with the children. "When?"

"Next week. Tuesday afternoon, I believe they said. They're renting a car in Santa Fe and driving up, so no one needs to meet them at the airport. She told me to tell you they'll be staying at the Morning Light. I offered my spare room, but she says there is no way your father will sleep on a futon again in this lifetime.''

Devon let the statement pass without comment. Lydia and Myrna had been butting heads since Myrna had learned to talk, maybe before, or at least that was what her uncle Bradley always said. Thank goodness he and Irene hadn't decided to come to town early, too.

The door to the birthing room opened, and Celia Brice stepped out. Her long blond hair, held back by tortoiseshell clips, swung free halfway down her back. She looked poised and sophisticated, but the illusion of coolness dissolved with one look at her warm blue eyes and compassionate smile.

''How's she doing?'' Devon asked as the three women moved toward the reception area of the clinic.

''She's sad and feeling very fragile, and a little apprehensive about going to the hospital. I told her you would stay with her as long as she wanted. Was that all right?''

''Of course,'' Devon replied. ''Hope has agreed to see my last patient for the day, so we can go over to Arroyo as soon as she feels strong enough to walk to the car.''

''I think she'll do fine. I explained that people will react to her loss in various ways. Some will want to know all the details. Some will want to pretend it didn't happen. I've suggested short-term grief counseling. I think she and Rick are open to it.''

''I'm glad.''

Suddenly Celia smiled again, but this time it was a smile so dazzling that Devon blinked and turned instinctively to see who or what had brought such joy to the other woman's eyes. "Patrick." Celia held out her hand to her fiancé. "What are you doing here? I didn't expect you until tomorrow."

"I finished up my business ahead of schedule and decided not to hang around another day in rainy, gloomy San Francisco when I could be here enjoying the sun and the mountain views. I thought I'd take you and Trish to Angel's Gate for dinner this evening if you're free."

"I am and I'd love to go. I know Trish would love it, too. I can't believe you got past her at the front desk." She attempted to look over his shoulder. "Where is she?"

"My mother is absent from her post. Shall we form a search party?" he asked with a grin so sexy it even raised Devon's pulse a beat or two.

"She had to make a trip to the post office," Lydia said. "She should be back at any moment."

"Wonderful. Hello, Lydia." He held out his hand. "How are you feeling?"

"Very well, thank you." Her haggard looks said otherwise.

"I'm glad to hear that." Patrick's eyes sought Devon's and for a moment she saw concern before he banished it with another sexy smile. "Devon, it's good to see you again."

"Hello, Patrick."

Trish's voice preceded her around the corner. "I'm back, Lydia. You can switch the calls back through—

Patrick!'' She came forward with outstretched hands, her face flushed with pleasure. ''We weren't expecting you until tomorrow.''

''I couldn't stay away.'' He took her hands in his and leaned down to kiss her cheek.

Trish's eyes sparkled with happiness. ''I'm so glad you're back. Will you be staying long this time?''

''I think I can manage a week or maybe two.''

''Wonderful. Then you'll be here for Kim and Nolan's wedding.''

He looked at Celia. ''I wouldn't miss it for the world.''

Trish's smile was radiant. For thirty years she'd suffered the abandonment of her baby in guilt and shame. Now she was reunited with the man he'd become, and the healing for both of them had begun.

''Excuse me,'' Devon said. ''I need to return to my patient.''

Patrick stepped back so that she could pass. As she moved down the hall, she could hear the conversation resume again. The low rumble of Patrick's voice, the pleased murmur of Trish's replies. But it was the look in Celia's eyes that stayed with her as she opened the door to the room where Carla and Rick waited.

It had been a look of love, deep and abiding, and it had echoed in Patrick's dark gaze. Patrick and Celia no longer had any secrets that must be kept. They were free to love—and Devon was not.

CHAPTER THIRTEEN

DR. OCHOA HAD BEEN CALLED away to do an emergency C-section by the time Devon arrived at Arroyo County with Rick and Carla. The two hours' wait before he made it to the E.R. had been tense and stressful. Carla had called her mother's house to talk to her little boy, and he'd started crying apparently. Then Carla had started crying, and by the time Devon had talked her through another bout of exhausted tears, she was wound so tightly herself she thought she might never relax.

When she returned home, Sylvia made her dinner—chicken breast and salad—but she ate only a little. Jesse was still at Manny Cordova's as he had been every day since the fire. Devon tried not to worry. Manny would send him home before dark, since Jesse was adamant that he wouldn't accept a ride from the old man every night. If nothing else, Jesse was resourceful. He'd gotten his sisters from Phoenix to Enchantment and kept them safe along the way. Still, Devon didn't like the idea of the teenager riding the old Schwinn along the twisting mountain roads between her place and Manny's in the dark.

Jesse's safety on the road wasn't her only worry. She suspected Manny was paying the boy in cash, and the first day he had free, he'd take the bike and head up to Silverton to work on his truck. He'd agreed to remain in Enchantment for Sylvia's sake, but he was wary and watchful, and Devon was aware that it wouldn't take much to spook him—all three of them—into running again.

She wished she'd been able to find their aunt that night at Angel's Gate. She'd been too busy since to go back. A phone call to the resort had gleaned little information beyond the fact that, yes, Lucia Molina did work there, but she was not on duty that day, and, in fact, not scheduled for the rest of the week. It was against resort policy to give out employee addresses or phone numbers, the polite but adamant voice on the other end of the line had told her. She would just have to check back at the beginning of next week.

Sylvia sat down at the table with Devon while she pretended to eat. Maria climbed onto the chair next to her sister and leaned against her. She knew Sylvia was going to have a baby. Now and then she put her hand on her sister's stomach to feel the baby kick, and Sylvia didn't discourage her. But other than that, she didn't ask many questions about the birth. She was a smart little thing and had picked up on the tension between her siblings. She must have realized the baby had something to do with it.

Devon, too, had bided her time these past few days. It would be Sylvia's decision whether or not to keep the baby when it was born. There were ways that help could be arranged for her, day care, medical assistance. But it would be much better if her immigrant status wasn't in doubt. Immigration would have to become involved no matter what decision she made. If Sylvia decided to give the baby up for adoption, it would become very complicated. If she kept the baby, would she be able to care for it properly? She could be sent back to Mexico, even though the baby would be an American citizen. The legal questions surrounding the birth made Devon's head spin.

Maria wanted an apple, and Sylvia got up to go to the refrigerator to get her one.

Devon looked out the window. The sun had already disappeared behind the mountain. She'd been inside all day, she realized, first at Carla and Rick's home, then at the birth center and the hospital E.R. Suddenly she needed exercise and fresh air. ''I'm going for a walk,'' she said.

''I'll come with you,'' Maria piped up, an apple slice poised halfway to her lips.

Sylvia placed her hands on the little girl's shoulders and turned her around. ''No, you won't. You are going to take a bath and wash your hair.''

''I don't need to wash my hair.''

''Yes, you do. You and Sammy were playing in the sand all afternoon.''

Devon had forgotten that Maria spent the afternoon with Nolan's niece. ''Did you have a good time at Sammy's?'' she asked.

Maria's pigtails bobbed up and down as she nodded. Seeing Maria so full of energy and happiness made Devon feel a little better. She *had* done the right thing in bringing the children to her home; she just had to remember that when the complexities of the situation conspired to overwhelm her. ''Yes. We

played with Brady. He's almost two.'' Brady was
Faith Tanner's little boy. Faith was Hope Reynolds's
sister. She lived with Hope and Parker, baby-sitting
for Sammy and other children during the day and taking college classes at night and on weekends.

''I'm glad you had a good time.''

She nodded emphatically again. ''I want to go back
to Sammy's house.'' Her sunny smile disappeared. ''I
know she can't come here.''

''Of course she can come here,'' Devon said.
''We'll invite her one day soon.''

''Really?''

''Really.''

''*¡Mil gracias!*'' She skipped out of the kitchen.

''Thank you,'' Sylvia said. ''But do you think it's
wise?''

''There's no reason she can't have a friend over if
you don't mind baby-sitting them. I'm sure Kim and
Nolan won't mind. I should have thought of inviting
Sammy sooner.'' It's what she would do if the children were hers. Except that they weren't hers. She
had always wanted a large family, brothers and sisters, children of her own. But these children had family, at least an aunt they cared enough about to uproot
themselves and come looking for. She, Devon, was
only a substitute, a good Samaritan. She wasn't family. She had no claim to them now or in the future.
The thought made her heart heavy. She stood and
picked up her plate and silverware. ''I'll help you
with the dishes.''

''No, go for your walk,'' Sylvia said. ''It will soon
be dark. You might twist your ankle or step in a hole

if you wait too long and can't see where you're going."

The sky had darkened slightly while they talked. "All right, I will. I'll take my cell phone with me in case the clinic calls or in case you need me."

Sylvia nodded. "Enjoy yourself."

Devon changed into her running shoes and stepped out into the clear, calm twilight. She jogged down the driveway but when she reached the road she slowed her pace. She didn't need physical exercise to tire her body, she needed peace of mind to rest her brain. Below her, she could hear cars on the more traveled roads leading into town. Above her, the sighing of night breezes in the pines were the only sounds to compete with her own soft footfalls.

Sunset had come and gone quickly as it always did in the mountains. It was high summer now, so the evening had not yet cooled enough for her to wear the light sweater she'd tied around her waist. Dust tickled her nose and somewhere off to her right a small animal scurried through the dry grass at the side of the road, heading home before night-hunting owls and larger predators became active.

She was abreast of Miguel's driveway now and she glanced through the screen of pines that hid his house from the view of passersby. No lights flickered through the webbing of pine boughs. He was probably still on duty. The Enchantment force was small. Even if he was chief now, Miguel often had to fill in an extra shift.

She hadn't seen him since the morning after the fire at Manny's place. The days had passed quickly, but now she realized how much she missed him. The sound of a powerful engine coming up the grade intruded on her thoughts, and moments later Miguel's SUV pulled into sight, as though her musings had conjured him from the thin mountain air.

He made the turn into his driveway, then stopped, waiting for her. She moved to the side of the truck. He rolled down the window. "Want a ride home?" he asked.

She shook her head. They hadn't been alone since that night on the mountain. She didn't think it was prudent they take up where they'd left off. Besides, the only time she'd seen him since had been the altercation with Jesse. She was still a little miffed with him for the way he'd treated the boy.

His thoughts must have been tracking along the same lines. "How's the kid working out at Manny's place?"

"Fine."

"You're still mad at me for giving him a hard time, aren't you?"

"No."

He grinned. Her stomach tightened with longing. God, his smile could turn her senses upside down in a matter of seconds. "You always were a lousy liar, Devon." He might have meant the comment in jest, but she took it seriously, a warning of how easily he could read her mind and her heart.

She focused on his words, not on his smile. "Manny says he's been a real help. He should have his new coop ready for the chicks by the end of the week."

"Then what's the boy going to do with his time?"

She didn't have an answer. He leaned his forearm on the window frame, and her eyes were drawn to the bandage on his hand and wrist. All thought of finding a suitable answer to his last query fled her brain. "Where have you been? That bandage is filthy."

He looked down at his hand, then back at her. "I was nosing around up at Silverton awhile this afternoon. Must have happened then."

A shiver skated up and down her spine, as if Teague Ellis's ghost had walked over her grave. "Silverton?" What had he found "nosing around" the old ghost town? The kids' pickup? The things they had left behind? The things Jesse had taken from Daniel's place? Was there anything in the pitiably small accumulation of stuff that could identify them? She longed and dreaded to ask him more. Instead, she touched a finger to the dirty gauze. "You need that changed. Did they send supplies home from the E.R.?"

"I have everything I need. Bandage, tape, antiseptic cream."

"I can help you—"

"I'll do it later, after I shower."

"Oh." She hadn't thought of that. And she wasn't going to run like a scared rabbit just because the thought of him coming out of the shower naked made her pulse pound in her ears. "I'll catch you on the way back…after I finish my walk…"

His hand closed over her fingers so quickly she couldn't pull them away. "Don't run away. Come with me now, Devon. We never finished what we started up there on the mountain Sunday night.'' She didn't know if he meant the conversation or the kiss. Repeating either was dangerous.

"I'm not running away." But of course she was, or should be, as fast and as far as her legs would carry her. Except that her traitorous feet were still planted firmly on the dusty roadway.

Miguel apparently wasn't taking any chances. He reached to his right and opened the passenger door of the Durango. "Get in." He wasn't asking her, he was ordering her. She didn't move for a moment, just held her gaze. The heat and challenge in his eyes called to something primitive and female in her. She might be a dozen times a fool for not turning her back and walking away, but she'd be damned if she let him think her a coward.

She walked around the hood of the truck and slid in beside him. "I can't stay," she said with a hint of challenge of her own. "The kids will miss me. I told Sylvia I was only going for a walk."

"You've got your cell with you, right? They can call you if they need you." She had no rebuttal for that and he knew it. "I won't make you stay one minute longer than you want to," he said, and put the truck in gear.

HE HADN'T TAKEN THIS FAST a shower since boot camp, Miguel thought as he ran a towel through his hair, then tossed it toward the hamper. He squinted at his face in the mirror above the sink. He needed a shave, but he wasn't going to stop for that, either. Devon was as skittish as a fawn caught in the open without its mother. He wouldn't be surprised if she'd hightailed it for home as soon as he'd shut the bathroom door, thinking he was bent on seducing her.

He *was* bent on seducing her, he thought as he pulled on his jeans. Maybe consuming her was more accurate. He had to put a tight rein on himself not to get hard just thinking about being with her, inside her, loving her. He did love her, damn it. Had loved her for almost as long as he'd known her. He'd just been too young and too stupid to recognize it for the enduring passion it clearly was.

She loved him, too, or was on the verge of it, he was convinced. But she had too many other things on her mind right now to let her heart overrule her brain.

He wasn't going to be able to walk into his kitchen, sweep her up into his arms and carry her to his bed like he wanted to. He was going to have to be more subtle. Besides, he didn't only have lovemaking on his mind. He was too much a cop for that. He needed more information about the Molina kids from her. He'd have to be as subtle going about that as the lovemaking. He slid his feet into a pair of moccasins his mother had picked up on the big reservation and pulled on a flannel shirt. Not bothering to button it, he scooped up the sack of supplies the hospital had sent home with him to bandage his burn and headed for the kitchen.

She hadn't bolted. She was sitting at the pine table staring out at the summer sunset that had turned the sky a dozen shades of purple and orange. She didn't look up, and he had a moment to study the clear, sweet lines of her profile. Her hair was pulled up into a knot on top of her head. She'd fastened it with some kind of clip that looked like tortoiseshell, all the same soft golds and brown of her hair. Tendrils had escaped to curl around her cheek and the nape of her neck. Faint lines bracketed her mouth and the corners of her eyes. She looked tired. Since his scouting mission up at the old ghost town, he knew it wasn't only the pressures of her job that had caused the worry.

She turned her head and her eyes widened a fraction in surprise to see him standing there. "I didn't hear you come in."

He lifted his foot to display the doeskin moccasin. "Stealth shoes."

"I've never seen you wear them before."

"Have you ever seen any Indian outside of the movies wear them?" he asked with a grin as he set the sack of bandages in front of her on the table.

She thought about that, then shook her head. "No, I guess not."

"That's because moccasins make great slippers, but they're useless for anything else. In this country you need boots. And good ones."

"Hmm…like your grandfather told me once. The Navajo have thrived when other tribes didn't because they take the best of other cultures and adapt it to their own."

"Damned straight," he said. She didn't seem too skittish, so he sat down beside her and laid his hand on the table. "You look like you had a rough day."

"I did. One of my mothers miscarried this morning. It was the woman who my grandmother called about the last time I was here. Do you remember?"

"I remember," he responded with a wry smile.

"It turned out there was a problem with the pregnancy, after all, although it seemed to be progressing normally." She looked past him out the window. He felt a little jab of pain near his heart. Babies were her business. She would be feeling the loss of this potential life almost as acutely as the mother. "It couldn't be helped, but still…"

"You aren't blaming yourself, are you?"

She shook her head. "No. There was nothing anyone could do. The baby wasn't developing properly. It leaves an empty hole in your heart, though." She looked up at him and her smile was sweet and sad. "They're not just little blobs of tissue, you know. They're babies, even then, arms and legs, eyes, a beating heart."

And babies grew up to be children, homeless on the run, in need of care and loving. Devon had a big heart. She'd take them all in. Hell, she probably hadn't given it more than thirty seconds thought. Not just big-eyed cuties like Maria, but the ones that were trouble on the hoof like Jesse, or an almost-woman having a baby of her own like Sylvia.

"This woman can have another child, right?"

"Yes." Her smile widened. "I'm sure she will. A healthy beautiful baby. Or two. Or three."

She always talked of babies in multiples, he'd noticed. Did she want a big family of her own? Like so many other important things, he couldn't remember ever having discussed the matter with her. He had lost so many years with her. He would regret that to his dying day.

"And you'll be here to deliver them?"

The smile faltered. "I hope so." She wiggled her fingers. "Let me see that hand."

The subject was closed. She wasn't going to let him closer to help ease the hurt. A shiver crawled over his skin, a tendril of doubt that he wouldn't let take root. He didn't know how to get past the roadblocks she kept throwing up in front of him, but he was damned sure going to try.

Her fingers trembled slightly as she turned his hand palm up. She slid the point of the scissors he'd brought to the table with the medical supplies beneath the soiled, wet gauze. "Sing out if I hurt you," she said. The kitchen was warm with the leftover heat of the afternoon sun. He could smell her hair, the flowery scent of her soap. There were tiny gold studs in her ears, and he remembered the feel of them from their night together as he had nibbled the soft lobes. She was wearing a pale-yellow T-shirt and cutoffs, which let him gaze his fill at the long, smooth length of her legs. He gave an involuntary jerk at the thought of those legs wrapped around him in the darkness of his bedroom as he drove himself into the heat of her body.

She stopped immediately. "Did I nick you?"

"No. The blade's cold, that's all."

"I'm almost done." She unwound the last of the bandage and turned his hand over, laying it flat on her own. He held himself very still. She lifted the medicated squares the E.R. doc had placed over the blistered skin on the back of his wrist. A little frown appeared between her brows. She touched the reddened skin on the back of his hand with a gentle pressure. Her nails were round and unpolished, her touch gentle. He suppressed the urge to sweep the tape and bandages off the table and make love to her right there and then. ''Is it still painful?'' she asked in a voice that wasn't quite steady.

''It's not bad unless I forget and twist my wrist too quickly.''

''It'll be tender for a while yet. It looks like it's healing well, though. You should probably keep it covered for another few days.'' She slipped her hand from beneath his, and he had to stop himself from closing his fingers around hers and holding her close, pain or no pain. He waited as she applied the antiseptic cream to a sterile square and placed it over his blistered skin. Then with quick, deft movements she replaced the wrapping, and the warmth of her touch was lost under the layers of gauze.

Once more she turned his hand palm up and secured the bandage with two short strips of tape. ''Keep it clean and dry for another day or two and it'll be fine.'' She laid down the roll of tape. ''All done,'' she said, and the words came out a breathy sigh.

He lifted her chin with the tip of his finger. ''No,'' he said. ''We're not all done.''

She didn't pretend to misunderstand his intent. ''I can't stay here, Miguel. I need to get back to the children.''

''They seem pretty self-sufficient to me,'' he said as she whisked the soiled bandage and paper wrappers into the empty sack they had come in.

"They'll be worried about me if I don't get back before dark." She stood up. "I...I should wash my hands."

He took the sack from her hands and pointed to the sink. "There's soap and a clean towel." He disposed of the plastic bag while she ran water over her hands and dried them with the towel. She turned around, her back to the sink, her eyes large and the color of the rain clouds that seemed to have vanished from the sky over Enchantment forever.

"I should be going."

"Not before we settle something between us."

"What?" A trapped looked came into her eyes.

"I'm not going to ask you about the kids, Devon," he said, moving toward her.

"You're not?" She faltered for a moment and he saw the muscles of her throat move as she swallowed. She lifted her chin and gave him back look for look. "I mean, why should I mind if you ask me about the children? Their mother was a good friend. They needed someone to watch over them. I volunteered. Lots of people would have done the same thing." She recited her reasons as though she'd memorized them for just such inquiries.

"I think we both know that's not the whole story." She took a step sideways as though to move past him. The words came out in a low growl, although he hadn't meant them to. He was losing her, he could tell. She was pulling back from him little by little, retreating into herself the way he'd done when he came back from Somalia. He wasn't going to let history repeat itself. "Devon, you can trust me. There are hundreds of things going on in this town I know about that I keep to myself.''

Surprisingly his words brought a smile to her lips. ''I know I can trust you,'' she said, reaching up to touch his cheek, the brush of her fingertips as light as dandelion fluff. She looked deep into his eyes. He sucked in his breath and held it. Her eyes were filled with tears, bottomless pools of gray. ''I can trust you to be exactly what you are. Loyal, honorable, a man of your word. Honest to a fault.'' Her voice dropped to a whisper. ''An officer of the law.''

She was right. His duty was clear—if he followed the letter of the law. But in reality he wasn't sure exactly what he would do if she came clean about the kids. He would have to notify the protective services and the INS, that was for sure, and he didn't want to do that. A good percentage of the citizens of Arroyo County were undocumented aliens, holding down jobs, raising families. He didn't bother them; they stayed out of his way.

At the moment he wasn't sure what the best course would be. They could work it out together if she trusted him, but right here, right now, she didn't, and that hurt. Maybe he should go at it from another direction? Maybe she needed commitment before she could trust him? ''We won't talk about the kids. We'll go back to that night on the mountain and we'll talk about us.''

She shook her head. ''I don't want to talk about us,'' she said. ''I know all about you that way, too. You're part of this town. Your roots are here. Your future's here. Mine may be, too, but my life isn't my own—''

He caught her around the waist and pulled her close. ''I'm in love with you, Devon. I wanted to tell you up there above Angel's Gate where we could almost touch the stars and you kissed me like you couldn't get enough of me. Enough of us.''

''We've always struck sparks from each other.''

''I'm not talking about some rekindled teenage crush, the kind of love that's as much sex as emotion and can't stand up to the test of time and the kind of raw deals life gives you sometimes. I mean the real thing. The forever kind of love.''

She lifted her hand to his mouth to silence him. ''Don't say any more, please.''

''I know what's coming next. Don't ask me to just be your friend, Devon.'' This time he made no attempt to keep the rawness out of his voice. He bracketed her face with his hands, smoothing the pads of his thumbs across the velvety softness of her cheeks. ''We've got too much history to be just friends.'' His heart was beating hard in his chest, as much from fear that she would still bolt and run, as from desire.

Her smile was a little lopsided this time, a little sad. ''No, I won't ask you to be my friend. I won't ask you for anything, Miguel. Only this.'' She closed her eyes and lifted her face to his.

CHAPTER FOURTEEN

HE CLOSED HIS MOUTH over hers, urging her lips apart. It wasn't a gentle kiss, but like their night of lovemaking in the spring, like the kiss on the mountain, it was a melding of body and soul that seared the senses. She slipped her hands inside his shirt and splayed her fingers across his chest. His skin was warm and smooth and she wrapped her arms around his waist so that she could press her breasts against the solid wall of muscle and sinew that lay beneath.

She had told herself she didn't need this, didn't need him, but she'd lied about that, as she had lied about so many things these past weeks. She did need him, desperately, wantonly, and she feared that would be the case until the last breath she drew into her lungs. She traced the outline of his ribs, the indentation of his spine, the flatness of his buttocks. She felt the heat and strength of him along every inch of her body, and deeper to the very depths of her soul.

His hands moved, too, unhooking the snap of her shorts, lowering the zipper, sliding them down her hips. The contrast of callused fingertips and soft gauze on his bandaged hand was momentarily distracting, erotic and sensual. His hands dipped below the waistband of her cutoffs and cupped her bottom through the thin silk of her panties. She moaned and pressed against him, leaning into the kiss and the intimate caress.

She ached to be wrapped in his arms, to sleep with the strong, steady beat of his heart beneath her cheek. She was tired of being alone, of having no one to confide in, to lean on...to love. "Ah, Miguel, don't stop." She reached down and urged his hands beneath the thin cotton of her T-shirt, upward to the aching fullness of her breasts. "I want you. I need you just like I did that night Lydia was so ill." She almost added, *Just like I've needed you every night of my life,* but she caught herself in time. She bracketed his face with her hands, urging him into another soul-searing kiss.

But he resisted. He covered her hands with both his own and held them at her sides. "No, Devon," he said, his eyes as dark as the high country night stealing down the mountain toward them.

"No?" She was utterly confused. Ten seconds ago he'd been ready and willing to make love to her. He was still hard, she knew, but he raised his head and stepped back. Cool air rushed into the space between them, chilling her skin, as his next words chilled her heart.

"No sex. Not like this. I'm not going to be your escape valve, Devon. That's not what I want from you."

"It's not like that." She was so breathless with desire, with need, that no words came. How dare he stop what he'd started, what he'd made her want so badly?

Miguel looked down at her. His face was a mask, but he couldn't quite hide the misery in his eyes. "Isn't it?" he asked, and waited for a reply she couldn't give. "Unless you can convince me otherwise, that's what I have to believe." His voice roughened around the edges. "Do you love me, Devon?"

She wanted to say yes. Dear God, how she wanted to! But she couldn't. The guilt that lay so heavily on her heart had formed itself into a lump lodged firmly in her throat. He knew she was lying to him about the children, and if he believed that, he would question everything else she told him. Maybe not here, not now, but soon. And possibly for the rest of their lives. She had a glimpse of a hellish future. Miguel's love dying by inches because he could never trust her word or her actions. He would question and he would doubt, and sooner or later it would destroy the love between them.

"I...I don't know exactly what I feel right now. I told you..." But she hadn't told him. Not what he wanted to hear. She shut her mouth. She couldn't tell one more lie, not even to gain what she wanted most in the world. And she couldn't tell the truth, for the children's sake. She stepped out of his arms and attempted to straighten her clothes. She could feel the color rise in her throat and cheeks, but she didn't look down, didn't look away. Mustering what dignity she could, she moved toward the door. "I'd better be going. It will be dark soon."

His fingers curled around her wrist. "It is dark. I'll take you home."

His voice was even but implacable. Any thought

she might have harbored of throwing herself into his arms to pour out her hopes and fears died before it could take its first breath, just like Carla's baby. She wouldn't beg him to understand. There were limits even for the love she felt pushing against the edges of her heart. "That's not necessary."

"Yes, it is." He buttoned his shirt with impatient fingers and fished his car keys out of his pocket. He was still aroused, his erection pushing against the fabric of his jeans, but he ignored it. He held the screen door open so that she could pass through. It thumped shut behind them. Their footsteps on the wooden porch echoed in the quiet evening.

She climbed into the SUV and waited while he started the engine. Little more than a mile separated the two cabins on the curving mountain road. They made the trip in silence.

Miguel pulled to a stop outside her cabin. Light shone from every window. With a sharp jab of longing, Devon realized she wanted to come home every evening to that beckoning warmth. She knew that the children might not always be there, but she also knew that in the deepest recesses of her heart, she had dreamed Miguel would be one day.

She got out of the truck and inclined her head so that she could see his face in the faint glow of the dashboard lights. She swallowed hard and concentrated on keeping her voice even, devoid of any trace of unshed tears. "I'm sorry, Miguel."

He didn't turn his head to look at her. His profile was straight off a Remington bronze, proud, defiant. "I'm sorry, too," he said, finally turning to look at her, although the darkness hid his expression as effectively as a mask. "I love you, Devon. Not the girl you used to be, but the woman you are now, with the life you have now. I'll be here if you need me. But I won't come begging for your trust."

He shifted into reverse and drove away, leaving her standing alone in the chilly mountain air. She stayed where she was for a long few minutes, seeing nothing, her arms wrapped around her to hold the chill out and the misery inside. Then she turned and went into the house.

Jesse was waiting for her at the bottom of the loft stairs. "Where have you been?" he said bluntly.

"I went for a walk," she replied, throwing her sweater across the back of a chair.

He watched her through narrowed eyes. "The cop brought you home," he said, and for a panicked moment she wondered if her appearance showed some sign of what had almost happened between her and Miguel. She fought the urge to adjust her hair, taming the curls that her passionate kiss with Miguel had dislodged from the tortoiseshell clip. "Yes, he did offer me a ride home."

Jesse looked over his shoulder. Devon could hear the television in the loft. It must be on Nickelodeon— the nasal twang of SpongeBob SquarePants floated down the stairs, along with Maria's delighted laughter. He lowered his voice. "You got a thing for him, don't you?"

Devon fought for control. She wanted nothing more than to go to her bedroom and curl up in the dark and cry. It had been a lousy day. First Carla had lost her baby and then Devon had denied a love she'd only become aware was hers to lose. "That's none of your business, Jesse."

"The hell it isn't." He took a step toward her, his voice low and almost as strained as hers. "Manny says he was a Marine. He says he's one hell of a cop. That means he's going to go snooping around that old ghost town sooner or later. He's going to find our truck and come after us."

"He's been up there, but he didn't even mention the truck to me," Devon said. It was chilly in the cabin now that the sun was down. She moved to close the small windows on each side of the room.

"He didn't ask you about us?"

She looked at him over her shoulder. "No, he didn't."

"I don't believe you. That's bullshit. He's probably already trying to trace the truck. Damn it, I wish I'd known the old Indian was his grandfather before I took the junk from out behind his barn."

Devon had had enough. "Lower your voice," she said as calmly as she could manage. "You'll upset your sisters."

She sensed the stark fear behind his bravado. His hands clenched and unclenched at his side, but he did as she asked, attempting as always to spare his sisters more upset.

He punched the back of the couch, than flopped onto the arm, his elbows on his thighs, his head between his hands. "What am I going to do? I'm all they've got. Maria was born here, but I don't know how to prove it. Sylvia will have her baby and he'll be a citizen. But maybe they'll still send them both back. Me, I go for sure. I don't care for myself. I'll make it back across the border somehow. I was little, but I remember how we came here. I know how the Coyotes work. But the girls…'' His voice broke. ''We should leave. I can have the truck running by tomorrow night. It only needs new spark plugs, and I've made enough money working for Manny to buy them now. *Vamanos*. Now before *la migra* shows up at the door.''

''Jesse.'' Devon pushed her own heartache aside. She was responsible for him, for all of them, of her own free will. Nothing of what had transpired between her and Miguel changed that. ''Give me a little more time. I'll go back to Angel's Gate as soon as I can to talk to your Tia Lucia. And the baby. It will be coming soon. We have to think of Sylvia's welfare, and the baby's.''

''I know.'' He stayed where he was, his dark head bowed. Devon moved away from the window and put her hand on his shoulder. He didn't shrug it off.

''We'll get through this somehow, Jesse. I promised you that at the beginning. I won't go back on my word.''

He nodded. The sounds from upstairs changed, a cereal jingle replaced the cartoon voices of Sponge-Bob and his starfish sidekick, Patrick. Maria's face appeared over the half wall of the loft.

''Devon. You're home. I'm hungry. Can I have a snack? Please!''

Jesse twisted around on the couch and dragged his fists across his eyes. He stood up. ''Come on, little pig. You're going to be *muy gorda* if you keep eating like this.''

''*Muy gorda*. Like Sylvia,'' Maria giggled, hopping off the bottom step into her brother's arms.

''Like Sylvia.'' His voice cracked, and once again Devon realized how very young he was, not even legally old enough to drive the old pickup that represented everything they had in the world.

Sylvia came down the stairs in time to hear their last remarks. ''Jesse, she *can't* be hungry again.'' She laughed. She did it so seldom that Devon was surprised by the sound. She placed her hand at the small of her back as she crossed the room toward them, moving slowly as though not quite sure of her balance.

''I *am*,'' Maria wailed.

''Then let's get her a snack.'' Devon stretched her mouth into a smile and began to move toward the kitchen.

Sylvia looked from Devon to Jesse and back again. ''Is everything okay?'' she whispered, her left hand moving to her stomach. A tiny frown appeared between her eyebrows. ''Devon? I saw from the upstairs window. It was…it was the policeman…Miguel, who brought you home.''

Jesse answered before Devon could form a reply. ''Everything's fine,'' he said, swinging a giggling Maria up off the floor until she squealed with excitement. His tone was as upbeat as his words, but his eyes were as bleak as Devon's heart. ''Everything's just fine.''

"DEVON, I'M SO GLAD you're already at the center," Hope said over the phone. "I knew Serena Cartwright was ready to pop, but I was hoping she'd wait until this afternoon." Hope's voice sounded raspy and faint, not because she was catching cold, but because her cell-phone reception was poor. She was halfway to Taos, taking Dalton to the orthodontist. "But there's no way I can get back to Enchantment for at least another couple of hours."

"Don't worry about it, Hope. I'm glad to help out." Devon smiled at Trish in her accustomed chair behind the reception desk, even though it was barely eight o'clock and they weren't scheduled to start seeing patients for an hour and a half.

"This connection is awful, isn't it?" Hope fussed. "Wait a moment. I'll pull over when I top this rise and see if it clears up. Hang on."

Trish popped the last bite of a bagel into her mouth and pantomimed pouring a cup of tea. Devon nodded. She put her hand over the mouthpiece. "Two sugars." She needed the burst of energy. She'd spent a restless, almost sleepless night and was up before the sun.

"Devon?" Hope again. Her voice was clearer now, the static banished.

"I can hear you fine, Hope. Serena's contractions are eight minutes apart and regular. She should be here within the hour. She's going to drop her kids off at her mother's place in Red River first."

"I'll fill you in on the details," Hope said, rushing her words a little in anticipation of the next round of static. Trish set the steaming cup of tea on the counter and placed Serena's chart beside it. Devon opened it to find the page filled with Hope's neatly printed notes. "Serena's thirty. Thirty-eight weeks gestation. She has two great kids. Lydia delivered them both, so she can back you up on this one if I don't get back in time. I saw her, um..."

"Wednesday morning," Devon supplied from the chart.

"Has her water broken?"

"Not yet. You're starting to break up again. Anything else I need to know?" Devon asked quickly.

"She's very eager for a water birth."

"I'll make sure she's in the Jacuzzi suite," Devon teased. She tried to remember if she'd left an extra set of scrubs in her locker in the break room. One thing was always certain with a water birth. The midwife got just as wet as mother and baby.

"Serena's a trooper, Devon. You two will hit it off just fine. I'll be back by lunchtime to give you a hand."

"It's a deal, Hope," Devon said, and handed the phone back to Trish.

The older woman was perusing Serena's chart. "Water birth, huh? I'd better get some extra towels."

The front door of the clinic opened to the bright morning sunlight, and Kim Sherman entered. She walked briskly to the reception desk, her low heels clicking on the tile floor. She was wearing a silky-looking, buttercup-yellow blouse and a dark skirt. Her hair was smooth and sleek, tucked behind her ears. Devon's eyes were drawn to the rare rose-quartz earrings that had been a gift from the teenage Lydia to

Kim's mother. The stones matched Lydia's pendant with its Madonna and child likeness.

"You're here early this morning," Kim said, greeting Devon and Trish with a smile.

"So are you," Trish threw over her shoulder as she headed off to the storeroom for the towels.

"I have a mother in labor coming in," Devon explained. "What's your excuse?"

"I need to leave a couple of hours early today. I'm going shopping for some new towels and sheets for the guest bedroom. Nolan evidently missed Martha Stewart's checklist on what to keep on hand in your linen closet. My foster parents will be here at the beginning of next week, you know."

"Just in time for the wedding plans to swing into high gear. Have you borrowed Martha's checklist for that?"

"Not Martha's. My own." Kim opened her briefcase and selected a pale-green folder from the neatly arranged contents. "Flowers, check. Music, the organist for the church and the DJ for the reception. Food, Slim Jim's is providing all the barbecue and fixings. And the beer and wine. I'm making the punch myself. Trish gave me the recipe. The cake's coming from a baker in Taos. Father Ignacio's honorarium. The rings…"

She looked up at Devon's chuckle. "I thought the groom was in charge of the rings?"

"Do you honestly believe I'd leave a detail that important to Nolan?" Kim said with absolute sincerity. "The man hasn't bought a set of sheets since Bush Senior was in office."

"Right," Devon said.

"Besides, I believe it's the best man's responsibility to make sure the groom has the ring. I'm putting them directly into Miguel's hand at the rehearsal dinner. I love Nolan dearly, but he is a man, and a forgetful one."

"It sounds as if you have everything under control," Devon said a bit wistfully. Her life was so fragmented at the moment she couldn't help but envy Kim her situation.

"Well, *we* don't have everything under control," Trish said, bustling back into the waiting room. "Serena and her husband just pulled up in the back. Her water broke about twenty minutes ago. Her contractions are now four minutes apart and hard. They decided not to chance the drive over to Red River to her mother's. She's meeting them here to help with the older children." She glanced at the clipboard on her desk that listed the day's appointments. "Your grandmother has a home visit on her schedule for this morning. I imagine she's already left her house. I'll call Gina for backup for you, Devon." The phone rang. Trish rolled her eyes as she picked up the receiver. "Ladies, I have the feeling it's going to be a very busy day."

IT *WAS* A BUSY DAY and by two-thirty in the afternoon, when Devon and Hope bundled Serena Cartwright and her new son into the back seat of their car, Devon was feeling the effects of her sleepless night. Her back and shoulders ached from kneeling beside the big tub where Serena had spent most of her short labor, massaging the woman's neck and shoulders, then later supporting her legs and knees as she gave birth. Hope had arrived in time to catch the squalling and red-faced little boy while Devon assisted. Serena's husband proudly cut the umbilical cord, and only minutes later the newest Cartwright was introduced to his awestruck sisters and doting grandmother.

For most of the morning the birthing room had been filled with the positive energy that always seemed to flow from a successful birth, and it had kept Devon's exhaustion at bay. But now that the happy family was on their way home, she felt fatigue drag at her again. She shielded her eyes with her hand against the afternoon sunlight as she waved the Cartwright caravan out of the parking lot.

Inside the clinic once more, the hallway leading back to the birthing rooms seemed dark in contrast to the outside. She stopped for a moment to let her eyes adjust, and that was when she heard a familiar imperious voice coming from the reception area. She knew there were at least half a dozen women scattered around the room waiting for appointments with one of the midwives or Celia Brice, but there was no mistaking her mother's voice. Devon hurried past the open door to the birthing room where Hope and Gina were finishing tidying up, and stopped just inside the archway leading into the reception area.

Her mother was talking to her grandmother, using the extravagant hand gestures that were so much a part of her personality. She'd told them she'd be here in the early afternoon, and as always, she was as good as her word. Myrna shared the same tall, rangy build as Lydia, but there the similarities ended. Myrna's body was toned and lithe. Her hair was cut in a sleek curve that fell just below her chin. It was a lighter blond than Devon's without a single strand of gray.

Myrna was the senior vice president of West Coast operations for a Fortune 500 company. She had worked hard to get where she was in life, and she didn't mind flaunting her success. But to give her mother credit, she had never once faulted Devon for not following in her footsteps.

From the set of her grandmother's shoulders and the slight frown on her father's face, she could tell that Myrna had already said something that Lydia disagreed with. Devon didn't immediately step into the fray. She stayed where she was, just out of Myrna's line of sight, to study her father's face for a moment. Sam Grant, now in his mid-fifties, was balding and round faced. Not a big man, he stood only a few inches taller than Devon in his stocking feet, but in her eyes he was ten feet tall and always would be. He was a partner in a small but prestigious architectural firm. He enjoyed his work, but it wasn't the focus of his world the way Myrna's had always been.

Born while both her parents were struggling through college, Devon had grown up an only child. If her father had been as driven to succeed as her mother, Devon's childhood would have been far less happy than it was. He'd always been home when she came through the door after school, always there for her basketball and soccer games. The few times her mother had volunteered to chaperon a school dance or field trip, it was because Sam insisted she do so.

Patients were beginning to take notice of her standing quietly in the archway. Her father turned his head and his eyes met hers. "Devon," he called, smiling and opening his arms for a hug.

"Hi, Dad." She let him wrap her in a big bear hug, pressing her cheek against his.

"You're right on time."

"Did you think your mother would let me miss her ETA by more than fifteen minutes?" he asked, holding her at arm's length.

"You always get her where she wants to be on time," Devon said, one hand still held in his.

"We've already checked in at the Morning Light." Myrna held out her arms for a hug of her own. Her mother may have looked as if she stepped out of the pages of a fashion magazine, but she paid no attention to her clothes or hair as she folded Devon into her embrace. "We've missed you, baby. You look so tired." She studied Devon worriedly. "Have you been getting enough sleep? Are you sure taking care of those children on top of all the hours you spend here isn't too much for you?"

"I am tired," Devon said, having learned long ago not to try to bluff her mother. By phone she'd explained as truthfully and succinctly as she could to both her parents the reasons she'd taken the children under her wing. They had been surprised, somewhat apprehensive, but for the most part supportive, as they always were. "But it's not because of the kids." At least not completely. It was because of a certain lawman, but she wasn't about to let her mother get an inkling that she had trouble with her love life on top of everything else. "It's because I've been up since five and I just got done delivering a baby."

"Boy or girl?" Sam asked.

"A bouncing baby boy." Devon grinned. "With lungs like a rock star."

"How many does that make for you now? Four hundred?"

"I...I'm not sure. I'd have to look it up."

"Well, it's the three who are living under your roof I'm interested in," Myrna said. "I want to meet these kids, you know. What if we all go out to dinner tonight? Angel's Gate, maybe? There was a write-up in the travel section of the *Chronicle* a few weeks ago. I've been dying to see the place."

Angel's Gate. Devon had intended to drive up there herself today to try once more to contact Lucia Molina, but Serena's labor had derailed her plan.

"We'll be at Angel's Gate next Friday for the rehearsal dinner," Lydia inserted.

"I don't want to wait that long," Myrna said impatiently.

"It's not exactly geared for children," Devon cautioned. The kids would find her mother overwhelming enough without subjecting them to the added strain of dinner in the trendy Angel's Gate dining room, even if they did come across their aunt Lucia at the resort. *Especially* if they came across their aunt Lucia.

"She's right, Myrna. And we've been traveling all day. How about carryout from Slim Jim's? I've been thinking about their barbecue since we got off the plane.''

"Sam, your cholesterol,'' Myrna warned.

"One sandwich won't hurt. I'll eat chicken the rest of the week.'' Sam gave Devon a wink, the private signal they'd shared for years when he knew her mother was threatening to run roughshod over anything or anyone in her path and he was aiming to slow her down.

"Slim Jim's? Well, I suppose—''

"Thank you, Mom. That's a great idea. The kids will enjoy it,'' Devon said. "And it will be less stressful for them to meet you at the cabin than in a public place.''

"All right. But tomorrow the four of us are going to Angel's Gate for lunch. That's what Mother and I were discussing before you arrived, Devon. A family lunch.''

Lydia squared her shoulders, a sure sign she was ready to do battle. "I was telling Myrna that I don't know what Kim's plans might be for tomorrow. It's getting close to the wedding. She might have last-minute details to attend to.''

"Surely Kim can spare two hours for us tomorrow? We're her family.'' Myrna's lips narrowed and her gray eyes took on the color of an approaching thunderstorm. The same obstinate expression was mirrored on her grandmother's face.

"You know I won't be able to make it if one of my patients is in labor, or Devon, either, for that matter.''

Myrna raised an eyebrow. "*Et tu,* Devon?'' she

said, and sighed with exaggerated resignation. "Mid-wives. I know you might have to cancel at the last minute, Mother. I learned that lesson long ago."

"I'm sure Kim will be honored by the invitation. I know she has plans for today, but I think she'll probably be able to work lunch into her schedule tomorrow," Devon said hastily before Myrna's oft-repeated lament escalated into a real quarrel.

"I've got a tee time tomorrow at eleven," Sam reminded his wife.

"I know, dear. Go play golf." Myrna smiled, content now that the world was once more ordered to her satisfaction. "I want this to be just the four of us. The Kane women together at last. Now where is my niece? I want to meet her."

CHAPTER FIFTEEN

"THIS PLACE IS REALLY VERY NICE," Myrna said the following day at lunch, as she settled into her seat. "I was expecting lots of antler chandeliers, Navajo rugs, pottery bowls everywhere. You know the whole Southwestern, après-ski sort of thing. "The artwork is really quite exemplary. It's far more sophisticated than I imagined, rather stark, actually. I suppose they decided to underplay the interior to take advantage of the view."

"Angel's Gate *is* beautiful," Kim said, unfolding her napkin to place it in her lap. For a woman who had been alone most of her life, it must be slightly overwhelming at times to suddenly find herself part of a family, Devon thought. Yet Kim radiated a quiet happiness, a serenity that hadn't been there when Devon first met her a year earlier. Finding Nolan and Sammy, the family of her heart, had obviously given her the confidence she needed to take the appearance of long-lost blood relatives in stride.

"Outstanding," Lydia agreed, looking out the window over the top of her reading glasses. They were occupying a table near the fireplace, not far from where Devon and Miguel had been seated the night they'd come here. This afternoon there was no fire on the massive stone hearth, but it looked as if there'd soon be fireworks outside. A low-pressure system was set to collide with unusually cool air coming down from the plains states directly over the Sangre de Cristos. Thunderstorms were predicted for the nighttime hours. Storm clouds were already attempting to form to the south, but the air was so dry that little if any of the rain that fell from them would reach the ground. It wasn't the rain that worried Devon—it would be welcomed—but the lightning strikes that were sure to accompany the storms.

"The views from this room are breathtaking, Devon," Kim said, leaning a little forward to catch Devon's attention. "Now I see why you wanted to have the rehearsal dinner here. Thank you so much for arranging it."

"It's our pleasure," Devon said, giving Kim's left hand a quick squeeze before she could object.

"Did you know they did a feature on Angel's Gate in *The San Francisco Chronicle* a few weeks ago?" Myrna asked as she perused the wine list, nodding approval of the choices.

"You mentioned that the other day." From the corner of her eye, Devon watched the waitstaff as they went about their duties, just as she'd noted the desk clerks and the office personnel as they'd come through the lobby. None of the women she'd seen looked like the children's description of Lucia Molina. But what if she was part of the kitchen staff, or housekeeping? It would be harder to find her in those off-limits parts of the hotel.

"Oh, I did, didn't I. The chef's said to be first-class."

Devon could have affirmed the chef was first-class, but that would mean admitting she'd been here before. And that admission would elicit more questions from her mother. She wasn't ready to speak of Miguel, might never be able to say his name again without choking up.

"We should know soon. I'll have a diet soda," Kim smiled at the waiter who came to take their drink orders.

"Lemonade," Devon said. She had two patient exams scheduled for later in the afternoon.

"Ice water, please." Lydia gave her order and picked up the leather-bound menu.

"No one's going to join me in a glass of wine?" Myrna asked.

"I don't want to fall asleep in front of my computer this afternoon," Kim demurred.

Myrna held up her hand to forestall Devon's explanation. "I know. I know. You and Mother have patients to see. Very well, I'll have a glass of chardonnay. I don't mind drinking alone."

For once Devon could find no fault with her mother's tendency to take charge of any conversation she was engaged in. She suggested they order salads and then splurge on a truly decadent chocolate dessert that the *Chronicle* article had recommended, and permitted herself a satisfied smile when everyone agreed. She pronounced the venue absolutely perfect for Devon and Miguel's prewedding party, and then she turned her attention fully on Kim and demanded to be told everything there was to know about her wedding plans.

Devon joined in the conversation when she was obliged to do so, toyed with her fruit salad and watched the staff come and go from the corner of her eye. The hour passed surprisingly quickly, but when the attentive waiter had cleared their coffee cups and laid the bill folio by her mother's plate, she still hadn't spotted any woman that might be Lucia. She was going to have to detach herself from the group and go looking for her. She simply couldn't waste the opportunity.

"Excuse me, Mom. I need to use the rest room."

"Go ahead, dear. Kim and I are going to go out on that marvelous terrace and enjoy the view. Mother, do you want to join us?"

"Uh, yes, of course." Devon could feel her grandmother's shrewd gray eyes on her as she walked away from the table. She did use the rest room, but only to see if there was an attendant who might be the woman she was looking for. The gleaming tiled room was empty. She walked into the lobby, deciding to find someone in the business office who might be able to tell her if Lucia had returned to work, or at least agree to deliver a message to her when she did return.

She came to a halt before the gleaming copper-and-teak reception desk, unsure which of the branching hallways might lead her to the personnel office. "May I help you?" asked one of the smiling clerks. She was a beautiful young woman, perhaps a couple of years younger than Devon. Her name tag said Felicia. Her raven-black hair was pulled back into an elegant twist at the back of her head. Silver droplets dangled from her ears. The charcoal-gray blazer and skirt that all the female front-desk employees wore complemented her olive skin and dark eyes.

"Uh, yes." Devon stepped forward and took the opportunity offered. "I'm looking for someone actually. An employee. Lucia Molina? Would you perhaps know her?"

Some of the warmth left the girl's smile. She looked down at the Rolodex on the counter in front of her. "I'm sorry, *señorita*. I don't know anyone by that name who works here."

"Perhaps I could talk to someone in your personnel department. I do know that she's employed by the lodge. But she was off duty when I called to inquire last week. I need to find out if she's working today. It's very important."

"I'll ask if our human resources director has a moment to speak to you."

Devon turned her back on the desk. She could see her mother and Kim and Lydia strolling along the terrace, the backdrop of mountain and storm cloud behind them echoed in its soaring ceilings and walls carved from the living rock of the mountain. The young woman returned with a middle-aged African-American woman. "This is Mrs. Greencastle, our human resources director."

"How may I help you?" she asked in a voice with a Caribbean lilt.

"I'm Devon Grant." Devon held out her hand. "I'm looking for a woman who works here. Lucia Molina."

"It's nice to meet you, Ms. Grant." She returned the handshake. "Yes, Lucia works here, but I'm afraid that's all I can tell you. It is our company policy not to reveal information about our employees without their permission."

"But I have news from her family. It's important that I contact her."

"I'm sorry." The smile was no longer quite so polished or polite. "Lucia has taken a leave of absence. That is all I can tell you."

"But when will she return? Surely you can tell me that much?"

"I'm sorry. My hands are tied. Now, if you will excuse me, I have a very important meeting to attend." She turned away, moving back behind the reception desk.

"May I leave her a message?"

"What?" Mrs. Greencastle looked over her shoulder. She frowned as she considered if a message might be another breach of policy she couldn't condone. "Yes, I suppose I could put it in her mail slot. But as I said, I can't tell you when she is scheduled to return. You'll find writing supplies in the desk in the alcove to your left. You may leave the letter with Felicia. She'll see that I get it."

"Thank you." Devon felt renewed discouragement hit her like cold rain. The woman could be away for three more days. Or three weeks. Or three months. Could she keep the children safe and undetected by the authorities for that long? It would seem she had no other choice. Dejected, she turned around.

Her grandmother was standing in the archway that

separated the dining room from the lobby. She approached Devon, her sandals tapping lightly on the stone floor. "I saw you talking to that woman," she said. "Is there a problem with the party plans?"

It would be easy to let her grandmother think she'd been talking about the party and walk away. "I...I was just trying to get a message to someone who works here."

"Who would that be? I didn't think you knew anyone in Enchantment these days."

"I...it's a friend of a friend."

"A friend of the children, you mean?" Shrewd gray eyes bored into hers.

"No. Yes." Suddenly Devon longed to lay it all before this wise woman. "Their aunt. I've been looking for her for the past few days. She's taken a leave of absence. They won't tell me where she's gone."

Lydia nodded. "Surely the children know how to contact her?" When Devon didn't answer, she went on, "There's more to your taking care of these children than you've told me, isn't there."

"Yes." Devon was relieved to have it out in the open at last. "There is more."

Lydia nodded. "I thought so. They're undocumented, aren't they."

"Yes."

"I was afraid of that. And they aren't a friend's children, either, are they."

"They're runaways. I found them hiding out in the Silver Jacks mine. They'd been living there for at least two weeks."

"Poor things." Lydia motioned to one of the huge,

overstuffed leather sofas that beckoned guests to sit and talk and enjoy the view. "Your mother and Kim are discussing wedding plans. Weddings are filled with detail and scheduling. Myrna and Kim are soul mates in their love of both. They won't notice we're gone for another ten or fifteen minutes. Sit down and tell me everything."

Devon and Lydia had come a long way back in their relationship over the past few weeks, but it still wasn't the way it had once been, would never be again. Devon was no longer a starry-eyed little girl. She was a woman, with an aching heart and a secret that had already possibly destroyed what might have been the love of her life. Letting herself be that loving little girl again, even if only for a short time, meant telling her grandmother she was in love with Miguel. And that she couldn't do—it hurt too much. But she did tell Lydia everything she could about the children's situation as she stared unseeingly at the ever-changing pattern of cloud shadows on the mountain slopes beyond the lobby's huge plate-glass windows.

"Jesse trusts no one," she added when she finished. "He lives in fear of the three of them being separated, of being sent back to Mexico, penniless and alone."

"We should contact a lawyer," Lydia advised. "One who's versed in immigration law. You could do it privately. The children wouldn't have to know."

"I've considered that." And the cost. She would have to go to her parents and borrow money. She couldn't ask Lydia for a loan. Her grandmother had little enough that wasn't tied up in The Birth Place.

"Jesse will surely bolt if I bring a lawyer into the equation. I was worried enough about introducing him to Mom and Dad last night."

"The evening went off well, though, didn't it?"

Devon braced her elbow on the back of the sofa and rested her cheek on her palm. "Mom and Maria hit it off really well. She bought ice cream and all the fixings for banana splits. Mom is Maria's friend for life. They're going shopping together to buy toys. I don't have enough, she told Dad, in what she thought was a whisper." Devon smiled at the memory of the little girl, her face smeared with chocolate, her eyes sparkling with happiness. "Jesse was on his best behavior. Dad tried practicing his Spanish on Sylvia. He's not very good—he had her laughing so hard I was afraid she'd have the baby right then and there."

"She's very close to delivering, Devon," Lydia said quietly. "Have you been able to get her to talk to Celia?"

"No." Devon's anxiety returned, too strong to be banished by the warm memory of the evening just past. "She's opened up to me a little, but not much. I wish she would talk to Celia. Perhaps after the baby is born..."

"It will be a hard decision for her—keep the baby or give it up for adoption."

"I know."

"She'll be tempted to keep the baby as an anchor to stay in this country."

"Actually, I think she'll be even more inclined to keep it because she's a loving, giving young woman." Was Sylvia mature enough to raise her baby on her own? Devon would do everything in her power to support Sylvia in that event, but would her best be good enough?

A couple came out of the restaurant hand in hand, laughing, heads close together, and headed for the elevator. A married couple on a summer getaway? Honeymooners on their way to their room to make love in the afternoon? A sharp pain stabbed through Devon's chest. Love in the afternoon. She had made love to Miguel once when they were young under the summer sun on the banks of Silver Creek. She couldn't let herself think about Miguel now. Perhaps not ever again.

She turned her head. "Here come Mother and Kim." Myrna and Devon's cousin were advancing toward them along the stone wall that bordered the terrace. Myrna was talking, though lecturing would be a more accurate description. Devon could tell by the way she moved her hands. Kim was listening attentively, her head bent at a slight angle toward her aunt. They halted momentarily and Myrna raised a hand to touch the rose-quartz earrings Kim wore.

Lydia was watching them, too. Her own hand went to her pendant. "They are very alike, your mother and Kim. Have you noticed?"

"Yes, I have."

"Does it bother you?" she asked.

Devon didn't hesitate. "No. I'm happy for them. And I've always wanted a sister. Perhaps one day Kim and I will be that close. I hope so."

"I'd like that, too."

Lydia's eyes went once more to her daughter and

granddaughter. Myrna and Kim, both smiling, continued to approach.

"I...I should write my note to the kids' aunt," Devon said. "Can you divert Mom's attention for another five minutes or so?"

Lydia made a face. "I'll try, although I haven't been very successful diverting your mother from something she's interested in since she was about two." She rose from the couch and moved toward the huge sliding doors that opened onto the terrace. "Be quick," she advised.

Devon hurried toward the little alcove where Mrs. Greencastle had indicated she would find paper and pen. She didn't have time for a detailed explanation of how she came to have the children in her charge. She simply supplied her name and all the phone numbers she could think of. In both Spanish and English she asked Lucia to contact her as soon as she received the note, day or night, as she had important information about her nieces and nephew. Perhaps the woman was even looking for them herself? That might explain why she'd left her job at Angel's Gate at this precise moment in time. Devon hoped that was the case. She folded the single sheet of paper, sealed it in an envelope bearing the resort's name and took it to the desk where Felicia waited.

Felicia looked over her shoulder, down the hallway where Mrs. Greencastle had disappeared. "The lady you were talking with, the elderly *señora?*"

"My grandmother," Devon said. She could hear her mother's imperious tones filtering through the open doors from the terrace.

"She is *la comadrona,* no?"

"Yes, my grandmother is a midwife. Do you know her?"

"Señora Kane delivered my sister's baby. She came all the way out to her house on Saddleback Road in a snowstorm. She didn't care that my sister had no money."

"Your sister and her baby, they're doing well?"

Felicia smiled, and the polished politeness of the well-trained employee vanished, to be replaced with a brilliant smile. "Yes. Very well." She leaned slightly closer over the counter. "I know Lucia Molina," she said quietly.

Devon felt her heart rate accelerate. "Do you know where she is?"

"I think she went to Phoenix. There is a problem in her family. She was very upset when she left."

"Do you know what kind of family problem?" Had Lucia learned that the children had disappeared and gone in search of them while they were making their way to her?

"I'm sorry, *señorita.* You must realize that it is...difficult...for some of us here. We must be very discreet, not draw attention to ourselves. I can only tell you that she was very worried when she left."

"Can you tell me how to get in touch with her?"

She shook her head. "I'm sorry, truly. I don't have a number or an address where I can reach her. But she might call me." Her eyes dropped to the envelope, then lifted to Devon's face once more. "To see how the wind is blowing, you know? To make sure that management is not growing impatient with her being away.''

''I see. Of course. Please. If she calls, tell her to get in touch with me. It's very important. I'll leave you my name and number.'' Devon scribbled both on the back of a business card she took from a holder on the counter. Felicia slipped it into her pocket just as Mrs. Greencastle reappeared.

''You're still here.''

''Yes. Here's the letter.''

The woman held out her hand. ''I'll see that it's placed where Señora Molina will find it if and when she returns.''

''Thank you.'' Devon had no doubt the woman would be as good as her word. But she was also certain she wouldn't go out of her way to let Lucia know Devon was trying to contact her. She just hoped that the young desk clerk would.

MIGUEL CLIMBED out of the Durango and reached back inside for his hat. If the meeting with the Angel's Gate management team to discuss their fire evacuation plan went smoothly enough, he might have time for a sandwich before he left on patrol. Enchantment had a mutual-aid pact with the county sheriff's department, so getting the guests and employees of Angel's Gate down off the mountain in case of a fire emergency was his responsibility. He damned well wanted to make sure they had a workable plan in place. The doorman hurried up. ''Good afternoon, Chief Eiden.'' He motioned to the valet who was already trotting toward them from his stand at the far curve of the brick-paved, half-timbered entry.

He recognized the kid in the white shirt, red vest and bolero tie as the star fullback of the high-school football team. Angel's Gate had provided a lot of jobs for the town, even though there had been some resentment when it was built. "Leave it here, Randy," he said, waving the valet off. The doorman, done up in an ersatz Beefeater coat and top hat, looked pained to see the dusty SUV parked in the middle of his domain. "Official business," Miguel growled. The doorman backed off with a hasty tip of his hat.

Halting a moment just inside the lobby doors, Miguel removed his sunglasses and tucked them in the pocket of his shirt. He let his eyes rake over the huge sweep of stone floor, vaulted ceiling and picture-postcard view of mountain and ski slopes. He just hoped it still looked that good in another twenty-four hours. The storms that were predicted to roll in during the night wouldn't bring much rain, but they would mean lightning strikes. A lot of them. The fire danger was almost off the meter. It would be a miracle if one or more of them didn't set off a blaze somewhere on the mountain.

He flexed his left hand and winced. Not from pain, although the healing skin was still uncomfortable at times. He no longer wore a gauze bandage, hadn't for a couple of days. It was bulky and interfered with his work, but mostly because it reminded him of the gentle touch of Devon's fingers. And that always led to the truly painful realization that he might never experience that pleasure again.

Of course, damned near everything he did reminded him of Devon in one way or another. Like right now. The woman walking across the lobby toward the dining room—he could swear it was her. She was wearing khaki slacks and a pale-green, silky-looking shirt, open at the throat, sleeves rolled up to just below her elbows. Her honey-toned hair was braided close to her head in that complicated way he'd never understood how a woman on her own could accomplish.

She looked casual and feminine, her blouse clinging to the soft curves of her breasts, the khaki molding itself to her rounded bottom with every step. Sexy as hell. If he'd come across her up here a hundred years ago, he could have thrown her across his saddle and ridden off into the hills. Of course in those days he would probably have been hunted down by the U.S. Cavalry or her outraged male relatives and strung up on the closest tree branch, but it would have been worth it.

Today he'd probably settle for scooping her up into his arms and carrying her to one of the posh suites on the top floor of the hotel, stripping her naked, sliding into the hot tub with her... The woman must have sensed his scrutiny, because her steps faltered and she half turned, glancing over her shoulder in his direction.

Miguel blinked in surprise. It *was* Devon. He should have known his libido wouldn't get this revved up about just any woman. She didn't seem any too pleased to see him. From the look she gave him, she wouldn't have had to rely on the cavalry to rescue her from his advances, she could damn well do it herself. But as he moved closer, he imagined there was as much sorrow as anger in her storm-cloud gray eyes.

"I didn't expect to see you up here on a Thursday afternoon," he said, making a preemptive strike as he came to a halt a safe three feet from her. She smelled as good as she looked, like wildflowers and meadow grass. His chest tightened and he found it hard to take a full breath. He hadn't seen her for a week. Seven long days. Seven interminable nights.

"No more than I expected to see you," she said, and her voice wasn't quite as steady as her gaze. He hooked his thumb in his utility belt and the movement drew her eye. "Your hand. It's healing okay?"

"It's coming along." He held it up for her to see. He'd covered the blistered area with a wide adhesive bandage.

She reached out as though to touch him, to reassure herself, then stopped with her fingers inches from his hand. She stuck her hand in the pocket of her pants. "That's good," she said. "Why are you here?"

"I need to go over fire-evacuation plans with the management."

She nodded, needing no further explanation. "We're here for lunch."

"We?"

"Yes. My parents are visiting, and it's a chance for Mother and Kim to get to know each other."

Movement behind her made him glance over her shoulder. Lydia Kane and Kim Sherman were walking toward them with an elegant, sharp-eyed blond woman between them. An older, more sophisticated, version of the woman he loved. Myrna Grant. He hadn't seen her since he was a teenager, but she hadn't changed much in the past twelve years. He was glad *he* had, though. She'd intimidated the hell out of him as a kid.

"Devon, who have we here?" she asked as the trio came to a halt beside them.

"It's Miguel Eiden, Mom. You remember him, don't you?"

"It's a pleasure seeing you again, Mrs. Grant." He took off his hat and resisted running his hand through his hair to make sure it wasn't plastered to his skull. He nodded toward Lydia and Kim. "Ladies." Lydia returned his greeting with a slight inclination of her head. Kim smiled a hello.

"Miguel Eiden? Devon, is this the boy you had such a crush on all those years ago?"

"Yes, Mother. But that was a long time ago. These days we're just…friends," Devon responded before he could form a neutral answer. He was a Marine and a cop, pretty good at not letting what he felt show on his face, but the words cut like a knife. *The boy she had a crush on all those years ago?* What about the man who loved her now? *Just friends?* If he looked over at her, would he see pain and hurt that equaled his? Or merely embarrassment and relief that their uncomfortable affair was ended?

"You're Elena Elkhorn's son. I remember her from high school. She was a senior the year I was a freshman, I believe. She's well, I hope?"

"Yes, ma'am, she's well."

"The last I heard you were in the Marines." Myrna spoke into the silence that had descended on the group.

"I'm still in the reserves, ma'am."

"Miguel's Enchantment's chief of police," Devon said. She had herself under control now. He might have thought she wasn't bothered at all by his showing up if the hand she'd shoved into the pocket of her pants wasn't balled into a fist. "He's here to go over the resort's evacuation plan if there's a fire in the area."

"Are you worried the storms I hear predicted will start a fire, Chief?" Myrna asked.

"As dry as it is around here, ma'am, it's always a possibility."

Myrna's gaze traveled to the view beyond the windows. "Maybe we'll all be lucky and there'll be a lot more rain than the weatherman has predicted."

"Yes, ma'am. We can always hope." But he wasn't going to bet his life on it—or anyone else's if he could help it.

CHAPTER SIXTEEN

DEVON AWOKE, feeling weary and drained again. She'd slept very little, spending most of the darkest hours of the night watching the play of lightning patterns above the mountains, wondering if one or more of the white-hot strikes would find the fuel it needed to smolder away until a stray gust of wind fanned it into hungry flame. But it wasn't only fear of wildfire on the mountain that had kept her awake. It had been seeing Miguel again.

She'd had no idea it would be such a shock, a jolt of pure physical awareness and need that had weakened her knees and made it hard to catch her breath. She had wanted to touch him so badly she had to stuff her hand in her pocket to keep from doing so. The effort to keep her voice and expression pleasant and normal when she'd introduced him to her mother had been intense. And hearing the echo of her own words when she'd lied and said they were only friends had cut like a knife. She didn't want to be his friend. She wanted to be his wife. His love. If she was going to react like that when all he did was walk into a room, how was she going to get through the wedding celebrations next week? *The rest of her life?*

She showered and dressed for work. It wasn't light

enough yet to see if there was smoke spiraling up among the pines in the higher elevations, but she hadn't heard the emergency sirens go off during the night. That was a good sign. She hoped the wind she heard sighing among the aspens in the yard would die away with the sunrise, leaving the morning still and quiet.

Devon was pouring milk into a bowl of cornflakes when she heard someone coming down the stairs. Sylvia. There were dark circles under her eyes. Her face was puffy and so were her fingers. She moved with the ponderous grace of a very pregnant woman. The baby had dropped in the past few days, Devon had noted. The girl could go into labor at any time, still without plans for what she wanted to do once the baby was born.

In order not to put any more pressure on Sylvia, Devon had quietly begun acquiring a few of the most basic newborn supplies. If Sylvia kept the baby, she would say they were a gift. If she gave the baby up for adoption, they would stay on the top shelf of the closet. There would be more important things to think about than diapers and receiving blankets.

Devon had told both Jesse and Sylvia what she'd learned about their aunt the night before. Sylvia had nodded, tears in her eyes. ''She's looking for us,'' she said. ''But even if she goes to our cousin, he won't be able to tell her anything.''

''Then she'll come back here,'' Jesse had said, his jaw tight.

''And we'll be waiting here for her,'' Sylvia repeated. Jesse had stalked off into the bathroom and shut the door, quietly, so he didn't waken Maria, but there was anger in the restraint.

"He wants to go," Sylvia had said. "He's getting worried. Tomorrow is the last day Señor Manny has work for him. He doesn't know if there's enough money to fix the truck...and to help you pay for what it is costing you to let us stay here."

"You don't owe me anything."

Sylvia had shaken her head, a tear slipping down her cheek, before she'd turned to climb the stairs. "We owe you more than we can ever repay."

Devon banished the memories of the night before and smiled a greeting. "Good morning," she said, doing her best to hide her worry from the young mother-to-be. "Did you sleep well?"

Sylvia went to the refrigerator and poured a glass of orange juice. "Maria couldn't get to sleep because of the lightning. I stayed up with her." She put her hand to the small of her back, a slight frown marring the smooth skin of her forehead.

"How are you feeling this morning?"

"I don't know. Tired and achy. My back hurts."

"No cramps, no spotting?"

Color drained from beneath her skin. "No. No, I'm just tired. The baby isn't coming. I'm sure of that." Her voice rose a little with each word.

"You're probably right," Devon said. The baby would come in its own good time. But if, when she returned in the afternoon, Sylvia's face and fingers still looked so puffy, she was going to insist on taking her blood pressure. There was always the possibility she might develop toxemia, and Devon didn't want to take any chances.

Maria walked into the kitchen next, her hair sticking up all over her head, the doll Devon had bought for her clutched in her arms. "I'm still sleepy," she complained. "But my tummy is hungry and wanted to get up."

"You can eat breakfast and then go lie down and watch television for a while," Devon suggested. "How does that sound?"

Maria yawned hugely. *"Bueno,"* she said. "I want cereal and toast."

She sat down beside Devon and placed her doll on the empty seat beside her, rested her elbows on the table and put her chin in her hands. "There was too much noise to sleep last night. Like guns in the sky," she said. "They shoot guns where we lived with Cousin Rodrigo. I didn't like it."

"It was just thunder and lightning, honey," Devon said as Sylvia placed bread in the toaster and took a bowl out of the cupboard. "No guns."

"I didn't like it, anyway. And I don't want to go back to Rodrigo's. I like it here. We're going to stay here, aren't we, Sylvia?"

Her sister didn't turn around, but the spoon she'd taken out of the silverware drawer jangled against the china bowl. "I hope so, Maria."

Maria was quick as always to pick up on the emotions of those around her. Her lower lip trembled. She looked at Devon with tears in her eyes. "I want to stay."

"Of course you can stay," Devon said, forcing a

smile to her lips. "And if you're a good girl today, we'll go for ice cream after supper, okay?"

"I'm going to be very good. Will the *señora*, your mother, come, too? I like her." Sylvia set her toast and cereal in front of her. Maria picked up her spoon and began to eat as she waited for Devon's answer.

"I think she would like that, too. I'll call her from the clinic and invite her and my father to come with us."

"We can split another banana split." The hint of tears had disappeared. Maria tipped her head, waiting to see if Devon caught the play on words that Myrna had taught her the first night they met.

"Ha, ha. Very funny." Devon rolled her eyes and made a face, just as Maria wanted her to do. "That's a good one."

Maria giggled, her mouth full of toast. "I know. A good one."

They heard Jesse coming down the stairs. His feet pounded across the main room of the cabin, and the front door slammed back against the wall with a bang. Devon and Sylvia both hurried out of the kitchen. The sun had risen while they were eating, and morning light flooded through the big uncovered window.

Jesse was out on the porch, barefoot, his shirt hanging open. He was staring out at something Devon couldn't see. From the town below, emergency sirens had begun to wail. The sound of an engine being gunned to life came from the direction of Miguel's place, followed by the flash of red-and-blue lights as he headed into town. She knew what she would see even before she stepped across the threshold into the cool morning air.

"Madre de Dios," Sylvia whispered, making the sign of the cross.

Off in the distance a ribbon of white smoke spiraled into the blue-gray dawn sky. Across the ridge a second thicker column rose toward the sun.

Her nighttime fears had come true. There was fire on the mountain.

HE MADE IT to the station in seven minutes. Lights but no siren, no use waking those citizens of Enchantment still asleep in their beds. Miguel had no doubt he'd spend enough time over the next hours and days, and maybe even weeks, soothing jangled nerves and ruffled feathers if the fires got out of hand. No need to start before he had to.

He'd come awake a split second before the phone began to ring. That happened more and more often since he'd become chief, just the way it used to back in the Marine Corps. How he'd hated being awakened by the blinding overhead lights and bellows from his drill instructor. Later, in Somalia, it evolved from habit to a survival skill, one he'd honed to perfection. He'd looked out his bedroom window and knew without hearing Doris's voice on the other end of the phone that there was fire on the mountain.

He shouldn't have been surprised after last night's lightning display, but he'd hoped against hope they might somehow make it through until the winter rains. He counted two columns of smoke in his line of sight. "I see it," he told the dispatcher without preamble. "Give me ten minutes."

Hank Jensen and Lorenzo Cooper were already at the station when he arrived. Three of the town's auxiliary police followed him through the door. Doris was at her console in the cubbyhole radio room. "The mayor's on line two, but I put him on hold. I figured you'd want to talk to the fire chief and the state boys first."

"Thanks, Doris. What's Chief Michaels got to say?"

"He's already out trying to pinpoint the locations of the flare-ups. He's mobilized all four engines and the tanker trucks, but he thinks they're both too far off-road for him to get very close."

"We need aerial spotters. Get me the Forest Service guy over in Taos. This is really their bailiwick. Our job is to keep this town calm and under control. While you're raising him, I'll talk to the mayor. He should be in on this. We'll wait for the spotters' reports to come in, but my guess is they'll want to set up their command post higher up the mountain. Probably at Angel's Gate. Better give the manager a call and tell him to prepare for some unexpected guests."

Seventy-two hours later, he still hadn't found time to shave, but none of the other men grouped around the metal folding tables in the lobby of Angel's Gate looked much better. By his count, there were fifty or sixty people all told. The place was so damned big it didn't look crowded, just busy and purposeful. The feds had arrived early in the afternoon of the first day and pretty much taken over the show. Miguel was glad they had once the wind picked up and the two fires merged near the base of Silver Canyon. He leaned one shoulder against a pillar where he could see pretty much everything that was going on and still keep an eye on the dark wall of smoke that spiraled skyward across the valley, turning the sunrise a thousand shades of pink and orange. Smoke could do that, make hell on earth and glory in the sky.

A tall Native American woman was getting ready to give a press conference. Her title was information officer, and since she was with the Incident Management Team from North Carolina, he figured she was probably Cherokee. She was dressed in a khaki jumpsuit and combat boots and looked as if she could handle just about anything anyone threw at her. Miguel had liked her on sight. Some of the feds were a damned pain in the butt, but she knew her business and she didn't take guff from anyone.

To his left a couple of TV reporters were doing run-throughs of their lead-ins for the noon newscast. They seemed oblivious to the fact that they were creating an obstacle for the dozens of U.S. Forest Service personnel, New Mexico State Highway Patrol officers and volunteer fire crews from half a dozen states. And now just being ushered through the main door by the unflappable doorman, were a score of ranchers in jeans and dusty boots, members of Arroyo County's mounted search-and-rescue team, whose skill on horseback and knowledge of the mountain were being put to good use.

Miguel saw Ben Carson across the room accepting a cup of coffee from one of the members of the Enchantment American Legion Auxiliary. His clothes were dirty, his face shadowed by a three-day growth of beard and his eyes bloodshot from too much smoke and too little sleep. He lifted a finger to the brim of his hat to acknowledge Miguel's presence, and Miguel returned the salute.

He'd give the guys a chance to get something to eat before he got their report. They were doing a hell of a job keeping overzealous reporters, amateur photographers and just plain nutcases out of the danger zone. He was going to owe Ben and his group a big thank-you when this was all over.

There were other civilian volunteers milling around with trays of coffee and fruit juice and bottled water. They came from all over. Enchantment and Red River, Taos, Albuquerque and Santa Fe. Some from as far away as Denver and even Montana.

But no matter how many there were, they seemed outnumbered by the media. They were everywhere, print and network and cable-TV affiliates. From dawn to midnight their satellite trucks were parked end to end on the scenic turnouts along Desert Valley Road, the closest his men and the state patrol had allowed them to get. They'd taken every available room in the hotel and every available inch of space in Enchantment they could wheedle or bribe their way into. Slim Jim's and the Sunflower Café's tables were packed with them morning, noon and night. Miguel had the uncharitable notion that some of them were going to be disappointed if the whole town didn't go up in smoke.

The only people who looked as if they had nothing

important to do at the moment were the impeccably groomed hotel desk staff, still on duty, even though most of the guests had chosen to check out early, rather than be unceremoniously rousted from their rooms in the event the wind shifted yet again and sent the fire heading toward the hotel.

"Ladies and gentlemen. I'll begin the briefing in five minutes." It was the IMT woman speaking again. Miguel couldn't resist glancing at his watch. If she said five minutes, she meant five minutes. The media crews scrambled to get into position.

"Hey, Miguel. As usual I need a quote from law enforcement for the special edition of the *Bulletin* I'm putting out tomorrow." Nolan McKinnon detached himself from the gaggle of reporters ringing the information officer and headed over to Miguel.

"Don't you want to hear what she has to say?" Miguel asked, inclining his head in the IMT woman's direction.

"I can listen and talk to you at the same time. I've got a pretty good ear for picking out the important stuff. Besides I've already got the handout." He glanced down at the sheet of paper in his hand. "The fire's involved thirty-five hundred acres along upper Silver Creek. They're using four helicopters, a Super Huey 205, a Bell Jet Ranger…"

Miguel only half listened to Nolan's recitation; he was due to be briefed along with other law-enforcement personnel by the feds after the press conference. But suddenly Nolan's words registered. "What did you just say?" He reached out and grabbed the sheet of paper from Nolan's hand. "Jump the line if the wind changes direction." He looked up. "They know damned well the wind is going to pick up and swing around to the south this afternoon. The weather guys have predicted it all week. Damn those feds. Why am I always the last to know this stuff? It's my town and my people out there."

Nolan switched off the tape recorder he held in his hand. "Hey, don't shoot the messenger. But if the fire does shift, that means it'll head up the canyon. Doesn't your granddad live out that way?"

THE AFTERNOON SUNLIGHT WAS MUTED by the pall of smoke that hung over the valley. From where she was standing in her grandmother's office, Devon couldn't see any flames on the mountain, but that was little consolation. They were there whether she could see them or not. Later, when the sun set in a surreal kaleidoscope of oranges and reds, the flames would appear once more, a menacing counterpoint to the beauty in the sky.

Lydia came to stand beside her. Devon turned her head and gave her grandmother a smile. "You should be resting," she said. "You've been up since three."

"I just wanted to check on mother and baby one more time," Lydia said. Bridget Escalante had delivered a small but beautiful baby girl during the night. She and her husband were still in the birthing room. They had nowhere else to go at the moment. The highway patrol had closed Silver Creek Road above their homestead, and evacuated them just before dawn.

Lydia crossed to stand beside Devon at the window. "Since the baby's so small, maybe we should have Dr. Jo look her over before they leave."

"I'll give her a call and ask her to stop in on her way home," Devon said. "How is the new family doing?" She'd spent the past half hour making her report and updating charts in the office across the hall that seemed to have become hers by default.

"Mother and baby are getting to know each other. The father is snoring away in the chair. It's a shame Bridget's first labor had to take place under such trying circumstances, but she did well. I hope the authorities will allow them back into their home soon. In the meantime they can stay here for as long as need be."

They were silent for a few moments, and Devon realized it was the comfortable silence of old friends, not the awkward gap in conversation that had so often been their lot these past years. Things had changed between them the afternoon she had told her grandmother the truth about the children's circumstances. They were united now in their attempt to protect them.

"Have you and Miguel decided what you're going to do about the rehearsal dinner?" Lydia asked, still watching the smoke rise into a gloriously tinted sunrise. "The fire team has set up headquarters there."

"I haven't had a chance to talk to Miguel about it." She had to force the words past a sudden lump in her throat. Would she ever speak to Miguel again?

"I'm sure Kim and Nolan will understand if you decide to cancel."

"I know they will, but there's still a day or two to make up our minds."

"Yes, I suppose there is."

In her heart of hearts Devon wanted to cancel the party. She would get through Kim and Nolan's wedding because she wouldn't let her cousin down. But hosting the party with Miguel at her side, polite and withdrawn, would be more than she could bear, and then knowing she had to turn around and do it all again the next day...! "The wind's picking up," she said to change the subject.

"I felt it switch a while back. The window in the green birthing room always rattles when the wind's from the south. It's nearly seven. Why don't I turn on the radio and see if there are any updates while you make us a cup of tea?"

Devon raised her hand and massaged the tight muscles at the back of her neck. "That sounds like a good idea. Do you want herbal or English breakfast?"

"English breakfast, I think. I need a pick-me-up."

The morning passed quickly. The midwives were determinedly cheerful, going about their business as though nothing was very different from any ordinary summer day. But of course, everything was very different. The usually blinding sunshine was hazy and diffused. There was a smell of smoke in the air that hadn't been there the night before.

More than once Devon caught herself glancing out a window when she walked by, watching the plumes of smoke that rose into the thin mountain air veer off on a tangent as the wind came more strongly from the south.

She'd just finished lunch—a package of wheat crackers from the vending machine, a piece of cheese and an apple from the break room fridge, washed down with a glass of sun tea that Trish had made the day before—when her cell phone rang.

"Devon here," she said fishing the tiny cell phone out of the pocket of her lab coat.

"It's Jesse," the boy said without preamble.

"Hi, Jesse, what's up?" She'd half expected the call to be from Jesse or Sylvia. The girl had been having Braxton Hicks contractions at fairly regular intervals. Over the past thirty-six hours, they'd become more like real labor pains.

"I wanted to let you know I'm going to go up to Mr. Elkhorn's place with Manny Cordova and help him bring his animals down to his ranch. I guess the fire is getting pretty close."

"That's what I heard on the radio a few minutes ago." Devon stuffed the apple core into her empty foam cup with her free hand. "You be careful up there, okay?"

"Yeah, I'll be real careful not to get eaten by no billy goat," he said with all the machismo of his Latin heritage. "And, Devon?"

"Yes?"

"You'll be close by if Sylvia needs you, right?"

"I'll be here all day. Call me when you get back into town."

"*Sí,* I'll do that."

Devon snapped the phone shut. Maybe she was making progress with Jesse, after all. She sighed, or maybe not. No matter how often over the past few weeks he'd clashed with her, he'd always put his sisters' welfare before his own.

"Devon." Trish's head, then the rest of her, appeared in the break-room door. "Jenna Harrison is on line two. She says Kyle is nursing every two hours and crying all the time in between. Her breasts are sore and she's sobbing harder than the baby." She rolled her eyes in sympathy. "Poor thing. She sounds like she's at the end of her rope. Do you have time to see her this afternoon?"

"Can she be here in an hour?" Devon asked, pitching the remains of her lunch into the wastebasket.

"From the sounds of that baby's howls, she can probably be here in ten minutes. I can move Carrie Simpson back a half an hour. She won't mind."

Devon chuckled. "Okay, ten minutes, then."

Jenna was indeed in a state. It took Devon almost forty-five minutes to calm her down and assure the nervous woman that she wasn't being a bad mother if she supplemented one or two breast feedings a day with formula from a bottle. It would be better for both her and Kyle, Devon explained patiently. Her breasts wouldn't be so tender. The baby wouldn't be so hungry and suck so hard. Everyone would benefit.

By the time Kyle had been coaxed to take his first ounce of formula and readied for the trip home, Devon was a half hour late for her next appointment. It was three o'clock before she had a chance to leave the exam room and go in search of a glass of iced tea.

The main phone line began to ring. After the fourth peal Devon realized Trish wasn't at the reception desk to answer. The receptionist must have gone up to the second-floor records room for a moment. Her grandmother was with a patient, the other midwives also occupied, so Devon ducked back into her office to answer the phone.

"The Birth Place. How may I help you?"

"Señorita Devon Grant, *por favor,*" a gravelly voice said.

"This is she."

"*Señorita,* this is Manny Cordova."

"Yes, Manny. Is there something wrong?" Jesse's helping the two old men bring Daniel's menagerie down off the mountain had been at the back of her mind all day. It wasn't particularly dangerous work under normal circumstances, but a wildfire less than two miles away wasn't normal circumstances.

The old man hesitated. "Yes, there is. After we unloaded Daniel's goats and chickens and he headed off for his daughter's place, Jesse stayed to help me put a new lock on the gate. Then, when I was busy feeding the horses, the boy, he drove off with my old truck. Left me stranded here at my place."

"What?" Devon leaned against the desk and closed her eyes. "He stole your truck?"

"Well, I guess you'd have to say that. I thought maybe he just needed something real bad from town, but he didn't come back, and it's been an hour."

"Did…did you call the police?" She couldn't bring herself to say Miguel.

"No, ma'am. Not yet. I wanted to give the boy a chance to come back on his own. He's a good kid. Been a real help to me. I don't want him to get into trouble and maybe have Immigration come sniffin' around about it.''

''You guessed the kids weren't here legally, too?'' she asked. She had been a fool to think she could keep their undocumented status a secret. Who else had guessed? The answer was obvious and sharp as a dagger in her heart. Miguel, of course.

''The boy let some things slip, but it's none of my business how he got here, ya know.'' But it was Miguel's business, and yet he had said nothing, done nothing to separate the children from her. Was he staying silent for her sake?

''Thank you, Manny. I'll find him. I'll get your truck back, good as new.''

The old man chuckled, low and gruff. ''She's got two hundred and forty thousand miles on her. She hasn't been new since my oldest boy was in boot camp.''

''I'll get her back, Manny.''

''The boy brings the truck back and we'll forget this ever happened, okay?''

''Okay, Manny. Goodbye. And thank you.''

''*Adios.*''

''Manny wait.'' Devon stood up clutching the phone receiver with both hands. ''How close was the fire to Daniel's place?''

''Too close. Miguel, he stopped while we were loading up Daniel's horse. He said the fire crew, they would send in a bulldozer to clear the brush from around Daniel's buildings. He said they were going to close the road soon. Maybe even today if the fire jumps the line anywhere up there.''

''How long ago did he tell you that?''

''Before the wind changed.''

CHAPTER SEVENTEEN

DEVON CLOSED HER EYES and tried to decide what to do next. She rested her weight on her hands, but she paid no more attention to the feel of the cold metal desk than she did the sight of mismatched chairs and the empty bookcase on the far wall.

She needed to get to Jesse. She had no doubt he was headed back up the mountain to the old ghost town. The most valuable thing in the world he and his sisters possessed was the truck they'd hidden at Silverton. But he would need help, a second driver, unless he planned to abandon Manny's pickup on the mountain—and Devon didn't think he would. And for that there was no one he could turn to...but Sylvia.

She picked up the receiver again, her heart beating hard in her chest. Before she could begin to dial, she heard her name called. "Devon?"

"I'm in here, Trish."

The receptionist appeared in the doorway, her cheeks pink from hurrying. "I was putting some files away upstairs and I forgot to take the portable phone with me."

"It's okay. The call was for me."

Trish nodded, looking back down the hallway now, not at Devon. She seemed a bit distracted. "Look who I found in the play area.'' She held out her hand to someone Devon couldn't see. "C'mon here, sweetie. Devon's in here.''

Devon put the receiver back in the cradle and took a quick couple of steps toward the door. "Maria." The little girl was wearing a new T-shirt in a striking shade of hot pink that Myrna had bought for her the day before when they went shopping in Taos. Her sandals were pink, too, as were her toenails and fingernails and the ribbons in her pigtails. Maria had brought all Myrna's latent grandmother traits to the surface with a vengeance, her father had noted at dinner.

Devon dropped to her knees and Maria rushed into her arms. She buried her face against Devon's shoulder and wrapped her arms around her neck, holding on for dear life. She gathered the little girl close. She felt strong and sturdy now, a comfortable weight in Devon's arms.

"Maria, sweetie, how did you get here?" Devon looked at Trish over the top of Maria's head. The older woman raised her hands palm outward to show she didn't know.

"Sylvia brought me. She told me to play nice until you could come and get me."

"Where is Sylvia?"

Maria rubbed her fist across her eyes. "With Jesse.''

"Where is Jesse?" Devon asked patiently, working hard to keep her growing fear from seeping into her voice.

"In a truck. An old, noisy truck.''

"Where did they go in this truck?"

"Don't know."

"Did they go up the mountain, Maria?" she coaxed gently.

"Jesse said the fire was going to get our truck and all the things we left in it." She leaned close to Devon and whispered so that Trish couldn't hear. "I think he and Sylvia went up the mountain to get it."

Trish gasped. "Devon, do you think—"

Devon closed her eyes, fighting to keep from showing any fear. Maria was a bright child, and she would pick up on it immediately. "I think Maria needs a snack. And I bet that my mother would love to come here and take you out for ice cream. Would you like that?"

Maria nodded. "I guess so. Will you come with us?"

Devon shook her head. "No. I think I should go find Sylvia and Jesse, don't you?"

Maria's head bobbed in vigorous agreement. "Yes. I don't think Sylvia wanted to go anyway. She said her stomach hurt. *Muy mal.*"

Really bad, Devon translated. If she had any doubts at all what her next step should be, they vanished. Devon was certain, now, that Sylvia was in labor. "Trish, will you make that call to my mother at the Morning Light? I need to go speak to Lydia."

MIGUEL LEFT THE COMMAND center at Angel's Gate and headed for the fire. As he drove, he watched a Forest Service plane disperse a load of fire retardant on a hot spot, then lumber off to the south to reload.

They'd already closed Silver Creek Road above the cutoff to the ghost town, but now he wanted Hank and Lorenzo to move the barricades down to his granddad's place. The old man and his animals were safe, but if there was a breakout anywhere along the fire line, it would jump the road and roar up the narrow valley faster than a man could run.

The radio squawked to life. He'd been monitoring the fire crews' communications, as well as the highway patrol's, but this one was for him. "Go ahead, Doris." The dispatcher had been pulling double shifts since the fire started, and refused to be relieved.

"Chief, can you take a call on your cell?" she asked.

Miguel fished the cell phone out of his belt and checked the signal. "Ten-four on that, Doris. Who's calling?"

"Myrna Grant. It's a ten-thirty-five," which meant confidential information. "Says she has to talk to you. It's urgent."

"I'll pull over so I don't lose the signal. Tell her to make the call." He couldn't imagine why Devon's mother would want to talk to him. He didn't have long to wonder about it, however. He'd no sooner steered the Durango onto the narrow shoulder that was all that separated him from a drop of 150 feet down the mountain than the cell beeped. "Eiden here."

"Thank goodness I was able to get through to you, Miguel!"

"What is it, Mrs. Grant?"

"It's Devon…and my mother." She was speaking

so quickly that Miguel had trouble keeping up with her words. "I'm at The Birth Place. They're gone. Both of them. The radio just said the fire jumped the line near Silver Creek Road. That's where we believe they were headed. To the ghost town."

"Damn, what the devil are they doing up there?"

"It's Jesse and Sylvia. They…borrowed—hang on a moment." Miguel waited impatiently while Myrna questioned someone on her end of the conversation. "He took a truck belonging to somebody named Manny Cordova and went up there for some reason. That's all I know, but I'm worried."

"How long ago?"

"Trish says Devon and Lydia left about an hour ago. I was away from our room. I only got the message a few minutes ago. What's going on, Miguel? My husband and I are very worried."

"What about the little girl? Maria?" So far he had four civilians in the danger zone, one of them a very pregnant girl. Did the little girl make five?

"She's with me. I'm taking her for ice cream. I'll have my cell phone with me."

"I'll take the number, but there's not much chance I can get a signal up around Silverton."

She rattled off the digits and he scribbled them on a notepad he kept on the floor of the unit. "I've been trying to reach Devon, but she's not answering."

"Like I said, Myrna, I'll do my best."

He disconnected the call, then keyed the mike and gave Doris his ETA for Silverton. "Tell Cooper and Jensen to stop anyone trying to get past my granddad's place."

"Roger, Chief. Do you want me to relay this to the feds?"

"Not yet. Let me see if I can round them up first." He knew what the boy was after—the truck, of course. He should have had the thing hauled down the mountain the day he found it. Now Devon was after the two kids, trying to get them back to Enchantment safe and sound, with no one the wiser. He didn't know who he was angrier at—Devon, or himself.

"IS THE FIRE GETTING BIGGER or is it just that we're getting closer?" Lydia asked as they drove up Silver Creek Road. They were about a mile from Daniel Elkhorn's place as the crow flies, farther on the twisting mountain road.

"I don't know," Devon admitted. "I hope it's just that we're getting closer." She pulled her eyes from the curtain of smoke that rose above them on the mountain and concentrated on the road. An hour earlier, when she told her grandmother where she was going and why, Lydia insisted on coming with her. Devon had done her best to reason with the older woman, but soon gave up. There simply wasn't enough time. And once Lydia made up her mind, there was little chance she'd change it.

Still, all the way up the mountain she'd been trying to find a way to get Lydia out of the car, drop her off someplace safe and continue on alone. Except they hadn't seen another human being since they made the turnoff onto Silver Creek Road under the incredulous eyes of a TV camera crew filming stock shots for the evening news. Devon hadn't expected to see any fire teams, but what about support personnel? Police roadblocks? Did that mean the fire was already contained, or were they driving into an inferno? The mere fact that they couldn't see any flames, only smoke, didn't make Devon feel any more secure.

At the turnoff to Daniel's homestead an Enchantment police cruiser blocked most of the road. As Devon and Lydia approached, a young patrolman got out of the driver's side. An older, heavier officer that Devon recognized as Lorenzo Cooper exited the passenger door. The younger man held up a restraining hand. Devon rolled down the window and slowed to a stop.

"Ladies, may I ask what you're doing up here?" the young cop, whose name tag said Jensen, asked.

"We need to get to Silverton. It's urgent."

"Sorry, can't let you do that. The fire's too close to the road between here and there to let you through."

"How long have you been here?" Lydia asked, leaning forward in her seat to look at the young cop.

"Just a few minutes, ma'am. We were set up a couple miles on up the mountain for most of the morning."

"Did you see anyone else on the road?"

"No, ma'am. Except for the old ghost town, only about two more houses on up that way. Those folks left yesterday or the day before."

"We have to get to Silverton."

"I can't let you do that, miss. We have to keep this

road clear for the fire crews to bring equipment up to the blaze.''

The cop twisted around, his hands still on the window frame, to confer with his partner. ''Have him contact Miguel, Devon,'' Lydia said quietly. ''He might give us permission to pass through if you tell him the truth.''

''No. I don't think that will work.'' Even if the young cop followed orders, she doubted Miguel would give them. Devon was tired of trying to be reasonable. She had to get to Jesse and Sylvia. ''Officer, has the fire crossed the road between here and Silverton?''

''Not yet, miss, but it might at any time. That's why you have to turn around and go back now.'' He stepped backward, his thumbs hooked in the webbing of his utility belt. ''Those are Chief Eiden's orders.''

If the two cops had been driving a big SUV like Miguel's Durango, she could never have attempted what she did next. But they were driving an older patrol car, a sedan, and if she got a good enough start, she could probably get past them without putting her wheels into the steep, narrow ditch beside the road. ''Hold on,'' she told Lydia. ''We're going to make a run for it.''

''Hey! Stop! You can't do that!'' both cops yelled, then jumped back out of the way as she rammed the rear side panel of the patrol car, shoving it sideways. The sound of metal crushing metal sent a shiver up and down Devon's spine.

The Blazer bounced in and out of the ditch, listing far to the right, throwing Lydia against the passenger door with a thump. Devon hung on to the wheel with both hands, remembering not to pump the brake when they skidded back onto the graded surface of the road and fishtailed toward the rock wall on the other side. The back bumper kissed the stone and caused her to make one more swerve before the tires straightened out and they shot forward up the steep incline toward the Silverton cutoff.

"Are you all right?" Devon asked, chancing one quick glance at Lydia before she turned her eyes back to the road.

"I...I think I sprained my wrist," Lydia said, holding up her right hand. "I hit the door handle when we bounced over that rock in the ditch."

"I'm sorry. I've never run a police roadblock before."

"That's okay, dear. I think you did a great job." Lydia was smiling, but her face was pale. She was in pain and in danger, and it was Devon's fault.

"I'm sorry, Grandma. I should never have brought you along with me."

"Nonsense," Lydia sniffed, flexing her fingers. "I insisted." She reached over and touched Devon's elbow. "Do you know how long it's been since you called me Grandma?"

"What?"

"You called me Grandma just now. You haven't done that in years."

Devon wanted to cry, but she didn't have time to waste on tears. "Well, now that I've started again, don't expect me to stop."

The higher they climbed, the more smoke they

could see. Lydia cradled her injured wrist on her lap. Devon drove with both hands clenched on the wheel. Wind bent the dry grasses at the side of the road—away from the direction of the fire, she noted gratefully, but the knowledge gave her little comfort. Wildfires made their own rules. The direction of the wind didn't always dictate their path.

The sign for the turnoff to Silverton was down again and Devon relied on her own well-remembered landmarks to guide their way. She maneuvered up the rutted track to the ghost town with one eye on the rearview mirror. She'd been looking back over her shoulder with every turn of the road, but so far she hadn't seen the patrol car following them. She was certain they'd radioed Miguel before the Blazer was out of sight, but evidently he'd ordered them to stay put.

Once more she wondered if she was driving into a death trap. It didn't matter if she was, not as long as there was any chance that Jesse and Sylvia were still on the mountain.

Five minutes later she had her answer. She rounded the last curve of the creek bed that had been obscuring her view, only to find Manny's commandeered truck blocking the plank bridge. The offside back wheel was over the edge, the whole truck leaning at a precarious angle over the water a good eight feet below.

"That's Manny's truck, isn't it?" Lydia asked peering through the dusty windshield.

"They must have given up on trying to get their truck running and decided to drive back down the mountain. The back wheel went off the bridge and they were stuck.''

''It sounds plausible, but I don't see any sign of them.''

Would they start overland on foot? Jesse must know his way around the area—after all, he'd scavenged there for at least two weeks. That would be an even more dangerous situation than they were in now. ''We'll probably find them in the town.''

''There's no way you're going to muscle your way past that truck like you did the police car. The bridge is too narrow,'' Lydia said.

''I know. I'll go look for them on foot. But first I'm going to turn around so we can make a quick getaway if we have to.'' She didn't have to look up at the curtain of smoke that now hazed the afternoon sun to know the fire had changed direction. She didn't have to. The smell of burned grass and pine was stronger here, and far off in the distance the rush of flames could be heard. She switched off the ignition. Lydia reached over with her left hand to try to open the door. ''Wait. Let me help you.'' Devon jumped out of the Blazer and hurried around to Lydia's side. She opened the door and put her arm under her grandmother's elbow, steadying her for a moment. ''Okay?''

''I'm fine.''

''You wait here.''

Lydia nodded. ''I'll monitor the radio while you're gone. But, Devon—'' she held out her hand and wrapped her long, strong fingers around Devon's wrist "—be careful, dear." She looked around. "And don't be any longer than you have to."

MIGUEL PULLED to a halt and stuck his head out of the window of the Durango. "What the hell are you guys doing?" he asked, giving Hank Jensen and Lorenzo Cooper the once-over. Both patrolmen were squatting beside the left rear tire of their unit, attempting to pull the dented fender away from the frame.

"She blasted right through our roadblock," Jensen said, looking miserable.

"Who? Two women in a Blazer?"

Cooper got to his feet. He was a burly, middle-aged, ex-Phoenix detective who had left the city behind to join the Enchantment force three years ago. "She didn't exactly blast through, Chief," he corrected his partner. "But I wasn't about to step in front of her. The lady was in a hurry and not in the mood to take no for an answer. Said there was someone at Silverton. We've been up and down this road since dawn, but we didn't see any other vehicles, and we got no radio traffic on it, either. Is she right, Chief? Is someone up there?"

"It looks like it." The wind freshened for a moment and drew their eyes to the fire line. Sparks and blowing embers, several as big as basketballs, sailed overhead. Somewhere, and too close for comfort, the fire was crowning, racing through the tops of the trees, instead of along the ground.

"Chief Eiden, this is Angel Base." He recognized the information officer's North Carolina drawl.

"Eiden here," he replied, toggling the mike.

"Chief, have you got any men up on Silver Creek Road? One of the spotter planes sighted vehicles near the Silverton area."

"Roger that, Angel Base. I'm here with one of my units now. We also believe there's at least one civilian vehicle farther north. Possibly in that vicinity. Over."

"I suggest you all get out of there ASAP, Chief. We've got a flare-up three-quarters of a mile north of the Silverton turnoff. It's already jumped the road in at least one spot. The other bad spot is directly south of a Daniel Elkhorn's. Are you familiar with the place?"

"I'm there right now."

"Get you and your men out of there, Chief. I've already called a chopper drop on it, but one of the Hueys is refueling and the other's grounded for some routine maintenance. Their ETAs are uncertain. Do you copy?"

"Roger, Angel Base."

Jensen went back to working on the dented fender with less finesse and more muscle than he'd been using before. "How long, Cooper?" Miguel asked.

"I think we can be out of here in five minutes."

"Make that two minutes. Get yourself down to the Desert Valley Road intersection and make sure no more civilians get up here, understand?"

Smoke began to rise from the tree line above his grandfather's place. Miguel watched it for a moment with narrowed eyes. Daniel's trailer and barn were ringed by meadow, and bulldozers had cleared a fire break around the buildings, so the place stood a good chance of surviving, unless one of the fireballs that had just passed over landed on the roof of the barn.

"Two minutes. Yes, sir." Jensen gave the fender one last yank, then climbed in behind the wheel. He moved the patrol car a few yards down the road and pulled it to a halt. Cooper picked his hat up off the road and slapped it on his thigh. "What about you, Chief?"

"I'm going to get those women out of there before they're cut off."

He didn't bother to add if it wasn't already too late.

CHAPTER EIGHTEEN

"JESSE! SYLVIA!" Devon was almost too breathless to call their names. She'd been running since she crossed the bridge, and the thinner air was getting to her. "Kids! It's me, Devon. Where are you?"

She slowed her pace, bypassing the derelict buildings along the main street, heading for the ruined stable where Jesse had stashed the pickup. The higher she climbed, the more smoke she could see, but still no flames. Devon took heart at that, although she wasn't sure why. Smoke meant fire. The flames were there somewhere beyond her line of sight, probably almost ringing the small valley that contained the little ghost town and the played-out silver mine.

Above her, the top of the mountain looked serene and untouched. The trees swayed in the breeze. If she kept her back turned to the fire, she could almost believe it didn't exist—except for the smoke and the smell of burning pine. But no birds called, no hawks circled high overhead. Around her there was silence, too, as if all the small, scurrying things that populated the ghost town had burrowed deep in the ground until the danger had passed.

"Devon, is that you?" Sylvia stepped from the shadows of the stable door. She leaned against the splintered wood of the side of the building. The skirt of her denim maternity jumper, one of several that Gina had given her, was darkened by a wet stain.

Devon sprinted the last hundred feet, coming to a halt just as the teenager dropped to her knees, moaning in pain. "Oh, honey," Devon crooned. "Are you in labor?"

"I don't know. I…" Sylvia plucked at the damp skirt of the jumper. "Yes, I think so."

"How often are the contractions?"

"I don't know. I don't have a watch." She held her stomach and rocked back and forth in misery. "I don't want this to happen now. It can't happen now." She covered her face with her hands and began to sob.

"It will be okay, Sylvia. I'm here. We'll get you back to Enchantment. To The Birth Place. You'll have the baby there. Everything will be all right, I promise you."

"Where's my sister? Where's Maria?"

"She's with my mother. She'll take good care of her. Don't worry."

"Jesse can't get the truck started. We tried to leave in Manny's truck, but the wheel went off the bridge. The door wouldn't open. Jesse had to pull me out. It hurt. I hurt…"

Devon pushed the girl's damp hair back off her face. "It's okay, Sylvia." Dear God, she hoped she was right. Had Sylvia harmed herself or the baby when the truck wheel dropped over the edge of the bridge? She turned her head, looking back in the direction she'd come, but the trees hid the bridge from view.

She heard the whining growl of an uncooperative engine from inside. "I'm going to talk to Jesse," she said, squeezing Sylvia's arm. The girl nodded but kept sobbing as if her heart would break.

Devon slipped inside the building and blinked. The roof was full of holes, and sunlight dappled the dusty interior. Jesse was sitting in the cab of the pickup, but the fading groan of the starter told Devon the battery was too weak to turn over the engine.

She called his name. His head whipped around.

"What are you doing here?"

"I came to get you and take you back to town. You can't stay here. The fire is too close." As with Sylvia, his next thought was of his little sister. Once more Devon gave the assurance that she was safe.

"I changed the plugs but the battery's run down. We can't leave it here. There's no insurance. It's all we've got."

"It's not worth your lives."

"I have to get it running. Manny's truck is stuck on the bridge. I need this one to pull it off."

"Jesse," Devon said, doing her best to keep her fear and impatience out of her voice. "It will take a tow truck to move Manny's pickup off the bridge. We have to get off the mountain. Sylvia's in labor. She needs to be back at The Birth Place, maybe even in the hospital."

He dropped his head onto the steering wheel in defeat. "Our things. All we have left…"

"We'll take what you can carry. The rest has to

stay behind. If we had more time, we could put it back in the mine shaft.'' She moved to the door of the truck and put her hand on the window frame. ''But, Jesse, I don't think we have that time.''

He looked past Devon, his eyes darting here and there in the shadows of the barn. ''Where is my sister?''

''Outside.'' He flung open the door and jumped out of the truck. He slammed it shut as hard as he could and pounded his fist against the frame. ''I've screwed up again.''

Devon reached out and grabbed him by the shoulder. He was young and scared, but they didn't have time for him to indulge in an orgy of self-recrimination. ''Jesse, my grandmother is with me. We could all be trapped here if we don't get off the mountain.''

''Trapped?''

''The last radio bulletin I heard said that there was a flare-up of the fire just below us. Do you understand what that means? It could jump the road and make it impossible for us to leave this place.'' She didn't add that it meant the fire could reach the ghost town itself. She didn't have to. The color visibly drained from his face. He dropped onto an old barrel as though his legs had lost the ability to hold him upright.

''*Dios*. The fire could come all the way up here?'' He buried his face in his hands. ''What have I done?''

''Jesse, we don't have time for you to beat yourself up. We need to get Sylvia down to my car and away from here.''

For a moment he didn't move. Devon reached out,

ready to give him a shake when he lifted his face. "I understand." He stood up, put his hand on the rim of the truck bed. "I tried, Mama," he said softly in Spanish. He turned away. "Okay. Let's go."

"Sylvia's very frightened. The less concerned about the fire we act, the better for her, okay?"

"Okay." He opened the door of the truck once more and grabbed a frayed and faded backpack from the seat and slung it over his shoulder. "A few things," he said, not quite meeting Devon's eye. "Some pictures and letters."

"If there's anything else you can get quickly, I'll carry it."

"No. This is all."

Sylvia wasn't slumped against the side of the building when they emerged. She was standing a few yards away staring out over the mouth of the small valley, her hands clasped around and beneath her distended stomach as though to hold in the pain. *"Madre de Dios,"* she said, casting huge, fear-filled eyes back at Devon and Jesse. "Fire. I can see the fire and it's coming this way."

ASH AND SPARKS WERE BLOWING across the road in front of him. Miguel gunned the truck forward through the low-hanging haze of smoke. Smoke that low to the ground was good. It meant the fire was staying along the ground, as well, not racing through treetops, outrunning fire crews and fire-retardant-dropping planes and helicopters.

But the situation was still bad enough. He wasn't going to be coming back this way any time soon. And neither were Devon and Lydia, or the Molina kids—if they were all together. That they might not be didn't bear thinking about.

Silverton, like his granddad's place, was relatively safe. It was true the buildings were all wood and dried out from years of sun and wind, but beyond that negative, if the fire jumped the creek, there were few trees in the little valley. They'd all been cut for firewood and garden plots generations earlier. The ground was stony, not much vegetation, and as a last resort the old mine would provide shelter if the fire got that far. As a defensive position he'd seen worse, but that was as much praise as he was prepared to give the place.

The turnoff to the ghost town was just ahead. Miguel took one last look in the mirror, and any hope he harbored of beating the fire back down the mountain died. Flame licked at the edge of the roadway and snaked up a pine tree, exploding and raining fire around it while he watched. He keyed the mike and relayed the coordinates of the flare-up to Angel Base, then switched channels to tell Doris where he was headed.

She took the news calmly enough, assured him that Cooper and Jensen had just checked in, had made it down the mountain and were setting up a roadblock at the Desert Valley Road intersection. She agreed he would check in again in ten minutes and ended the transmission as though he'd just called in a routine ten–thirty–five, a bathroom break.

He bumped along the neglected roadway as fast as he dared. Deep ruts and rocks that'd heaved out of the earth made the going difficult even for the sturdy Durango. A broken axle was the last thing he needed right now. The trees along the creek opened up—and Devon's Blazer came into view. Miguel felt his heart thud fast and heavy in his chest as adrenaline coursed through his veins.

She was safe. She was here and not farther up the mountain somewhere he couldn't go. A second look at the figure in the Blazer proved him wrong. It wasn't Devon, but Lydia sitting there, looking as cool and composed as if she was at her desk at The Birth Place. One more look told him the reason she was on this side of the creek: the road to the town was blocked by the wreck of Manny Cordova's old beater of a truck. So the kids were here, too.

He pulled up behind the Blazer and got out. Lydia did the same, coming toward him with one hand raised to shield her eyes from the hazy but still strong sunlight. "Miguel. I'm glad to see you. Devon is up at the town trying to talk Jesse and Sylvia into coming back with us."

"I figured as much. Are you hurt?" he asked, noticing she had a makeshift splint on her left wrist.

"I banged my wrist on the door handle—it's only a sprain. Will you go see what's delaying Devon? She's been much longer than I expected."

"We'll both go, Lydia," he said, watching her from beneath the brim of his hat. "The fire jumped the road between here and my granddad's place. We need to move to open ground, and the sooner the better."

Dismay deepened the lines around her mouth and

her eyes. "The vehicles? If we leave them here, they might be destroyed."

"Once we get settled, I'll see if there's some way to get Manny's truck off the bridge. I don't want to be cut off from the radio." He motioned for her to start walking.

"Ours isn't working," Lydia said. "It hasn't since we dropped into the valley."

"I was afraid of that."

"Will we need to be evacuated?"

"I hope not." The words came out too rough and hard-edged, like his thoughts. He took care to modulate his next words. "I don't think we're in immediate danger. The wind's supposed to die at sunset. Night is the best time to work a fire. And it's only a flare-up, not a breakout. There's a difference."

"Both seem equally dangerous at the moment."

"Watch your step." He held out his hand, but Lydia waved it off.

"I'm better on my own." She began to move carefully onto the planks of the bridge. Miguel wondered how long the bridge had stood at this spot. It was still sturdy despite years of weathering and flooding. It had probably been designed and built by the miners to carry the heavy ore wagons down the mountain. Still, he didn't think he'd trust it to take the weight of a tow truck, even if they could get one up here. Manny's truck was going to have to go over the side into the dry creek bed. There was no other way around it.

He looked up the overgrown pathway that had once been a street and saw Devon coming toward them.

Her arms were around Sylvia's shoulders. The girl was clutching her distended stomach, her face pale and streaked with tears.

"Oh, dear," Lydia said under her breath. "It appears Devon was right. She's in labor."

"In labor?" Miguel lost a step. Lydia halted and looked back at him over her shoulder.

"I'm afraid so."

"Damn."

Jesse trailed a couple of feet behind the women, looking scared, but when he glimpsed Miguel, his shoulders stiffened and his mouth tightened. Great, that was all he needed, Miguel thought. An angry, defiant kid to deal with.

"Sylvia." Lydia hurried forward to smooth the girl's dark, tangled hair from her cheek. "Are you all right? Were you injured when the truck went off the bridge?"

She shook her head.

"I don't think she was hurt," Devon said. "Jesse said the back wheel slid off because he came at the bridge at too sharp an angle, not because he was going too fast."

"I just hurt so bad here." She clutched her stomach and moaned. "And my back. The pain is terrible."

Devon looked first at her grandmother, then directly at Miguel. There was fear in her eyes, but it was buried so deep in the gray depths that he knew he, and probably Lydia, were the only ones who saw it. "We need to get her to the clinic."

Lydia had detached Sylvia from Devon's arms and, talking low and soothingly, began to lead her toward the porch of the abandoned hotel. Jesse gave Miguel a sidelong look and followed them.

"She's in labor. I'm not sure how far along or how fast it's progressing. She's too upset to answer my questions with any accuracy. She's at risk because of her age and lack of prenatal care. Do you understand? We need to get her out of here."

She didn't move closer or reach out to touch him, but he wished she had. He wanted to batter down the wall that had grown between them since the night he'd sent her away from him. He wanted to pull her into his arms and hold her close, keep her safe and soothe her fears. But she didn't want that, wouldn't accept it if he tried. He spoke quietly, although the others were too far away to overhear. "We're not going anywhere, Devon. The fire jumped the road behind me." He indicated the plumes of smoke now rising above the tree line on the ridge.

She turned her head, her eyes widening. "Oh, God. We're trapped."

"We're fairly safe here, at least for the time being. And there's always the mine."

"Oh, no. She's been through so much. I don't want Sylvia's baby to be born in that dark, filthy mine."

He bent his head toward her so that the brim of his hat shadowed his face. It was as close as he allowed himself to come to touching her. "We may have no choice."

Devon closed her eyes for a moment. He could see her gathering her composure, searching within herself for strength. "All right. We're staying here." She spun on her heel and moved toward the others. "I'll need my midwife's box from the back of the truck. And the blankets and flashlight, and even the seat covers if you have time to take them off." She stopped and turned back to him. "And I suppose you should get my registration...and insurance papers out of the glove box. I mean...in case—"

"I'll bring your box, and whatever else I can find. I've got some emergency equipment in my unit that should help get us through the night."

Devon looked up at the sun, now shrouded in smoke. It was hanging just above the ridge line, ready to drop out of sight. Night would soon follow. "I'd forgotten what time it was. I'll need light...and... some way to keep the baby warm."

He chuckled, a dry croaking noise that didn't sound much like a laugh even to him. "We'll build a fire."

"I suppose we'll have to. In the truck Jesse and the girls had a couple of blankets and an old..."

"Granddad's old mattress. And his lawn chairs?"

She didn't look away, but her chin came up just a fraction of an inch. "Yes. It's all still in their truck. In the barn."

"I know where it is. It'll come in handy. But first I'm going to do my best to get our vehicles across the bridge. I'll take Jesse with me and between the two of us, we might be able to heave Manny's pickup over the side and drive the others up here. I'm not looking forward to going to the city council and asking for a new truck because mine went up in smoke."

"I can see where that would be a little awkward." She wrinkled her nose and gave a small smile.

He straightened his hat, smiling back. "I wouldn't put it past them to take it out of my paycheck."

Lydia had settled Sylvia on the hotel steps. She was leaning against one of the listing porch posts, moaning in pain. Devon's steps faltered once more. She turned to him. Now tears glistened in her eyes. "You're certain there's no way out? A helicopter?"

"They're all tied up working the fire. If we had radio contact, we might get one up here from Taos, but we don't."

She pulled in a deep breath as though absorbing a blow.

"Devon." This time he did touch her, just a quick brush of his fingertip across her cheek. "You're good. You can do this."

She turned her head toward his caress, a movement so slight it might have been just his wishful thinking. "Can I? I'm not so sure."

Devon knelt on the top step of the hotel porch. The wood was sun-warmed and scoured smooth from years of wind and snow. "Sylvia," she said softly but firmly, tugging gently at the sobbing girl's clenched hands. Sylvia raised her head. "We can't leave this place, perhaps for many hours. Do you understand?"

Sylvia sucked in her breath on a sob. *"Sí."*

"It's possible your baby will be born here. On the mountain."

"No." The word was a wail of despair. "No, Devon, please. I want to go to the clinic. To our cabin. Anywhere but here. I hate this place."

"She's right," Jesse said, bending forward, looking almost as miserable and frightened as his sister. "She can't have her baby here. She needs to be at the hospital. Or the clinic.''

Devon felt tears sting her eyes again, but she held them back, just as she had when Miguel touched her and the urge to throw herself into his arms and sob out her fear and uncertainty had been almost more than she could bear.

''Women have been having babies outside for thousands of years,'' Lydia said calmly.

Miguel leaned over and smoothed a big hand over Sylvia's hair. She looked up at him from wounded eyes. ''It will be okay, Sylvia. You're in good hands. You'll do fine.''

Another hiccuping sob stole her words, but she nodded. Devon began to croon, speaking softly, encouraging Sylvia to watch her mouth and try to breathe as she did. The girl gripped Devon's hands so hard Devon almost cried out in pain herself, but finally Sylvia did as Devon instructed, and eventually the contraction passed, leaving her limp and gasping.

Devon realized that she and her grandmother were alone with the girl. She looked up to see Miguel and Jesse just disappearing into the trees that bordered the creek. She looked back at Lydia.

''Three minutes,'' Lydia said as the contraction eased. ''Let's move. We might find someplace more pleasant for Sylvia to labor.''

Devon stayed where she was for a moment, her insides knotted with fear. She couldn't do this. Not alone, not even with Lydia, out here so far from The Birth Place and Arroyo County Hospital. She wasn't the same kind of midwife her grandmother was, that

Hope and Gina were. She needed the reassurance of fetal monitors and medical backup. She didn't have the necessary instincts.

"Devon." Lydia's voice was firm. "This is what we are. This is what we do. It is woman at her most powerful and her most vulnerable. She needs you to guide her through. And you will."

"How?"

"Stop thinking so much, my dear. Listen to your heart, trust your hands. You are good. Very good. You have the instincts and the compassion—let them guide you."

"Okay. We've got this baby jacked up as high as it will go. Now. On the count of three, start rocking." Miguel had taken everything of any value from Manny's old truck before affixing the jack to the undercarriage where he figured it would give him the best leverage. Jesse didn't obey. He just stood with his hands balled into fists.

He'd been helpful enough so far, but now that it was actually time to dump the truck over the edge, he'd lost his nerve.

"Isn't there some other way?" he asked for about the tenth time.

Miguel hung on to his patience. He pushed his hat back on his head and looked at the kid. "We need the other vehicles up there. It's too big a gamble to leave them here for the fire to get."

"How will I pay him for it?" Jesse asked, his voice cracking, betraying the youth behind the macho facade.

"I don't know." Miguel wiped his hands together. "Is that what you're worried about? Compensating the old man?"

Jesse held his gaze for a moment, then looked down. "Yeah. He loves that damn old truck."

"Aren't you worried about being in trouble for stealing it in the first place?"

"I didn't steal it." He flushed. "I borrowed it."

"I'll have to hear that from Manny." No reason to bring up the underage driving. The kid was miserable enough.

"Are you going to turn me in to *la migra*?"

Miguel braced both hands against the truck. He turned his head and looked at the kid. He was wearing sunglasses and the boy was squinting against the sun. He outweighed him by at least fifty pounds. He was a lawman with all the power of New Mexico state law behind him, but Jesse didn't flinch or look away.

He was an officer of the law, but he was also a human being. "No," he said.

"What if Manny...? What if he...?" Jesse jerked his thumb toward the truck.

"We'll deal with that when it happens. But right now it doesn't make any difference how it got here. It's a hazard to health and safety and it's got to go. Now push."

Jesse braced his arms alongside Miguel. "Are you doing this because of her? Devon?"

Miguel stared at the faded green paint of the truck cab. Off in the distance he could hear a helicopter's rotors beating the air. "What makes you think that?"

"'Cause you're a good cop. Manny says so. You

wouldn't go against the law just for me and my sisters. You're doing it because of Devon. I see the way you look at her. She looks at you the same way.''

''You don't know what the hell you're talking about. Now start rocking this old crate. One. Two. Three.''

Jesse pushed, but he wasn't about to hold his tongue. ''You love her. And I think she loves you, too.''

His tone implied he didn't have the foggiest idea why, though. Miguel shook his head. Were his feelings so obvious that even a fifteen-year-old could see how much in love with Devon he was? It seemed they were. Maybe he ought to ask Jesse for his opinion on what to do to win her back. He was striking out big time on his own.

''Keep your opinions to yourself or I just might change my mind about turning you in.'' Miguel took a deep breath. Manny's truck had been made before Detroit started using aluminum and plastic, instead of steel. It was heavier than hell. He dug in his heels. ''No more analyzing my love life,'' he puffed. ''She's rockin' pretty good. On the count of three. Push.''

For a long few seconds the old truck teetered on the brink, threatening to slam back down on three wheels, then a last straining push sent it over with a crash that echoed off the rock walls for a full thirty seconds. They stood, breathing heavily, looking down at the exposed undercarriage with its slowly rotating wheels.

''I'm in big trouble,'' Jesse said mournfully.

"We'll both be in trouble if we don't get these other two cars up to where the women are."

"Okay." Jesse took off at a trot, then looked back over his shoulder. "I'll drive the Blazer. You go first."

Miguel swallowed a grin. The kid had guts. He'd make a good Marine one day, if he ever got his green card. He didn't even want to think of the red tape and strings he'd have to pull to keep the three of them— no, in a couple of hours it would be the four of them—in the country, but he was damned well going to yank on every one of them. For his sake and Devon's, as well as theirs.

CHAPTER NINETEEN

DARKNESS CAME EARLY, because the smoke blocked the last of the sunlight. Flames danced along the ridge, here and there illuminating the smoke from below, while untroubled by the fire on a mountaintop in New Mexico, the moon and stars shone above. Jesse and Miguel had gone to the disabled pickup and gathered the camping equipment the kids had scrounged during their stay in the mine. They'd taken it to the small spring-fed grotto above the town where the women were.

"We found it when we stayed here," Sylvia explained while resting between contractions. She was reclining on the old mattress that Jesse had "scavenged" from Daniel's place and Miguel had wedged against a boulder. Devon had covered it with a waterproof sheet from her midwife box, then added one of the thin cotton blankets she kept in a storage container in the back of the Blazer: "It's where we got our water," she went on. Suddenly she began to breathe heavily again. Devon knelt beside her and held out her hands for Sylvia to clutch. When the contraction was over, she said, "It's clean, not like the mine, or the buildings of the town."

"I never knew it was here," Devon said. "I don't

think Miguel did, either, and he used to come here a lot when he was a boy.''

The little grotto was pleasant and green, open to the sun, with thick grass, nourished by the life-giving moisture of the spring as it bubbled up out of the rocks before seeping back into the stony ground. The space wasn't much larger than a big room. The rocks that sheltered it from view were smooth and sun-warmed, and would hold that warmth well into the cool of the night.

Miguel and Jesse fashioned a curtain of sorts for Sylvia's privacy out of some lengths of old pipe and the blankets that Miguel kept in his emergency supplies. Along with the cotton blankets Devon carried with her, and the ones that were among Jesse and Sylvia's belongings, they would be comfortable enough during the chill of the mountain night.

And they *would* be staying the night. Miguel had finally made contact with both the firefighting crew and the police dispatcher after he and Jesse drove the vehicles onto the open ground near the mine entrance. The flare-up was contained, but the road was blocked between Silverton and his grandfather's place, and it would be morning before bulldozers could be spared to clear it.

"Devon," Lydia said, "I'm going to send Miguel back here to help you while I warm a couple of blankets beside the fire." She'd been sitting half behind, half beside Sylvia on the mattress supporting her as she labored, periodically massaging her neck. It was fully dark now, and the temperature was falling quickly.

The smell of smoke in the air was strong, not because the fire was coming closer, Devon had assured Sylvia over and over again, but because the air was heavier, holding it closer to the ground. Off in the distance now and then they could hear the roar of chain saws and the growl of powerful engines as the fire crews worked their way closer to the little valley.

"She's fully dilated," Devon said to her grandmother. "The baby's moved well down in the birth canal." Because the temperature was dropping, Devon had only removed Sylvia's ruined panties. They'd found an old sweater in the truck and put that on her for extra warmth.

"I know. That's why we need the warming blankets ready," Lydia reminded her.

Devon managed a smile. "No microwave or autoclave to do the job out here."

"I'll hold them close to the fire and then fold them over on themselves. It'll work fine, you'll see. We can do our work without those things just as midwives have for hundreds of years."

Oddly enough Devon agreed with her grandmother. Something had changed inside her over the past two or three hours. Always before, she'd felt comforted by the beeps and whooshing sounds of monitors and automatic blood-pressure cuffs, the ringing of phones, the calls of nurses moving up and down the halls, the background noises of a busy hospital obstetrics department. Now she found herself welcoming the silence. She was more than ever aware of the laboring mother, attuned to the changes in Sylvia's breathing patterns, the building of the urge to push that she needed to talk her out of until the time was right. Her sense of touch seemed more finely honed as she palpated the distended uterus, her hearing more acute as she listened for any change in the rhythm or strength of the baby's heartbeat as the contractions ebbed and flowed. This was right and natural, and for the first time she understood fully what Lydia had always known. She shouldn't try to control the power of the birth force, but let it work through her for the benefit of mother and child.

"You're doing fine, Sylvia," she crooned, bracing the girl's knees as she rocked through another wave of pain.

"I'm not," Sylvia whimpered. "I'm going to die. And there's no priest."

"You're not going to die. It won't be much longer, I promise you. Just a little while and you can push. And then you won't feel so helpless. You'll be working to bring your baby into the world."

The privacy blanket was moved aside and Devon glanced up to see Miguel. He looked as strong and solid as the mountains surrounding them. A rush of pure joy flowed through her veins. Would she ever not feel this way when she first saw him? She thought not. "How's my grandmother doing with the blankets?" she asked him. Lydia was so strong and uncomplaining, so staunch a partner, that Devon had forgotten for a few hours how recently she had been ill.

"Jesse's warming them while Lydia takes a break. I told her to stay by the fire and keep Jesse company. The kid's about at the end of his rope with worry.

She might be able to explain what's going on in here to him a little better than I've been doing.'' He dropped to the balls of his feet and brushed back Sylvia's matted hair with a gentle hand. ''How are you doing, Sylvia?''

''I hurt so bad,'' she said, but she choked back her tears. ''I…I'm afraid I will die.''

Miguel shook his head and moved around so that he was sitting with his back to a boulder. Sylvia turned a little sideways and he began massaging her neck, just as Lydia had been doing before she left. ''You won't die. You've got the two best midwives in Enchantment here with you.''

''I'm still scared. And what will I do with the baby? Oh…oh…Devon…''

''Breathe,'' Devon said. ''Whoo….whoo. Just like I showed you.'' The light of the kerosene lantern etched Sylvia's features in lines of pain and stubborn determination as she attempted to follow Devon's instructions. The contraction was long and hard, but when it was over, she didn't immediately begin sobbing again. Instead, she lay her head back against Miguel's shoulder and closed her eyes, gasping for breath.

He returned to the gentle massage, encouraging Sylvia with low words of praise.

''You're good at that,'' Devon said.

''I'm a Meals-on-Wheels Marine, remember?'' But the bitterness with which he'd used the reference in earlier conversations wasn't there. ''When the folks in Somalia weren't shooting at us, they were begging for our medics to help them. I spent a lot of time with the docs. I've seen a baby or two born.''

''Just keep on doing what you're doing. It's working. She's as relaxed as I've seen her.'' Once more relying on touch, Devon slipped on a pair of surgical gloves and checked Sylvia's progress. The cervix was totally dilated and the baby had moved well down into the birth canal. ''Excellent, Sylvia. A few more like that and you'll be ready to push.''

But by the third long, hard contraction Sylvia was once more agitated and afraid. ''I can't,'' she whispered, not opening her eyes, rolling her head back and forth on Miguel's shoulder. ''What good will it do for my baby to be born? I can't keep her if they're going to send me back to Mexico.'' Devon sensed she was now too exhausted even to cry.

''You're not going to be sent back, Sylvia. I promise.''

Miguel's big hands had moved to the middle of the girl's back, working in slow circles to ease the knotted muscles. ''You and the baby will be able to stay here. I promise, too.''

''You do?'' Sylvia was trembling, not only with emotion but with the power of the birth force. ''And Jesse?''

Miguel looked over the top of Sylvia's head and held Devon motionless with the intensity of his dark gaze. ''All of you,'' he said, and Devon's heart skidded to a halt before it began to beat again. ''You have my word.''

''I want to believe—arghhh.'' Sylvia screamed with the intensity of the contraction, straining against

Devon's hands as she braced her knees. She didn't need any monitors to tell her that Sylvia had made the transition into the final stage of labor. Miguel sensed the change, too. He rose to his knees, supporting Sylvia with both hands spread flat against her shoulders. Lydia appeared from around the makeshift curtain with another flashlight and Jesse, who carried warmed blankets.

"Do you have everything you need?" she asked Devon, after first positioning Jesse and Miguel to help hold Sylvia's shaking legs. Devon nodded.

Sylvia grabbed Jesse's arm with both hands. He winced at the strength of her grip but didn't pull away. "What should I do?" he whispered.

Devon spared him a quick smile. "Just support her leg so that I can see to catch the baby. And be there for her." He nodded, his eyes fixed on Devon, away from what was happening between Sylvia's legs. "*Sí.* I'll do that. But she's cutting off the blood to my arm."

"You can handle it," Miguel growled, and Jesse nodded.

"That's good, Sylvia. Go ahead. Push." The baby's head crowned, then receded back into the birth canal. Devon caught herself holding her breath, and released it. "Once more, Sylvia. Just like the last time. Don't worry about anything else. Don't think about anything else, just push." But once more the baby's head slipped back. Sylvia fell back against Jesse's arm, sobbing and discouraged.

Devon kept up her soft, encouraging croon of almost meaningless words. She knew it was the sound of her voice that would be an important touchstone to Sylvia, not what she said. With the next contraction the baby's head slid free, but as the infant rotated so that the shoulders could be born, Devon's blood ran cold. The cord was wrapped around the baby's neck. Lydia saw it, too. She rested her hand on Devon's shoulder and gave a slight encouraging squeeze.

Devon looked up and saw Miguel watching her, and the quiet confidence in his eyes sent the momentary beat of panic winging back into the darkest corners of her mind. She could do this. She had done it before. "Sylvia, I need you to slow down just a bit. Don't push through this contraction."

"I can't do that. Why do I have to stop now? It hurts too much." Sylvia struggled to sit up so that she could see what was happening.

Devon studied the frightened young woman's face, saw the exhaustion and fear, and beneath it all the strength that had gotten her, gotten all of them, this far in their journey. She decided to tell her the truth. "The cord is wrapped around the baby's neck. You must work with me so that I can slip it over her head. Do you understand?"

"Yes." Sylvia didn't have the breath or the energy to say more.

Carefully Devon worked her fingers between the baby's neck and the gently pulsing cord. She could feel another contraction beginning. She willed her fingers to stay steady and calm. Slowly, deftly, she worked the cord over the scrunched little face and the top of her skull. It came free just as the baby's head rotated and the shoulders were born. "One more push, Sylvia. One more, that's all."

"One…more…" Sylvia's cry faded away to a low, satisfied moan, as the rest of the tiny body slipped out into Devon's hands.

Tears filled her eyes and Devon did nothing to stop them falling. "Oh, Sylvia, it's a girl! A beautiful little girl."

Lydia immediately suctioned the infant's mouth and nose with a syringe from Devon's box and a few seconds later a faint but indignant wail of protest issued from the new arrival. Devon looked at her grandmother and they both laughed in joy and relief at the most wonderful sound a midwife could hear. "She's breathing well. Her color's good. She's perfect."

"A very beautiful little girl," Lydia seconded. Devon wiped the tiny body with a towel and handed her to Lydia. Her grandmother clamped and cut the cord, then wrapped the baby in a warm receiving blanket, while Devon delivered the placenta and examined it. It was intact and complete. She let her breath out in another sigh of relief.

"Here is your daughter, Sylvia." Lydia laid the baby in Sylvia's arms.

"Oh, Jesse, look at her! *Mi hija. Mi* Estrella. I want to name her that because there are so many stars in the sky tonight. She's as beautiful as they are." Sylvia fell silent, then held the baby out to Devon. "But I can't keep her." Tears flooded her eyes once more. "I…I want to give her to you."

Devon heard her grandmother draw in her breath. She halted with her hands still supporting the baby she'd just placed in Sylvia's arms. Devon pulled off her gloves and leaned toward the distraught new mother. "Sylvia, if you want to give the baby up for adoption, we'll discuss it later. But now you should rest."

"But if I give her to you, she will be able to stay here, even if I am sent back to Mexico." Tears continued to roll down her cheeks as she cradled the child to her breast. "I know you love children. That you want children of your own. Look at her. She is beautiful, is she not? *Muy linda.*"

Devon's heart contracted and pain filled her chest. Sylvia should be enjoying these first few moments of her daughter's life; she should be bonding with her baby. Instead, she was attempting to make one of the most painful decisions a woman ever had to make. "We'll work this out tomorrow. When everyone is rested and off the mountain." Devon reached out and touched the baby's tiny fist, which lay beside her cheek.

Sylvia wasn't comforted by the words. "I can't keep her if she will be sent back to Mexico with me. She is a citizen. She's an American."

Jesse remained on his knees behind her, supporting Sylvia's weight, his eyes fixed on his niece. It was Miguel who made the next move. He, too, reached out to touch the baby's silky cheek. "You won't have to give up your baby, Sylvia. Not unless you decide that is best for her welfare. It won't be because you have to leave the country."

"Can you do that? Can you make *la migra* let us stay?"

"I'll do my best. But it will take some doing. You have to be strong. And patient."

She looked up at Jesse. "God and the Blessed Virgin will help us. I can be strong and patient. Can you?"

Jesse was watching Miguel. Devon waited for his answer. "Do you mean what you said?" he asked. "That you'll help us, or are you only saying this to make my sister feel better right now?"

"I give you my word."

"You'll break the law to let us stay here?"

Devon watched Miguel's profile, the lines and angles of his face, a mixture of races and backgrounds that blended together into an individual of strength and character as he formed his answer. "I'll work with the law to make it legal for you to stay here. As far as the INS is concerned—" he hesitated a moment and Devon saw the muscles of his jaw tighten before a smile twisted up the corners of his mouth. "What they don't know won't hurt them."

DEVON CLOSED THE DOOR of the Blazer very quietly behind her. She held the precious weight of the baby in her arms, letting her eyes adjust to the darkness. Lydia and Sylvia were asleep on the old mattress in the back. Jesse and Miguel were bunked down in the Durango. Sunup was only an hour away, but Devon couldn't sleep.

Sylvia, dressed in the extra pair of scrubs Devon always kept in her midwife's box, had attempted to nurse her daughter with only one or two false starts, and then fallen into a sound sleep. Lydia, also, was too tired to stay awake all night. Devon had taken the baby so that the other women could rest without worrying about rolling over on her in their sleep.

She walked carefully toward the little grotto and settled into Daniel's rickety folding chair. The lantern, set on a rocky shelf, cast enough light for her to see the sleeping baby's face. Her eyes were screwed shut. Her little nostrils flared with each breath. Her hand lay fisted against her downy cheek. Her hair was thick and black, although not as black as her mother's, and her nose was more aquiline than Sylvia's, a feature inherited from her absent father? *Estrella.* Little star. It was a beautiful name, and it suited her. She was fragile and tiny, like the pinpricks of light in the sky.

Devon's stomach growled with hunger and she fished in her pocket for a peppermint to lull it into submission. They'd feasted on half a Snickers bar each, and peppermints from her emergency supply. There was fruit juice for Sylvia, to help rehydrate her after the delivery, and Miguel had contributed a couple of cans of soda he kept in the back of the Durango. There was water from the spring. They wouldn't starve before they could get back down the mountain, but everyone would be ready for a meal.

Devon held the sleeping infant close to her heart and laid her cheek against the top of her head. The wind had dropped at sunset. The sounds of men fighting the fire had continued all around them throughout the night, but as the hours passed, the chain saws and bulldozer noises had receded into the distance. Miguel's last radio check with Angel Base had promised rescue just after dawn.

"We don't need rescuing," he'd grumbled as he helped wrestle the old mattress into the back of the Blazer.

"Consider it an escort down the mountain then," Lydia had said. It'd been too dark to see her face, but Devon knew she was smiling. Miguel must have known it, too, because he'd chuckled and hadn't mentioned the matter again.

"Are you warm enough out here?" His voice came out of the darkness. Devon's heart accelerated and her arms tightened around the baby.

She looked up and saw him silhouetted by the dying flame of the fire. "Miguel. I thought you were asleep."

"I was dozing. I can't sleep in the front seat of that damned truck. I heard you come up here. Is everything all right?"

"I couldn't sleep, either. But now that I'm here, I'm not sure this was a good idea. The fire's nearly out and I'm a bit chilly." She'd wrapped one of the cotton blankets around her shoulders like a shawl, and the baby was swaddled in a cocoon of receiving blankets.

"That's easily fixed." He pushed the cotton blanket off her shoulders and draped them with his soft leather jacket. Devon drew in a deep breath. Sunlight and sagebrush filled her nostrils, the scents she would always associate with him. Miguel threw a couple of the boards he and Jesse had torn from a ruined building on the embers, and they both watched as a shower of sparks spiraled into the sky.

He perched himself on a boulder beside her chair

and stretched his booted feet toward the fire. The moon had set, but the star shine and the fire gave enough light for her to see his face. "Is she sleeping?" He leaned over to look more closely at the baby in her arms.

"Sound asleep. It's tough work being born, you know."

"You did a great job with Sylvia." His voice was a low, soothing rumble that warmed Devon as much as the flames. The baby stirred and turned her head as though listening to his words. "The kid was scared to death and you talked her through it like a pro."

"I *am* a pro." She caught him smiling at her. "No fair teasing a woman who's been awake for twenty-two hours," she said, smiling back. Maybe it was because she was so tired, or maybe it was because she had missed him so much the past few days, but she reached out and touched his cheek, a fleeting caress, all she would allow herself. "Thank you for coming after us. You came riding in like the…"

"The U.S. Cavalry?"

"No. Like the U.S. Marines." She had wanted to say, *"Like the man I love,"* but she lacked the courage.

"Did you think I could just stand by and leave all of you out here alone?"

"I knew you would do what was right and courageous and honorable."

"Bull," he said, and the baby screwed up her face and whimpered before settling back to sleep. "Devon, where are you going with this?"

She touched the newly healed burn on his wrist. "How long have you known the kids were illegals?"

"Your hands are like ice," he said.

She was shaking, but as much with emotion as cold. He scooped the baby up in one arm, as though it was something he did every day of his life, and then clasped his free hand around her wrist and tugged her into the V of his legs. He wrapped the blanket she'd been wearing on her shoulders around her legs, then settled her against his chest, sheltering both her and the baby.

She let herself relax against him for a long moment, inhaling his scent, absorbing his warmth. "How long?" she asked again.

"I suspected from the beginning. For sure since the day I found that damn pickup." He gestured in the direction of the barn. "I should have had it towed back to town then and there, and none of us would be out here tonight."

"Did you mean it when you said you'd help them stay in the country?"

"I always mean what I say, Devon."

"They have an aunt, but if we can't find her, or if she can't care for them, I'll adopt them to keep them here."

"Adoptions usually go easier if there are two parents in the equation," he said quietly.

Two parents. He didn't move, his breathing didn't change, but she felt the quick acceleration of his heartbeat as he waited for her answer.

"I'm glad I'm here right now." She was going to have to take this slowly, one step at a time, or she would lose her courage and fall silent again.

"Why are you glad? Tell me what you're really

thinking. Talk to me, Devon. Not talking to each other is what kept us apart for ten years. Don't let it happen again.'' She may have wanted to take this one step at a time, but Miguel, obviously, was not so cautious. He identified an objective and he went after it.

She could have said because Sylvia's baby had been safely born. She could have said because they were all safe and sound. That would have been the prudent, risk-free course the old Devon would have followed. ''Because of what you just said.''

He splayed his hands over her ribs. She could feel the warmth of them through the supple leather that separated them. ''Is that the only reason?'' he asked. His breath warmed the back of her neck.

She twisted slightly in his arms so that she could see his face. The sky was turning from black to gray to the silver of dawn's light. ''A few hours ago I might have said yes. But not now. I want to be with you because I love you. I tried to tell you that night at your cabin, but I...I couldn't.''

''Because you'd lied to me about the kids?''

He was looking down at her with just a flicker of a smile curving his mouth. She sensed that he already knew what her answer would be. ''Yes, I lied to you. I intended to keep on lying to you and I thought you would come to hate me for it. I couldn't have lived with that, so I kept silent and almost lost you.''

''God, Devon. For such a smart, brave woman, sometimes you're dumb as a box of rocks.'' The love in his voice took the sting from the words. He cupped the back of her head, being careful not to crush the baby in her arms, and kissed her. Kissed her long and thoroughly until she grew dizzy and weak with need and desire. When he raised his head, his eyes were glittering and his voice wasn't quite steady. "Loving someone means you stand by them. You trust them. You honor their confidence."

"I didn't want you to have to choose between me and your duty to the law."

"There wasn't any choice to make, Devon. You will always come first in my life. And as for my honor as a lawman, I'm not some movie-hero cop. This world's made up of hundreds of shades between black and white. Rounding up kids and turning them over to the feds isn't in my job description. I'm sworn to take care of the citizens of Enchantment, not enforce immigration laws."

"Why didn't you tell me all this that night?"

"Why didn't you trust me enough to ask me that night?"

She traced her finger down the line of his cheek. "Because I was afraid of all the changes in my life. Everything between us has happened so fast."

"Not fast enough. Ten years is a long time between acts."

"I wanted to tell you how I felt about you. How I've always felt about you. But I was afraid to trust my heart. I'm not afraid anymore. I love you, Miguel. I have always loved you. I will always love you."

"Do you know how long I've waited to hear those words?"

"As long as I've waited to say them?"

He kissed her again, because from that moment on, there was no more need for words.

EPILOGUE

"YOU'VE DONE AN EXCELLENT JOB with this party, considering all the distractions you've had this week."

Devon took a sip of wine to hide her smile. "Distractions" was putting it mildly. "Thank you, Mother. It is going well, isn't it?" She and Myrna were standing on the terrace outside the private dining room at Angel's Gate. The sun had just set. The sky was a riot of orange and pink and purple, and entirely free of smoke.

The Silver Creek fire had been declared one-hundred-percent contained two days after their night on the mountain. The recovery team had already begun its work, stabilizing denuded slopes, planting seedlings to speed the recovery of the burned-over areas. The view wasn't quite as beautiful as it had been on her last visit, but in a few years, the scars from the fire would be gone.

"Do you want to go back inside, Mom?"

"Not unless you do. I love it out here." Myrna adjusted her cashmere shawl and took a deep breath of the clear, cool air. "Did I tell you I approve of those shoes?"

Devon glanced down at the strappy high-heeled

sandals that Kim had picked for the wedding. She'd worn them to the rehearsal to practice walking on the stone floor of the little mission church where the ceremony would take place. She'd had no idea her very conservative cousin had such decadent taste in footwear. Pink-tipped toenails peeked back at her. She'd actually found time for the pedicure and manicure she'd needed, thanks to her mother.

Myrna had volunteered to watch over Maria and help Sylvia with Estrella while she and Kim went to the spa in Taos the day before. Myrna's grandmotherly instincts, first roused by Maria, had kicked into high gear when she held Estrella for the first time. "It's the way she's always been about something that interests her," Sam had said with a chuckle as they waited in their rented car for her to finish up a few last-minute details before they left for the church. "Damn the torpedoes. Full speed ahead. You and Miguel better be planning on a big family."

"Actually, we are," Devon had said.

"I wouldn't mind a couple of grandkids, myself. Of course, it appears you've got a good start with the kids you've got now."

"It would help if we could find their aunt. She's their closest relative, and if she's here legally—" She broke off. "I'm sorry. I promised myself to take this whole thing one step at a time."

"That's easier said than done for you Kane women. All four of you, Kim included. You're more like your mother—and your grandmother—than you want to admit."

"I'm noticing that, too," she'd said, and they'd both laughed.

"You made the right decision coming back to Enchantment, didn't you?" He'd reached out and taken her hand between both of his.

She'd turned her hand in his and squeezed back. "Yes, Dad, I did."

"Your father and I are thinking about buying one of the condos the resort's going to build. Did he tell you that?" Myrna asked, breaking into her thoughts.

"No, he hasn't."

"We've been thinking about a place to get away from the city for a couple of years now. Somewhere the sun shines a lot more than it does in San Francisco. We talked about Albuquerque, you know, since you were living there. But it will be much nicer here."

"Yes, it will." Devon touched the pendant at her throat. Lydia had given it to her just hours ago. It was a token of her grandmother's love, and with Devon's acceptance, it was also a symbol of Devon's commitment to The Birth Place.

And to the new life she would make for herself in Enchantment.

Devon couldn't stop herself from seeking out Miguel with her eyes. He was talking to his parents near the fireplace. He was wearing charcoal-gray slacks and a black sports jacket over an open-necked shirt as white as the snow on Mount Wheeler. He was so handsome he took her breath away. After a moment he turned his head, caught her gaze and smiled. He headed in her direction, meeting up with Sam as he moved toward the terrace with a glass of red wine for his wife.

Myrna followed the path of Devon's focus, and a satisfied smile curved the corners of her mouth. "He has matured remarkably well."

"Yes, he has, hasn't he."

"Have you set a date yet?" Myrna asked, pitching her voice loudly enough for Miguel and Sam to hear as they came through the sliding doors onto the balcony.

"No, ma'am," Miguel replied, not missing a beat as Sam handed Myrna her wine. "We've got to get Kim and Nolan married off before we can make plans for our own wedding."

"I'll be happy to help with any arrangements for yours. I've been looking forward to being the mother of the bride for quite some time."

"Speaking of the wedding, I think we should start the group moving back down the mountain," Sam said.

Myrna glanced at the thin gold watch on her arm. "Good heavens, yes. It's later than I thought. Maria and Sammy both need to be in bed. It's going to be a long day for them tomorrow." Sammy had been given a reprieve from chicken/salmon menu of the rehearsal dinner. She and Maria were having hot dogs and ice-cream sundaes back at the cabin. They were "baby-sitting" Estrella, which mostly meant leaning over the crib Jesse and Miguel had set up in the main room of the cabin, oohing and aahing over the infant.

"Good night." Miguel slid his arm around Devon's shoulders and leaned back against the terrace wall. They watched as Sam and Myrna returned to the dining room and walked up to the table where Kim and Nolan and Lydia sat with Kim's foster parents. After a few moments they all rose and began looking for purses and jackets. Five minutes later Myrna had ushered them out of the dining room and into the lobby.

"My mother is an incredible organizer," Devon said, her back against Miguel's chest, her fingers twined with his.

"Formidable," he said, bending his head to nuzzle the nape of her neck. "I wonder what she'll say when I tell her that for the Diné, after the marriage it is forbidden for a man to speak to his mother-in-law, or even to be in the same room with her for the rest of their lives."

"Lucky for my mother you're not a traditional Navajo," she said, unperturbed by his teasing. He could tease her all night long if he just kept nibbling at her earlobe as he was doing now. They'd had so little time together since the fire. Miguel's days had been busy dealing with the aftermath, and hers with last-minute wedding details, moving into her office at The Birth Place and helping Sylvia settle into motherhood.

"Yes, but I'm a man who takes the best of all the cultures that make up my background, remember? I might have to give this one a—" She turned in his arms and silenced him with a kiss.

"She has promised to send us the name of the best immigration lawyer in the West," she said, when she got her breath back. "And a no-interest loan to pay the retainer."

"Okay, I guess I can make an exception in her case, since she's going to be the only mother-in-law I'll ever have." He bent his head again and their second kiss of the evening curled her toes and raised her blood pressure to dangerous levels.

"If we leave now, we could spend an hour at your cabin before I have to be home," she said, her mouth still touching his.

"That's the best idea I've heard all day, but I'm going to have to decline if all you can spare is an hour."

"Is that because what you have in mind will take far longer than an hour to accomplish?"

He caught his breath on a low, sexy growl, but instead of pulling her closer and kissing her again, as she intended, he stepped away and turned her a little so that she was looking at the service door that led into the hotel kitchen. "It will take a lot longer than an hour, you're right about that. But first there's someone I want you to meet."

A small, dark-haired woman of about forty, dressed in the gray uniform of a hotel maid, was standing just outside the recessed door. As she began to walk slowly toward them, Devon saw Sylvia's dark eyes and widow's peak and Maria's smile.

"Señorita Grant? I am Lucia Molina."

Devon stared at Miguel. "How?"

"I called in a couple of favors and tracked her down in Phoenix. She got back this morning, but they were short of help so she couldn't contact me until a little while ago. Devon, I'd like you to meet Lucia Molina."

"Hello, Lucia."

"The *señor* tells me you know where my nieces and nephew are."

"I do," Devon said, smiling up at the man she loved so very much, the man who had found the time in his busy week to do this for her. She offered her hand to Lucia. "I know exactly where they are, and I'll take you to them right now."

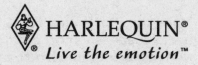

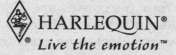

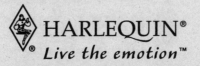

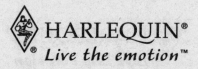

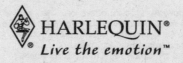